This book may be returned to any Wiltshire
library. To renew this book phone your library
or visit the website: www.wiltshire.gov.uk

Wiltshire
COUNTY COUNCIL

LM6.108.5

MENACE FOR DR. MORELLE

Doctor Morelle is a Harley Street Psychiatrist. His assistant, the timorous Miss Frayle, is walking to a party when she encounters a wounded man who collapses in front of her. She runs to get assistance, only to find he has disappeared — leaving nothing but a pool of blood on the road. Investigating, Doctor Morelle and Miss Frayle come up against a glamorous woman thief, a plot to rob a baron of millions of pounds — and a murderer.

ERNEST DUDLEY

MENACE FOR DR. MORELLE

Complete and Unabridged

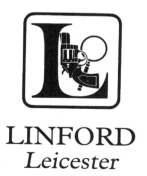

LINFORD
Leicester

First published in Great Britain

First Linford Edition
published 2006

All crooks, detectives and other characters, nice
and nasty, portrayed in this novel are merely the
wild imaginings of an author's delirium.

British Library CIP Data

Dudley, Ernest
    Menace for Dr. Morelle.—Large print ed.—
Linford mystery library
    1. Morelle, Doctor (Fictitious character)—
Fiction
    2. Detective and mystery stories
    3. Large type books
    I. Title
823.9'14 [F]

ISBN 1–84617–486–4

Published by
F. A. Thorpe (Publishing)
Anstey, Leicestershire

Set by Words & Graphics Ltd.
Anstey, Leicestershire
Printed and bound in Great Britain by
T. J. International Ltd., Padstow, Cornwall

This book is printed on acid-free paper

To the Film-Producer who
will buy the Film Rights

Extract from the *Medical Directory* (current year):

MORELLE (Christian names given) 221B, Harley St., W.1. (Tel. Langham 05011) — M.D. Berne (Univ. Berne Prize & Gold Medallist) 1924; F.R.C.P. Lond. 1932 (Univ. Vienna, Salzburg, Carfax, U.S.A.); Phys. Dept. Nerv. Dis. & Lect. in Neurol. Rome Academy, 1929; Lect. & Research Fell. Sorbonne, 1928; Carfax, U.S.A. Fell. Med. Research Counc. 1930; Research Fell. Salzburg Hosp. 1931; Psychiat. Carlos Hosp. Rome; Psychiat. Horgan Hosp. Baltimore; Pathol. Rudolfa Clin. Berne; Medico-Psychol. Trafalgar Hosp. and Clin. London.; Hon. Cons. Psychiat. Welbeck Hosp. Lond. Author, 'Psychol. aspects of prevent. treat. of drug addiction,' 'Amer. Med. Wkly.', 1932; 'Study of analysis in ment. treat.' Ib., 1930; 'Nervous & mental aspect of drug addict.', 'Jl. of Res. in Psychopathol.,' 1931; 'Hypnot. treat. in nerve & ment. disorder,' 'Amer. Med. Jnl.', 1930; etc

Extract from *Who's Who*
(current year):

MORELLE (Christian names, but no date, place or details of birth given). Educated: Sorbonne; Rome; Vienna. M.D. Berne, 1923 (for further details of career as medical practitioner see *Medical Directory* — current year); Lecturer on medico-psychological aspects of criminology to New York Police Bureau, 1934; Lecturer and medicopsychiat. to police bureaux and criminological authorities of Geneva, Rome, Milan and Paris, 1935 — 1937. Published miscellaneous papers on medical and scientific subjects (see *Medical Directory* — current year). Writings for journals include: 'Auguste Dupin versus Sherlock Holmes — A Study in Ratiocination,' 'London Archive & Atlantic Weekly', 1931; 'The Criminal versus Society,' 'English Note-book', 'Le Temps Moderne' & 'New York Letter', 1933; etc., etc., See also the Case-books

'Meet Doctor Morelle' and 'Meet Doctor Morelle Again' (published by John Long.) Address: 221B Harley St., London, W.1. *Recreations*: Criminology and fencing — European fencing champion (Epée) Switzerland, 1927–28–29. *Clubs*: None.

1

Mayhem in Mayfair

'I'm through.'

Sir Hugh Albany's mouth set in a line of finality. For the first time since the two others had known him they detected a sudden determination in the young, good-looking features which before had seemed a little weakly drawn. He went on:

'We're all washed up. You, Cleo and I. You've both got till this time tomorrow to get out of the country, or it's going to be too bad for you.'

Gresham tapped the ash off his cigarette. He said:

'It's not going to be too good for *you*.'

'That's my concern.'

There was a heavy pause. Gresham let his gaze flicker to the woman who was watching, a faintly amused smile touching the corners of her softly curving mouth.

Mrs. Cleo Latimer had contributed little to the conversation during the last half hour while the two men's voices, without growing louder, had become razor-edged with increasingly bitter hostility. In answer to his look she murmured:

'I think Hugh's being just a little thoughtless.'

Albany made no pretence at keeping the contempt out of his tone as he answered her.

'If you mean I don't give a damn what happens to you, or Charles' — he indicated Gresham — 'you're right.'

'I mean,' she corrected him gently, 'that, in this case, what's your concern is also ours.'

He caught the unmistakable threat underlying the quietly spoken words. He stared back at her long, thickly lashed eyes, that could change from brilliant blue to smoky, greenish-grey. They were blue and wide now as she returned his gaze over the cigarette she was lighting from a gold, beautifully made lighter. His spine chilled yet again as he realized behind that lovely face worked a brain that was utterly callous. He said between his teeth:

'I never thought it possible any woman could look like you and yet be so loathsome, so — horrible.' He nodded towards the other. 'He at least always made me think of something that crawled from under a stone, and I blame myself terribly for not guessing his game. But you —' He broke off, unable to find words to express his utter and complete revulsion for her. 'And if you imagine any veiled threats are going to stop me from washing my hands of you and the dirt you both stand for, you're mistaken.'

She smiled at him lazily through a puff of cigarette-smoke.

'Spoken like a gentleman,' she said. But he caught the sudden flame of murderous hate that had gleamed momentarily at the back of her eyes. She turned to Gresham and said: 'Don't you agree, Charles?'

A vein showed across Gresham's forehead. His voice came thickly. 'Before you're much older, Hugh Albany, I'm going to take pleasure in shooting the guts out of you and then kicking you

3

among the garbage-bins for the alley-cats to sniff round.'

'Very picturesque, but not likely to get us anywhere.' Cleo Latimer went on: 'I don't think, Hugh, you're going to get rid of us as easily as that. You've been useful to us and, for a little longer, you're going to remain useful, whether you like it or not. And you know as well as we do you can't help yourself.'

'I tell you —' Albany began, but she ignored his interruption. She said:

'Perhaps it *would* be a good plan for our association to end, but you've got to help us over the Baron Xavier business first —'

'I tell you I'm through!' Albany rushed on, and this time she was forced to listen. 'God knows how you kept yourselves out of it at the Travers' girl's inquest. But I know you and Charles caused her death just as if you murdered her with your own hands —'

'She was an attractive thing,' Cleo Latimer murmured. 'Pity. Weak, however. Just the type something was bound to happen to, sooner or later.'

'Delightful pair I've got myself mixed up with!' Albany said bitterly. 'But it's finished now.'

'Baron Xavier . . . ' the woman interposed softly.

'Yes, come on,' Gresham cut in, allowing a hint of amiability to creep back into his voice. 'Help us out with him and, as Cleo says, then we'll call it a day.'

'You'll have practically nothing to do, my dear Hugh. Just the little matter of Lady Tonbridge's reception tonight for Xavier, and that's all.'

'No! No!' Albany turned on her fiercely. 'I'm having nothing more to do with you —'

'Just a matter of introducing us to him, that's all,' the other man said.

'You keep away from Xavier —!'

But once more Mrs. Latimer's soft voice interrupted him. 'You want to marry Sherry Carfax, don't you?'

Albany flinched as if he'd been struck. She looked at him through a puff of cigarette-smoke and now her eyes were that smoky greenish-grey. 'You won't . . . unless I keep my mouth shut.

5

Which of course I shall, if —'

'You'll keep your mouth shut for your own sake and Charles',' he told her grimly.

'You're very sure of yourself,' she said slowly, and Gresham chimed in with: 'We've got the whip-hand, not you —'! He broke off as she turned to him.

'Give yourself a drink, Charles.'

At the peremptory note in her voice he muttered to himself and moved to a corner of the room where glasses and decanters glinted. She said to Albany:

'Now don't be foolish, Hugh. It'll be so much easier for us — and I mean you, also — if you co-operate. Such a little thing we want. Just for you to —'

'What are you after Xavier for?' he flung at her. 'He's got nothing for you. Just another Balkan prince living in exile, that's all!'

She laughed softly. 'You wouldn't hold anything out on us, would you? You wouldn't happen to know something about your friend which could be quite — useful?'

'I don't know what you're talking about.'

'No?' She shrugged and threw a glance at Gresham, who was staring at them over his drink. She went on:

'Anyway, that needn't bother you. All *you* have to worry about is the Tonbridge party tonight and see that we are introduced, very charmingly, to your friend Xavier.'

'I've given you both my answer. You're wasting your time. I only wish to hell I'd never set eyes on you, and the sooner I get myself out of here the cleaner I'll feel!'

Albany crossed to the door. Gresham started to say something and moved forward, but the woman gave him a look which stopped him. To the other she said unemotionally:

'I'm warning you not to go like this, Hugh. If you do, you're going to regret it.'

He turned and flashed back at her, his voice harsh with desperation: '*Tell* Sherry what the hell you like — or as much as you dare! I'd rather lose her than have to listen to you another second . . . '

She answered, her voice elaborately casual: 'Are you being deliberately stupid?'

'What d'you mean?'

'I mean this has gone beyond merely giving away your past to a girl you want to marry. We've reached the stage where we may decide upon action even more painful for you than that.'

'I'd like to beat the living daylight out of you . . . ' Gresham choked.

'Shut up . . . ' she said to him through her teeth. Then to Albany: 'I said, I'm warning you. If you take my advice, you'll think again.'

He stood and looked at them for a moment, his eyes narrowed his lip curled with unutterable contempt. Then, without a word, he went out and the door slammed after him.

With an exclamation, Gresham crossed quickly to the secretaire. Mrs. Latimer had exquisite taste in Empire furniture. The secretaire was of rosewood, ornamented with ormulu, and there was a drawer above the flap. Gresham pulled it open and grabbed a small black automatic. It was flat and ugly and made an unpleasant anachronism with the delicate piece of furniture in which it had lain. He looked up from the gun as the woman stood beside him. She said:

'Aren't you being a little crude, Charles?'

'Maybe,' he snapped back. 'But this is a time for something stronger than words!' and he slipped the automatic into his pocket.

2

Enter Miss Frayle

Miss Frayle was never fortunate with taxis. No doubt because she was slight and unobtrusive, meek of manner, soft of voice. No doubt because of the horn-rimmed spectacles over which she peered somewhat astigmatically and which seemed to be continually in danger of slipping off her nose. Or perhaps it was simply that taxi-drivers decided Miss Frayle was not looking for a taxi really seriously — at any rate, each and every one passed her by, flag up, flag down or flag covered.

With a sigh, and somewhat in the manner of an enthusiastic naturalist seeking a rare species of butterfly, she had at length set off in pursuit through sundry side-streets. Lured by a hoot here and a taximeter ring there, she presently found herself in the quiet back-streets of Mayfair. It was now about seven o'clock.

Miss Frayle had left her hairdresser's just after six, feeling vitally feminine as befitted a young woman fresh from the master hands of Louis. Then, as taxi after taxi sped by, her spirits had drooped and she now found herself making an uncertain way through a shadowy mews. She had the vague idea of taking a short cut in the general direction of Harley Street. Then, as the twilight deepened and she realized she was going to be later than she intended, or than Doctor Morelle would approve, her footsteps quickened.

Suddenly, from a shadow-filled turning in the mews, the figure of a man emerged. Miss Frayle pressed on steadily, not concerned with figures emerging from shadows, but intent on reaching her destination as quickly as possible. Then her heart gave an uncomfortable flutter and a horrid feeling of uneasiness came over her as she saw the man lurching towards her unsteadily. In her long association with Doctor Morelle she had witnessed many strange happenings, her spectacles had bent upon sights of varying degrees of unpleasantness and horror.

But if there was one thing in the world which dismayed her more than another, it was a drunk.

The individual approaching appeared to be very drunk indeed. The shadows were deceptive and made it difficult to see his face clearly. But he seemed to be a youngish man by the cut of his clothes and the slightness of his tall figure. He held a hand to his head and for a moment she thought he sounded as if he were groaning. But whether he was, or merely singing drunkenly to himself, she could not quite determine. She paused behind an open garage door, anxious only to be unobserved and hopeful the man would continue on his somewhat erratic way.

But it was not to be. He reached her and was about to pass, then — as she started to breathe a sigh of relief — his knees suddenly buckled under him. He gave a dreadful groan and pitched forward, flat on his face. He lay still. To her horror, Miss Frayle realized one side of his face was all blood.

'Oh, good gracious!'

It was an inadequate exclamation, one

she was given to making when confronted with the unexpected. For a moment she stood motionless, eyes wide behind her spectacles. What would Doctor Morelle do in such circumstances?

It was a question which in the past she had more than once asked herself in situations of varying emergency, and never once had she been able to provide herself with the answer. This was not altogether unaccountable, of course. The Doctor was inclined to react in a manner unpredictable. In such a case as this which now confronted her, for example, he could be expected to manifest an interest by ignoring the incident completely, proceeding on his way as if nothing had occurred, or on the other hand producing a policeman from the thin air.

However, it was not in Miss Frayle's nature to leave anyone obviously hurt, whether he was drunk or sober, and while she wished fervently she could induce a policeman to materialize one did not appear to be in sight. In fact, the surrounding gloom was empty of anyone except the now significantly still figure lying outstretched upon the cobblestones.

Heart thumping uncomfortably, she detached herself from the shelter of the garage door and approached the inert form. Stooping beside him she saw her first surmise had been correct. He was a youngish man, fair and, she noted, despite his ghastly pallor, good-looking. She glanced about her. Still the mews appeared empty. It seemed there was nowhere at hand either where she might get help. Suddenly she remembered a public house she had passed just before turning into the mews. The man gave another groan. His lips moved as if he were trying to say something. She could catch only an incoherent mutter. He tried desperately to raise himself and she restrained him with a hand on his shoulder.

'Try and lie quiet,' she told him. 'I'll get help.'

She hurried along the mews as fast as she could. Rounding the corner quickly, she saw a light glimmering through the glass doors of the public house. The abundantly bosomed character behind the private bar of the 'Mayfair Arms' viewed with some surprise the vision of a slim young woman rushing in, spectacles awry and somewhat breathless. Miss Frayle noted that, apart from the large person who eyed her over a glass she was polishing, the bar was empty.

'A man in the mews —!' she gasped. 'Badly hurt —! Could I have some brandy, please?'

Sympathetic understanding melted the stony expression on the other's face. 'Make you feel faint, dearie? Yes — I've got a drop.'

She reached out with a practised hand, grasped a bottle and tipped out a measure. Miss Frayle made haste to clear up any misunderstanding which seemed to exist as to who was to be the recipient of the reviving spirit.

'It's not for me. It's for him —Is there anyone — anyone who could help me? He ought to be moved.'

'Bit early 'ere, dearie, for customers,' the barmaid returned. 'Though someone should be in any minute.' She handed the

15

glass of brandy across the bar.

'Oh, dear!' Miss Frayle exclaimed while she produced the money from her handbag. 'I must get help.'

'*I* can't leave me bar, I'm sure. Take the brandy along to 'im, dearie, first. When 'e's recovered, perhaps you'll be able to manage 'im on your own.'

'I don't know,' Miss Frayle said doubtfully. 'But if anyone *should* come in, do send them along, please. It's the first mews on the right.' And clutching the glass tightly, she hurried out.

She was forced to make the return journey more slowly for fear of spilling the brandy. At last, however, she turned into the mews and hurried towards where she had left the young man. And now she almost dropped the glass in shocked amazement.

The Figure she had last seen lying, an inert heap on the stones, was no longer there.

3

Doctor Morelle Takes the Stage

Somewhat wildly Miss Frayle stared about her, then returned her gaze to the spot where the young man had lain, as if expecting he might in some miraculous manner reappear from out of the ground. But there was no-one. She forced herself to think clearly and, a frown marring her brow, began to wonder if this really was where she had left him. Could she have mistaken the spot? She looked around to reassure herself she had in fact returned to the right mews, although she was certain her sense of direction could not have misled her to that extent. There was the open garage door behind which she had sheltered when she had first seen the man approaching. She had not mistaken the mews, anyway. Nor had she mistaken the place where she had left him. For suddenly she gave a little gasp as she saw a dark stain marking the stones. There was no doubt it was blood.

Miss Frayle straightened herself, set her spectacles firmly on her nose, drew a deep breath — and gave a start as further up the mews she caught footsteps receding briskly. She picked up the brandy glass which she had deposited on the ground when she bent to examine the bloodstain and set off as quickly as she could after the footsteps. It was quite probable, she thought, that the young man, though he had obviously recovered sufficiently to walk away, might still welcome the stimulant. In a moment she glimpsed a shape in the shadows ahead of her.

'I say —!' she called out. 'I say —!'

The figure paused and turned and she called out again: 'Just — just a minute . . . I've got some brandy for you —'

She broke off, her gasp of surprise mingled with embarrassment. 'Oh . . .'

The man who was facing her a few yards away seemed shorter, more thick-set and somewhat older than the one she had last seen in a heap on the cobblestones behind her. Besides, he was wearing a hat, the brim pulled down, shading his eyes, and by now she was near enough to see there was no sign of blood on his face.

'I beg your pardon?' came his voice coldly out of the gloom.

Miss Frayle goggled at him, feeling somewhat nonplussed under his questioning gaze. She realized that to him she must appear slightly eccentric, to say the least, rushing about after strange men and trying to thrust glasses of brandy on them.

'But the other man . . . ?' she collected her wits sufficiently to ask. 'The one who was hurt . . . ?'

'Is anything the matter with you? Or is this a joke?'

'A joke?' Miss Frayle glanced round her wildly. 'Oh, no — not at all! I'm so sorry,' she apologized, and then felt she ought to offer some sort of explanation. 'You see, not — not ten minutes ago, I was coming through the mews when a man appeared, his face covered in blood, and collapsed. There was no-one about, so I — I went to get help. Then I came back with this brandy for him —'

She faltered and broke off. The man continued to stare at her unwaveringly. It occurred to her that her explanation was not, in fact, impressing him very favourably. She glanced at the glass of brandy she was still clutching desperately, started to put it on the ground, hesitated, decided perhaps she had better continue holding it, and faced the man again.

'I think you must be suffering from some delusion.' His voice was tinged with amusement. 'I myself have just come through these mews and certainly saw no-one, let alone this person you've described.'

'Oh, you *must* have seen him . . . I left him lying on the ground. I can't have been gone more than five minutes at the most. And as I say, when I came back with the brandy —' Again she broke off and looked at the glass she was holding. The stranger leaned forward and took it from her hand.

'You're slopping it all over you,' he said.

'Thank — thank you.'

A faint smile seemed to move across his

face and she said: 'You do believe me, don't you? I — I mean, I wouldn't be running about with — with brandy . . . '

He said quietly:

'I think you've been the victim of a trick. An old dodge. This man you saw undoubtedly spotted you coming along here alone and planned to snatch your hand-bag.'

Miss Frayle looked down quickly to see if she still carried her bag. She did. She noticed the strap was twisted round her wrist. The other nodded towards it. He said:

'Then he saw it was too securely attached to your wrist and he continued to pretend he was injured. When you went off for help, of course, he bolted.'

She could tell by the expression beneath the shadow of his hat what he was thinking. To him she was obviously the sort of person who could easily be deceived by this type of subterfuge.

'Oh,' Miss Frayle said. 'Oh . . . '

With a little frown she cast her mind back to her meeting with the young man. She found it difficult to believe he was the type that snatched hand-bags. She seemed to remember he had appeared well dressed — and then, there was that blood on his face. She shook her head and timidly expressed her disbelief.

'Evidently an artist at the game,' the other replied promptly. 'Made himself up for the occasion. Whitened his face and then stuck on plenty of red grease-paint.' Again Miss Frayle was conscious of his contempt — it almost amounted to that — for her naiveté. She said:

'I suppose so. I hadn't thought of that.'

Once again he allowed a tinge of amusement to creep into his voice. 'They think of everything, believe me.' There was a little pause and he said: 'Which way are you going?'

She explained she was taking a short cut to Harley Street, having given up all hope of finding a taxi. As she spoke, he turned his head and, with an imperious wave, suddenly called out: 'Taxi!'

To her astounded gaze a taxi-cab appeared promptly out of the descending darkness, to pull up with a jerk alongside them. Not without some bitterness, she reflected on the endless number of taxis which had swept past her that evening without so much as giving her a toot in acknowledgment of her appealing cries. Yet here was this individual to whom one had merely to breathe the word and, without the least exertion on his part, a taxi magically appeared at his beck and call.

Miss Frayle sighed gently to herself. No doubt about it, some people had that gift, ability, flair — whatever it was — for smoothing their way through life where others could pursue only a rough and jagged course. It was not the first time, she knew, she had been made conscious she belonged to the latter category. All the same she resented being reminded of it, and failed somewhat to stem the feeling of a certain ungracious irritation towards the stranger as he helped her into the taxi he had so easily conjured up.

'Where to?'

He gave her address to the driver and turning to her: 'I hope you get home safely without encountering any more nightmare adventures.' She caught the gleam of very white teeth as he smiled: 'Good-bye.'

She pulled herself together, contrived to dismiss the wave of resentment that swept over her sufficiently to answer him politely. 'Thank you very much. You've been most kind. I'm sorry if I've annoyed you.'

'On the contrary . . . It's been quite amusing.'

As her taxi moved off she glanced back through the window and saw him disappear into the shadows. He walked briskly, his head at an alert angle. She was left with the impression of a certain suaveness, a sort of streamlined air about him which, in some indefinable way, was slightly sinister.

It was only when she had dismissed the taxi and was closing the door of Doctor Morelle's house behind her that she suddenly remembered the glass of brandy left behind on the mews cobblestones. For a moment she thought of rushing back quickly to return it to the broad-bosomed barmaid at the public house. Then came the thought: Supposing she went back to find that, like the young man with the bloodstained face, the glass was no longer there?

Once again she frowned to herself and shook her head thoughtfully. Was it possible she had been the victim of an attempt to steal her hand-bag? Remembering the young man and his ghastly appearance, it seemed incredible. On the other hand, *could* she have imagined it all? That seemed even more impossible. Yet she knew that if she did hurry back to recover the glass and was unable to find it, she might begin to think it had all been a nightmare.

Anyway, she comforted herself, the barmaid had insisted upon a deposit on the glass. So if it were not returned it would not matter all that much.

Having in her mind cleared up this problem to her satisfaction, she glanced at her watch. With a gasp of dismay she saw it was twenty minutes to eight.

Doctor Morelle by now would have started the address he was giving to a distinguished gathering of doctors, scientists and, in particular, medical officials connected with police and prison institutions.[1] His lecture would be extempore, and it was Miss Frayle's duty to be present to take shorthand notes in order that the talk might be preserved among other erudite Morellia for posterity. To say the Doctor would be displeased with her nonarrival would be putting it mildly. He was due to take the lecture platform at seven thirty, and unpunctuality was one of the human frailties he seemed to find impossible to tolerate.

Her recent strange encounter had pushed her evening's routine temporarily to the back of her mind. To add to the wave of panic that now swept over her, not only had she to get to the lecture-hall as quickly as possible, but first she must change into an evening frock — she was accompanying the Doctor, who was going on to a reception Lady Tonbridge was giving for a certain Baron Xavier. Hence her hairdressing

---

[1] 'Psycho-therapy in Relation to Recidivism'. (See the files of *London Archive, Atlantic Weekly,* and *English Notebook*.)

appointment earlier with Louis.

It would be ironical indeed if her new hair-do — for which she had gone to great trouble and incurred considerable expense, and which had led her into the adventure of the mews — were to result in her being unable to appear at Lady Tonbridge's reception at all!

Quickly she put on the new dress got especially for tonight's occasion. She neatly arranged the clothes from which she had stepped, wondering how she would begin explaining to Doctor Morelle the reason for her delay. The more she tried to bring her hurrying thoughts to bear upon the incident, the more fantastic it seemed. Once again she began to doubt that her meeting with the first man, then the second, in the mews had really happened. Could it have been some sort of hallucination brought about by soporific effects attributable to Louis' ministrations?

'Oh dear, oh dear . . . ' she murmured aloud and sighed. This was an evening she had been looking forward to with more than ordinary anticipation, and now it seemed it was going to be spoiled before it had really begun. She picked up the gloves she had been wearing with her other clothes, telling herself all she could do was explain to Doctor Morelle exactly what had happened.

'Whether he believes me or not,' she added aloud. 'If he —'

She broke off, her trend of thought cut abruptly short. For a moment her mind was held in chill suspense as she stared down at the glove. Behind her spectacles her eyes grew more saucer-like. There, along one of the fingers, was a dull, brownish-red smear. She touched it timidly. She swallowed. Not grease-paint, or any other kind of paint. It did not require Doctor Morelle to tell her that much.

'It — it's blood! Then — then it *did* happen . . . '

* * *

Fortunately, the Wimpole Hall was not far from Doctor Morelle's house, and Miss Frayle ran most of the way. All the same, as she paused outside the lecture-room, a familiar intoning voice within told her Doctor Morelle was already half-way through his address:

' . . . directly concerned with etiology of crime in a general way, insofar as it affects the selection of cases for psychiatric study, psycho-therapeutic treatment and specialized training . . . '

In cold, pellucid phrases the Doctor, as was his invariable habit, was holding his listeners in his mesmeric grip. Miss Frayle, promptly choosing discretion as the better part of valour, decided it would be wiser to wait for him in the ante-room near by. To risk attracting his attention and consequent displeasure by making her arrival known at this moment was an idea which singularly failed to appeal to her.

Feeling guilty and uncomfortable, as if she were a schoolgirl late for class, she curled up forlornly in a deep leather armchair. From the jumble of mental pictures which crowded in on her from the past hour or two, she tried to sort out a coherent explanation in readiness for Doctor Morelle.

The more she reviewed the chain of circumstances which had entangled her, the more she seemed to be floundering in some half-world of fantasy and melodrama. Miserably she realized when the moment came to face the Doctor she would merely mumble incoherent excuses and goggle at him through her spectacles. Suddenly a ray of hope brightened her face. The bloodstained glove! That at least was proof conclusive enough to satisfy even him of the truth of her story. Then, as suddenly, she sank into gloom once more, murmuring.

'Oh, dear . . . Why didn't I bring it *with* me?'

It would have been the piece of vital evidence for her to produce in triumph and vindication of her excuse for being late, apart from bolstering up her courage from the start. And she had not thought to bring it with her.

She gave a heavy sigh. It would be little use showing him the glove on their return to Harley Street later that night. By that time, having dismissed her explanation as a phantasmagoria of her wild imaginings, nothing would induce him to give the subject his attention once again. Nothing, she reflected, biting her lip, unless perhaps she could lead him to the mews and show him a row of bloodstained bodies all neatly laid out for him.

She was about to permit herself a wry smile at the notion when, looking up, she saw him pause in the doorway before, hawklike, he bore down upon her. Hurriedly she stumbled to her feet, only just saving her spectacles from slipping off her nose, and, blushing violently, started to say something.

'My dear Miss Frayle,' he cut in, his voice like a whiplash, 'if I were to observe I am even remotely interested in whatever laboured form of excuse you are about to offer for your absence from my lecture, it would be an overstatement!' He gave a little cough and touched his tie, dazzlingly white against his saturnine features. 'What I am at pains to impress upon you, however, is the gathering of doctors and scientists, distinguished in their particular spheres, represented but a small proportion of the audience I wished to reach. In point of fact, they formed merely the nucleus. Because you deemed it of more importance to dally in a beauty-parlour, the larger proportion of those interested in my theme would have remained in darkness.'

'Would have . . . ?' Miss Frayle put in timidly.

'You are quick to seize upon the hint that — due entirely to the praiseworthy and disinterested enthusiasm, and ability to write shorthand, of one among this evening's gathering — my lecture has been preserved.'

'Oh, Doctor, I'm so glad. If you'd let me explain —'

But he waved her words aside. Remorselessly he proceeded: 'Your show of pleasure is little compensation for such flagrant neglect of duty.' He swept her with a narrowed gaze. If, instead of the simple little dress and modest hair-style, she had been wearing the most outrageous creation, plus one of Louis' more flamboyant efforts, his look could not have expressed chillier disapproval.

'It would seem my generosity in permitting you to accompany me to the reception has been misinterpreted as a form of weakness on my part, and advantage taken of it.'

He paused. Heart in the bottom of her shoes, Miss Frayle waited for him to add that, as punishment for her offence, she would not after all go to Lady Tonbridge's party. All dressed up and nowhere to go, she thought bitterly. That was how the evening was going to turn out for her. Obviously he guessed her fear for, sardonic twist at the corners of his mouth, he appeared deliberately to keep her on tenterhooks while he savoured the spectacle of her misery. Then, just when she felt she could no longer bear it, the cold austere countenance softened. He forced an elaborate sigh, and asked:

'Or is it possible you *can* furnish some acceptable explanation? Make it as brief as possible. We are due shortly at Belgrave Square.'

A wave of thankfulness swept over her and Miss Frayle plunged into her story forthwith. While she related her strange adventure, he lit a Le Sphinx and stared at her stonily through a cloud of cigarette-smoke. She painted for him as vivid a picture as she could of the events in the mews, ending up with a dramatic flourish as she recounted her discovery of the bloodstained glove.

'The other man — the man I ran after — thinking he was the one who'd been injured,' she finished, 'told me it was just a trick to snatch my bag. He was very kind and helpful, got me a taxi and — and . . . well —' She glanced up at his finely chiselled nose which, if anything, was an inch or two higher, and ended somewhat lamely: 'And here I am.'

'I had noticed your presence, my dear Miss Frayle . . . Though, as I believe I have already observed, the lateness of your arrival —'

'Better late than never,' she put in spiritedly. Her spectacles flashed resentfully at him as she realized her story had made as little impression upon him as water on a duck's back.

'That,' he retorted, 'is a debatable point!' He went on briskly: 'Allow me to indicate the hour is approaching 8.45 and we are due at Lady Tonbridge's at nine o'clock. I suggest you might care to hasten —'

'But — but, Doctor Morelle,' Miss Frayle cried, 'haven't you been listening to what I've just been telling you?'

'I think I may say I did not miss a word, so enthralling was your narrative . . . Do please hurry.'

'But isn't there anything we ought to do? Or do you think — that is — haven't you any explanation —?'

'Any comment I might make would be entirely superfluous,' he answered dryly.

'You mean you — you don't believe me?'

'On the contrary, I believe you implicitly. Even *your* imagination could not rise to such heights!'

She searched his face in an effort to read what lay behind its cold, mask-like expression, but it was as enigmatic as ever. His eyes, glittering and disconcerting, mocked her with sardonic amusement through a cloud of cigarette-smoke.

Flicking the ash off his Le Sphinx, suddenly he turned on his heel and stalked off, leaving her to trail after him, helplessly bewildered.

4

Baron Xavier Makes His Bow

Miss Frayle had been looking forward to this evening with eager anticipation ever since Doctor Morelle had — much to her surprise — accepted Lady Tonbridge's invitation to attend her reception given for a certain Baron Xavier. It was not a habit of the Doctor's to attend society functions. In fact, much to her regret, he almost invariably deplored them as a puerile form of exhibitionism, not to say waste of time. On a rare occasion, however, he did accept an invitation, as now. Usually, Miss Frayle would discover afterwards there had been some ulterior motive behind his acceptance, rather than any social pleasure it afforded him.

Whether that applied in this case, she did not know and, frankly, cared less. It was enough for her that the Doctor had accepted the invitation and, to her surprised delight, had informed her he expected her to accompany him. Though the keen edge of her anticipation had been somewhat blunted by her mysterious adventure and Doctor Morelle's subsequent displeasure, now, as the car bore them towards Belgrave Square, her spirits rose.

She remembered the Doctor had hinted that some time in the past — before her association with him — he had been successful in extricating a member of the Tonbridge family from some dangerous entanglement with an extremely attractive Continental confidence-trickster. As a result, Lady Tonbridge's regard for the Doctor was high.[1] Hence, she supposed, her invitation and his acceptance.

So far as Miss Frayle was aware, the Doctor was not acquainted with the one

---

[1] The case had international ramifications which made it indiscreet to publish at the time. It is hoped, however, it may be included in future memoirs of Doctor Morelle.

the party was in aid of — Baron Xavier. And her knowledge of him was confined to what she had gathered from those glossy illustrated magazines portraying Society: generally perched on a shooting-stick lugubriously watching something, or else in a night-club or restaurant, snapped in the act of taking an enormous mouthful. The Baron, Miss Frayle had gathered, was an ex-prince of an obscure mid-European royal family which once had its place in the jig-saw of international politics. Though what place it had been exactly she had never bothered to learn.

The Baron was young, good-looking and charming and was well liked in England where he had now made his home. That was the sum total of Miss Frayle's knowledge of the Baron Xavier. Combined, however, with the fact that a good number of other celebrities would also be present, she was warmly thrilled at the prospect of an exciting evening. She became aware Doctor Morelle was giving her a sidelong glance. She caught the chilling gleam showing momentarily in his eyes.

'It is apparent you are suffering from no after-effects of your adventure,' he murmured, as she turned to him.

He was still harping on her being late for his blessed lecture! She apologized again. 'I'm most dreadfully sorry, Doctor,' she began to mumble, then broke off. Feeling somewhat thankful for the darkness of the car, she realized she obviously did not appear in the least sorry. Any feelings on the subject she may have had were now entirely forgotten looking forward to the party.

'Hmmm . . . ' was his only comment.

And although she did not look, she knew instinctively his high-bridged nose was once again faintly lifted. She stifled a sudden and inexplicable inclination to giggle. Really, all this excitement was inclined to make her feel a trifle irresponsible!

The car turned into Belgrave Square, whereupon Lady Tonbridge's house immediately manifested itself by its brightly lit entrance and gay awning from doorway to pavement. Miss Frayle heard the hiss of a long-drawn-out sigh of resignation beside her and again wondered idly what had prompted Doctor Morelle to agree to come along tonight, since he was obviously disliking the whole idea so much.

As if reading her thoughts, his voice, tinged with faint irony, murmured in her ear: 'Judging from the number of opulent vehicles arrayed in serried ranks before us, I imagine quite a large proportion of Society's more flamboyant representatives will be present tonight, so *you* should enjoy yourself!'

She said: 'I hope you will, too.'

'I am hopeful there may be mingling with the guests a Scotland Yard official or two of my acquaintance with whom I *shall* be able to carry on an intelligent conversation. A sad reflection that generally there cannot be a gathering of this nature without Scotland Yard being in discreet attendance. The more notable the gathering, usually the more necessary the police.'

Miss Frayle was saved the necessity of answering this observation, for at that moment the car drew up, the door was flung open by a footman and she was at once caught up in the glittering whirl of Lady Tonbridge's party.

It was all immensely satisfactory from her point of view. Exactly as she had imagined it would be: the sparkling, scented atmosphere humming with voices and music, the ballroom glittering with crystal chandeliers, the ever-changing pattern of colour, brilliant uniforms plus decorations, white ties and tails and lovely evening frocks and jewellery.

'All in glorious technicolor!' she thought happily.

Now Baron Xavier was bowing over her hand as if she were the one guest of the evening he had been straining at the leash to meet. Tall and dark, very like the photographs she had seen of him, he spoke English with an almost imperceptible accent. His wide, dark eyes smiled into hers as if he were sharing a little joke with her.

Over his shoulder Miss Frayle saw with delight Doctor Morelle being led off by Lady Tonbridge. With amusement she watched the great, austere Doctor

Morelle being whisked off by the white-haired, shrewd-faced little woman who scarcely reached his shoulder, and was laughing up impudently into his face. A momentary pang caught her as she wished she, too, possessed that power apparently to bewitch the Doctor.

Presently she became aware of a young girl who stood some-what apart and seemed to be searching among the guests for someone. She looked attractive and rather nice, she thought. Without that spoiled, enamelled look which she observed so many of the young lovelies present wore. Miss Frayle was not sure what it *was* about her that attracted her attention, but several times her gaze seemed to be drawn towards the slim, blonde girl. And a little later, she found herself standing near when Baron Xavier hurried up to speak to the girl. She heard him say:

'Where *is* Hugh, Sherry? I've hunted high and low for him.'

'I wish I knew,' was the girl's answer. 'I'm quite worried about him.'

'Oh . . . ' the Baron smiled at her, 'he'll

turn up presently with some perfectly good excuse!'

Then someone came up to them, began talking animatedly to Baron Xavier and, with a mechanical smile, the girl he had addressed as 'Sherry' moved away. Without actually meaning to follow her, Miss Frayle seemed to continue to drift in her direction. She did pause for a moment upon realizing suddenly she had not seen Doctor Morelle for some time and, while she looked around for him, lost sight of the blonde girl. Then she glimpsed the Doctor's tall figure brushing through the crowd in company with a short, sturdy man with a bright, bearded face whom she recognized as a distinguished Doctor of Philosophy, As they moved away, she caught the bearded man's words:

'Well, it all depends what you mean, Doctor Morelle . . . '

With the secure feeling the Doctor would be happily engaged for some time, Miss Frayle once again felt herself looking out for the girl she had been unwittingly following. Then a young man with dark wavy hair came up to her and asked her to dance. She straightened her spectacles upon her nose, smiled back at him and moved into his arms.

'Er — you're Miss Frayle, aren't you?' the young man asked her after a moment, and she felt a glow of pleasure that he had recognized her. It seemed he had followed many of Doctor Morelle's cases with keen interest, and he chatted away about them as they danced.

And then suddenly she stopped in her tracks. She was not aware her partner was babbling apologies for climbing all over her toes. Instead she was gripping his arm and asking in a low, tense voice:

'Who's that?'

The other glanced in the direction she was indicating.

'That? Sherry Carfax,' he told her. 'Nice girl, too. Nothing snooty about —'

'No — not her —' Miss Frayle's voice was a taut squeak. 'I mean — the — the man talking to her.'

Her partner looked again. Shrugged his shoulders.

'Why?'

But Miss Frayle failed to hear his

question. Eyes saucer-like behind her spectacles, oblivious of the rest of the dancers hurrying past, she stood staring across at the man she had last seen face to face in the mews before he had got her the taxi and had walked off into the gloom.

5

Sherry Carfax is Scared

Brightly the young man steered the conversation back to Doctor Morelle. But Miss Frayle was no longer listening to him. Her mind was not even on the music as she followed his steps automatically. For a few moments everything was blotted out by the vivid memory of that inert figure lying on his bloodstained face in the mews. And then that other man — talking now to Sherry Carfax — who had appeared upon the scene and then vanished, leaving her with an inexplicable feeling there was something strange, sinister, about him.

True, she was unable to see him clearly at the moment. His face was half turned from her, but all the same, even though he was without a hat and in evening dress, she felt sure it was he. Over her partner's shoulder Miss Frayle saw the girl saying something to him. She caught the bitter expression that had appeared on Sherry Carfax's mouth and saw her eyes suddenly grow hard. Then the man laughed. As he did so he turned his head and, had Miss Frayle been faintly doubtful before, now she was certain. She had made no mistake.

For a brief fraction his eyes seemed to stare straight into hers. Miss Frayle held her breath. Did they flicker slightly with recognition? It might have been her imagination, but it was as if they did. Anyway, he turned his head away with a sharp movement. The girl spoke to him again, and he shrugged and moved off.

The music stopped. Miss Frayle's partner thanked her and she smiled at him absently, her gaze searching the group towards which the man had been heading. But he had disappeared. The girl, however, was where he had left her. Her expression was angry — or was it fear?

Impulsively Miss Frayle murmured an excuse to the young man at her elbow and crossed to the girl. Reaching her, she hesitated and then managed to stammer:

'Er — excuse me, Miss Carfax, but — that is — do you mind if I speak to you a moment?'

The other gave her a long, puzzled look.

'I'm Miss Frayle . . . I'm with Doctor Morelle . . . ' Miss Frayle mumbled in explanation.

'Doctor Morelle!' The girl's face lit up with sudden animation. 'I heard he was here tonight —' She broke off, then exclaimed almost involuntarily. it seemed: 'I wish he'd help *me* . . . ' And there was a world of bitterness in her voice. 'But he can't, even if he would.' She checked herself as she realized Miss Frayle was staring at her. In a calmer tone, she went on: 'You said you wanted to speak to me?'

Miss Frayle recovered herself sufficiently to say hurriedly:

'The man you were talking to a minute ago — could you tell me who he is? His face seemed familiar and I . . . '

Her voice trailed off as once again she saw the curious look of bitterness and fear on the other's face before she answered in a taut voice.

'Charles Gresham,' she said.

And to her increased bewilderment, Miss Frayle realized the other was almost on the verge of tears. In a low tone and voice only just controlled, the girl continued. She said:

'If you *have* met him before, Miss Frayle, I can only warn you to be more careful . . . in choosing your friends.'

Miss Frayle gulped.

Almost in a whisper, the other went on: 'I — I'm scared of him.'

'Scared?'

Sherry Carfax paused momentarily. Then suddenly: 'D'you know Sir Hugh Albany?'

Miss Frayle frowned. 'I've heard of him, of course.' Then she remembered something she had read in a gossip column a little time ago. 'Aren't you engaged to him?'

The girl nodded. Then said helplessly: 'But I don't know —' She broke off as if trying to pull herself together. 'Why am I telling *you* all this? Why should you be

50

interested in —'

Miss Frayle interrupted her. 'But I *am* interested. When I saw you just now I had a feeling we might be friends. If I can help you . . .'

Impulsively Sherry Carfax clasped her hand. 'You're very sweet. But there's nothing you can do. It's only that — that —you see, Gresham pretends to be a friend of Hugh, but he isn't. I *know* he isn't. And — and I — oh, it sounds silly — but I can't help feeling he's got some hold over him!'

Miss Frayle glanced round. They were in a corner of the ballroom that was away from the other guests who were watching the dancing, and the music made any danger of their being over-heard negligible. She recalled a precept of Doctor Morelle's that invariably the safest place to conduct a confidential conversation was in some crowded restaurant, or somewhere similar, under cover of music and other people's chatter. She turned back to the girl.

'If you really think that, why don't you ask him?' she said.

'I've so little to go on. I just feel instinctively —'

Miss Frayle nodded. 'I know,' she agreed. 'Intuition. I often get the same thing myself.' She frowned thoughtfully for a moment. 'I wonder if . . . That is — I'm sure if I asked Doctor Morelle —'

'No . . . ' Sherry Carfax shook her head slowly. 'It's something I've got to cope with myself. If there was anything tangible . . . ' She left the sentence unfinished and asked: 'You haven't seen him here this evening, I suppose?'

Miss Frayle managed to catch up with the sudden question.

'Sir Hugh Albany? . . . No.'

She looked at the other curiously. A tingling sensation was beginning to run up and down her spine. She was experiencing the uncomfortable conviction she was on the verge of something outside the ordinary run of things. Something carrying undertones of menace which she wanted to push away from her. She looked round quickly to gain some reassurance from the dancers sweeping past, all so romantically gay.

Was it possible anything menacing or sinister could exist in such surroundings?

Miss Frayle made an effort to laugh her apprehension away, turned back to Sherry Carfax. Again saw in her eyes that shadowed, frightened look which no bright music and gaiety could cover up. The girl was saying:

'I'll try ringing his flat again . . . There was no answer when I tried earlier, but . . . ' She paused, hesitated, then with a sort of hurried shyness: 'Would you come with me?'

They found a telephone off the hall and Miss Frayle waited while the other dialled a number. She could hear the burr-burr at the other end and there was something almost suspenseful in the sound as she waited for it to be answered. The burring continued and finally Sherry Carfax replaced the receiver.

'No answer.'

'You're sure he hasn't arrived here?'

But she seemed not to hear. Her mouth tightened. 'I'm going to his flat,' she said with a sudden resolution. Miss Frayle followed after her.

'Yes,' she agreed helpfully, 'perhaps he's left a note there or something.' She managed to mumble: 'Would you like me to come with you?'

The other smiled at her tremulously. 'I *would* like. Frankly' — she gave a nervous little laugh — 'I'm worried.'

'I'll just tell Doctor Morelle,' Miss Frayle said quickly. 'Shan't be two or three minutes.'

She realized almost at once, however, that to find the Doctor was easier said than done. There were far too many guests, and she could not see him or Lady Tonbridge anywhere. After questioning several people without any success she decided to give up the search and hurried back to Sherry Carfax, who was waiting for her in the hall.

'I'll explain to the Doctor later,' Miss Frayle told her breathlessly. 'I don't suppose we'll be long.'

'Oh no,' the other reassured her. 'It's only Jermyn Street.'

A footman whistled a taxi out of the night for them. As they got in the girl glanced at her jewelled wristlet-watch. It was just on eleven o'clock.'

Less than ten minutes later the taxi drew up outside a narrow old-fashioned block of flats at the St. James's end of Jermyn Street. A marble staircase spiralled upwards around the shaft of an ornate lift. From the basement ascended the faint acrid odour of central-heating boilers. Hanging on the open door of the lift as they approached was a card:

OUT OF ORDER.

'It always is!' Sherry Carfax smiled wryly. 'I'm afraid we've got six floors to climb.'

Miss Frayle laughed away her apologies and they started up the stairs, the other saying:

'I'm always trying to persuade Hugh to move from here, and he's always saying he will. But somehow he never does!'

She seemed more cheerful now, as if buoyed up with the assurance that Sir Hugh Albany would be waiting to greet her. They reached the sixth floor at last and, while Miss Frayle leaned breathlessly against the wall, she rang. There was no answer. She pressed the bell again. After a moment she produced a latchkey from her hand-bag and slipped it into the lock.

The light was on in the hall. Miss Frayle got the impression the flat was pleasantly furnished with an atmosphere of comfort about it. Good prints on the walls. A bag of golf-clubs slung in a corner. Ahead of them a door opened into a room that was in darkness. On the right was another door, and another faced it.

'Anyone at home?' the girl called out, but there was no response.

Miss Frayle followed her to the open door ahead. Light sprang up as she touched a switch.

'Gracious me!' Miss Frayle said in shocked tones, and other gave a sharp gasp.

'Oh, God!'

The sitting-room looked as if a hurricane had torn through it. A Queen Anne bureau against the wall had been burst open, the doors sagging. Books had been tumbled from shelves, papers scattered all over the floor. Drawers were wrenched wide, some tipped on to the floor. A rug was dragged aside, a lamp overturned. Pictures had been pulled down or hung crazily.

'What's happened? Hugh!' Sherry Carfax's voice rose hysterically. 'Hugh!' The echoes rang emptily through the flat, then silence. She turned suddenly. 'His bedroom — let's look there!' And Miss Frayle chased after her.

The bedroom was in much the same disorder as the other. Books, papers, were scattered over floor and bed. A dressing-table by the window had been shoved to one side and a lock on one of the drawers had been wrenched off. Drawers from a tallboy had been dragged out and their contents spilled everywhere. The wardrobe-cupboard looked as if a maniac had fought a way into it and out again.

A sudden draught blew through a door obviously leading into the bathroom. The scattered papers rustled and then, through the half-open door, came a faint, rhythmic creaking sound. Sherry Carfax turned a white, terrified face to Miss

Frayle, who gulped convulsively and caught her arm.

Together they advanced slowly and cautiously in the direction of the creaking noise. Suddenly Miss Frayle paused, relaxed, and gave a sigh of relief.

'The window in the bathroom! It's been left open and it's banging.'

'Oh yes! That's what it would be.' And the girl drew a deep breath and forced a smile to her lips. Then she added: 'I think the window leads to the fire-escape . . . '

Miss Frayle gave her a questioning look.

'They' — the other indicated the disorder around them — 'they probably went out that way.'

Miss Frayle nodded in agreement and moved forward. She switched on the bathroom light. Behind her came a shrill scream, while she herself could only goggle at the floor. Slumped against the bath, head sunk forward, was a man. A little tufted beard, grey-flecked, was buried in the whiteness of his shirt where a great crimson patch had spread over his heart. His pockets were turned inside out.

The lining of his coat was torn as if whoever had attacked him had frantically dragged at the inside pocket.

'Who — who is he?'

Miss Frayle's voice sounded, a far-away whisper in her ears.

'I don't know!' Sherry Carfax choked in reply. 'I — I've never seen him before.'

6

Shock for the Baron

During her association with Doctor Morelle, there were times when Miss Frayle had wished for an opportunity to deal, single-handed and alone, with a case of murder, mayhem or robbery, and present to the Doctor a *fait accompli*, the problem solved, before he himself had time to bring his massive intellect to bear on the mystery. It would have been a magnificent pin with which to deflate the balloon of his not inconsiderable egotism.

This was one of her favourite day-dreams: to find herself in such a situation with an unidentified corpse — preferably discreetly covered — the police baffled and Doctor Morelle himself utterly nonplussed. She, of course, would be in full command, not only of the situation but of herself. Speaking in a firm but modulated voice, she would reason quietly thus and thus, pointing out each clue that had been missed, linking together a chain of evidence which would lead unerringly to the criminal. All this while expressions of wonder and admiration would dawn upon the faces of the police, and even Doctor Morelle himself would be a veritable sun of respectful admiration.

Alas, her dream had never materialized. No such situation had ever arisen. If corpse there was, the police had not been baffled. Or if they had been, Doctor Morelle's ice-cold logic and reasoning had pointed to the solution of the crime while Miss Frayle was yet floundering, so to speak, on the outskirts of the mystery.

Now, as she goggled at the dead body of the stranger in the bathroom of Sir Hugh Albany's flat, her mind groped for some idea as to what course of action she should pursue. Her only positive reaction so far had been to communicate with Doctor Morelle at once. Alas! She could not think coherently of anything else but that.

Here, she realized, was a heaven-sent chance of bringing that favourite dream of hers to actuality — of showing the Doctor what she could do when the occasion arose. But for the life of her she had not the faintest idea how to set about it. The dead man was a stranger to her and, as she stared down at him, she could only think how pitiful and grotesque he looked lying there with his head against the bath.

Miss Frayle sighed tremulously. Behind her came muffled sobbing, and she returned to the bedroom to find Sherry Carfax crumpled in a chair. The girl turned a white, tear-stained face to her.

'I'm terrified,' she whispered. 'Let's get out of here quickly! I thought you were going to 'phone Doctor Morelle?' Without waiting for an answer, she went on agitatedly: 'Oh, where's Hugh? What's happened to Hugh?'

She was shaken and distraught, and Miss Frayle could see she was on the verge of collapse. She herself felt sick and faint, but the other's distress helped her pull herself together. She caught Sherry

Carfax's arm and said, in her most soothing voice:

'It's all right. Let's go into the sitting-room and I'll telephone from there.'

'Must we stay here at all?'

'I think we'd better — until Doctor Morelle comes,' Miss Frayle said, telling herself she would never again be able to enjoy her day-dream. For, instead of the calmly modulated tones, her voice had taken on a note that could only be compared to a nervous squeak.

They returned to the disordered sitting-room. The telephone was on a side-table which had not been over-turned. Miss Frayle turned to ask Lady Tonbridge's 'phone number but, as she opened her mouth to speak, the door-bell rang.

Both girls stared at each other a moment, and Miss Frayle felt a chill creep up her spine as the low trill of the bell echoed through the flat. Sherry Carfax swayed, her handkerchief pressed against her mouth, her eyes wide with terror.

The bell rang again, more insistently. For a moment Miss Frayle feared the other girl was going to break under the strain and cut loose with an hysterical shriek. Forcing herself to sound as calm as possible, she said quickly:

'We'd better go and see who it is.'

Her words had their effect on Sherry Carfax, who choked and managed to pull herself together sufficiently to gasp:

'It — it might be someone who can help . . . Please don't leave me! I'll come too!'

As they reached the hall the bell rang yet again, accompanied by a sharp knocking on the door.

'They — seem very per-persistent,' Miss Frayle said, trying desperately to prevent her voice from shaking. And with a sudden burst of courage she flung the door open violently.

Standing on the threshold were Doctor Morelle and Baron Xavier.

Miss Frayle gulped at the Doctor and then gave a little cry of relief. To her it seemed nothing short of miraculous that the Doctor should appear at this particular moment. In fact for a fleeting second she wondered if, by some uncanny power of telepathy, he had anticipated her telephone call and hastened to her assistance.

'Oh, Doctor Morelle! Thank goodness you've come!' she exclaimed. And added in the same breath: 'There's a dead man in the bathroom!'

The Doctor betrayed no emotion at her announcement. His calm features showed none of the mingled dismay, horror and consternation displayed by the Baron. He merely drew at his inevitable Le Sphinx and, stepping into the hall, observed quietly:

'Indeed, my dear Miss Frayle? Am I to assume that is the reason for your quitting Lady Tonbridge's without so much as hinting to me of your intention? Both Baron Xavier and I have been quite anxious about your and Miss Carfax's disappearance.' Turning to the other, he said; 'Miss Carfax, you appear some-what upset.'

'Where's Sir Hugh Albany?' she exclaimed. 'Something terrible's happened!'

The Doctor raised his hand. 'As I am unacquainted with him it is unlikely I should know anything of his where-abouts.'

'Baron Xavier,' the girl cried, 'you *must* know where Hugh is!'

If Doctor Morelle detected the desperate appeal in her question he appeared not to notice it. He awaited the other's reply. Beneath dark brows his eyes narrowed slightly and flicked a swift glance at the girl, then at the Baron and back to the girl again.

Baron Xavier shook his head.

'No, Sherry. I haven't seen him.' His voice was troubled. 'He hasn't arrived at Lady Tonbridge's. That was one of the reasons Doctor Morelle and I came along here. I was beginning to feel worried about him. Then I missed you and learned you had left with Miss Frayle. I found the Doctor and asked him if he knew where you'd gone — he said he didn't even know Miss Frayle had left. So I explained to him how you and I were anxious about Hugh —'

'Whereupon I assumed you had both

made your way to where you might naturally be expected to find him.' Doctor Morelle finished for him. There was a hint of impatience in his tone as he went on: 'However, these explanations for our being here are tedious and unnecessary. Miss Frayle —'

'Yes, Doctor?'

She answered him meekly. She was now beginning to view his advent with mixed feelings. Admittedly, she felt a tremendous relief at his presence. But while it seemed as if a great weight had been lifted from her shoulders, yet she could not help a feeling of chagrin that she had not one single constructive comment to suggest. All she had been able to offer was that there was a dead man in the bathroom. It was extremely galling.

'You referred to a lifeless individual in the bathroom,' he was reminding her. 'Instead of remaining rooted there, gaping first at Baron Xavier and then at myself, I suggest it would be more helpful if you led me to the body in order that I may make at least a cursory investigation.'

'Yes, Doctor Morelle.'

As she led the way he queried:

'Are you aware of the man's identity?'

'No,' she said over her shoulder.

'Have you telephoned the police?'

'No. You see, I —'

'Why not?'

Miss Frayle drew a deep breath. 'I was just going to telephone you when the door-bell rang and — and there you were.'

He made no comment, but Miss Frayle felt his eyes boring into the back of her neck were glinting with sardonic amusement.

'Good heavens, what's happened here?' the Baron exclaimed behind them as they entered the sitting-room. 'It's as if there's been a terrible fight or something! Look at the mess the place is in.'

While the Baron and Sherry Carfax remained in the sitting-room, Doctor Morelle followed Miss Frayle to the bathroom. The Doctor gave a mere fleeting glance at the signs of upheaval around him.

'In there,' Miss Frayle said, pointing to the bathroom. 'He's — he's on the floor.'

'Do not touch anything,' Doctor Morelle snapped over his shoulder. 'Inform the others not to touch *anything.*' And he went into the bathroom.

For a moment he stood surveying the inert figure before him. Then the open window attracted his attention and he stepped through it on to the fire-escape. It was an iron staircase zigzagging down the side of the block of flats to the darkness below. The adjacent building was but a few yards away, the space between them forming a black chasm. From where he was standing he could catch a glimpse of Jermyn Street.

After a moment he descended a few steps, paused, then turned and came back slowly and thoughtfully. On the threshold of the window leading into the bathroom he stood poised like some dark eagle, then stepped inside, his gaze on the door leading to the bedroom. Once more he turned his attention to the body.

Dropping to one knee, he peered closely into the bearded features, touched the forehead with the tips of his fingers, gently raised an inert hand and let it fall again. He stared closely at the crimson stain on the dead man's shirt-front, pulling the jacket away a little to examine it. He observed the wrenched-out pockets and began scanning the floor. A moment later he gave a little exclamation of satisfaction as, from under a fold of the man's coat, he picked up a small white square of pasteboard. It was the return half of a railway-ticket.

'Miss Frayle,' he called peremptorily.

She appeared in the doorway.

'Take these notes.'

'Oh, but — but, Doctor,' she protested, 'I've no notebook or pencil.'

'I might have known you would have come unprepared,' he remarked acidly.

Miss Frayle blushed faintly and replied in an aggrieved voice:

'Well, after all, I didn't expect to find dead bodies and have to take notes about them at midnight!'

But all she got from him was a dry 'Neither did I, my *dear* Miss Frayle!'

Whereupon he produced a slim note-book and slender gold pencil from his pocket and began writing.

'Time of death,' he murmured, 'between ten and eleven p.m. Cause: bullet entering the heart. Presumed victim travelled from Haywards Heath district.'

Miss Frayle cast him a look of admiration mixed with envy. It seemed so easy the way in which he had arrived at his conclusions. Yet, for the life of her, she could not have said whether the man had been shot or stabbed, any more than she would have been able to deduce the time of his death — and how the Doctor had reached the conclusion the stranger had travelled from Haywards Heath was completely beyond her.

Doctor Morelle replaced the return half of the railway-ticket under the coat where he had found it. As he straightened, there came a sudden startled gasp from the door.

'Stefan!'

The Doctor turned to Baron Xavier, who stood gripping the door as if for support. His face was deathly white, his horror-stricken gaze fixed on the dead

71

man. Then, with a broken cry, he knelt beside the body.

'Oh, my God!' he breathed. 'This is ghastly!'

Doctor Morelle eyed him through a cloud of cigarette-smoke, an enigmatic expression on his saturnine face.

7

Surprise for Miss Frayle

Baron Xavier turned to the Doctor.

'I know this man,' he exclaimed.

'So it would appear,' Doctor Morelle murmured, and Miss Frayle threw him a quick glance as she detected that familiar edge to his tone.

The Baron rose and grasped Doctor Morelle's arm. His good-looking features were drawn in hard lines, his mouth grim and set. Through his teeth he said:

'Doctor Morelle, you've got to find his murderer! Stefan Zusky was my greatest friend.'

'It will be of some assistance that you have been able to identify him,' the Doctor observed calmly. He fixed the other with a piercing gaze. 'Perhaps you would care to answer me some questions?'

The Baron hesitated almost imperceptibly, then:

'Anything!'

Doctor Morelle led the way back to the sitting-room. Sherry Carfax sank into a chair, her attention on Baron Xavier. A wave of sympathy swept over Miss Frayle at the grief that manifested itself on his face. He passed his hand across his forehead.

'I can't think,' he muttered, 'why this should happen to him. Stefan was such a *good* man. A most faithful friend and counsellor . . . ' Suddenly he burst out: 'I would have given anything — anything to have prevented this terrible happening!'

'Did you anticipate it, then?'

Doctor Morelle's query, quietly put as it was, cut through the room like cold steel. Amid the scene of disorder, in an atmosphere charged with emotions whose depths might be as illimitable as they were complex, the Doctor stood aloof, his tall figure imposing in his immaculate evening dress, his eyes narrowed with speculation.

Baron Xavier started slightly at Doctor Morelle's words. He flung him a quick, haggard look, then gave a despairing little shrug.

'Anticipate it?' he repeated. And went on bitterly: 'Why should I have done so?' He paused and again a frown darkened his face. 'On the other hand,' he said slowly, 'perhaps this blow was *not* entirely unexpected.'

'What do you mean?'

It was Sherry Carfax who spoke. He glanced at her, then went on in a troubled voice:

'Who knows what Fate holds for a man in these terrible times? Particularly a man like Stefan Zusky who remained staunch to me.'

'You are talking at quite considerable length, Baron Xavier, but saying little,' interposed Doctor Morelle. 'Are you suggesting the motive behind the murder may have some direct connection with you?'

The other nodded. 'It — it may have been a political enemy. I don't know.'

'I should wish to question you more closely,' the Doctor said precisely. 'I'm sure you will understand I do so only in the interests of justice.'

Baron Xavier bowed slightly.

'Was this man a personal friend of yours?'

The Baron's eyes were fixed intently on the Doctor as he answered: 'Officially he was my private secretary, as he had been my father's before me. But in reality he was more than that. He was the only friend I had left in the world.'

'In his capacity of secretary, what would his duties entail which might bring him into danger from your political enemies?'

Miss Frayle thought the Baron's attitude suddenly tensed before he made his reply. It was as if the question Doctor Morelle had put to him was one he found somewhat difficult to answer straightforwardly. He said, a certain abruptness in his tone:

'It is difficult to know exactly.'

'Can you not offer any suggestion?' the Doctor persisted.

'I — possibly while he was acting as a courier between my country and this, he might have put himself in danger from my enemies,' was the hesitant reply.

Doctor Morelle said quietly, 'Your ex-country, I presume you mean?'

Baron Xavier's jaw tightened. He seemed about to make an angry response, but the Doctor gave him no time.

'Do not misunderstand me, Baron Xavier. I merely wish to remind you to keep to the facts in this case, for it is when facts become coloured with extraneous embellishment that the truth grows more and more difficult to disentangle from fiction.'

The Baron made a little bow in acknowledgment of the Doctor's observation.

'You stated your secretary's duties included acting as courier between London and the Continent,' Doctor Morelle proceeded smoothly. 'When he was in this country, where did he reside?'

Again Miss Frayle thought she detected that almost imperceptible tension manifested by the other before he answered.

'At Stormhaven Towers —' he began,

and was interrupted by a sudden cry from Sherry Carfax.

'Hugh's home!'

He glanced at her and nodded, then back to Doctor Morelle. 'That is so — Sir Hugh Albany's home in Sussex.'

'In the vicinity of Haywards Heath,' the Doctor added.

Baron Xavier gave him a sharp look and was about to say something, but Sherry Carfax interrupted him with:

'Hugh never told me anything about it.'

The Baron turned to her. 'I'm sorry,' he said, and there was a new note of gentleness in his tone, 'but Hugh understood I wished to keep Stefan's presence there a secret.'

'Oh . . . ' the girl said, but a puzzled frown flitted across her face and lingered there.

'Why secret?'

It was Doctor Morelle once again who put the question quietly but incisively through a puff of cigarette-smoke. The Baron spread out his hands in a little gesture of helplessness.

'It is perhaps difficult for you to

appreciate the difficulties we were in, Doctor. The — country that *was* mine' — with an eye on Doctor Morelle he chose his words carefully — 'has been in a state of political chaos since the Royal House was overthrown. Those who drove me out undoubtedly have agents abroad. I didn't know whether there might be any in this country, and so Stefan and I agreed it would be wiser for him to remain under cover.'

He paused a moment, dabbed his mouth with a silk handkerchief from his breast-pocket, and then continued:

'He had contacts which made it possible for him to travel to and fro without his identity being in danger, but that was only so long as his association with me remained undiscovered.' He emphasized the words deliberately. 'That was why Sir Hugh so very kindly allowed him to stay at Stormhaven Towers while he was over here.'

Doctor Morelle eyed the tip of his cigarette abstractedly.

'Have you any suspicion regarding any individual or individuals who may be connected with this murder? Had the deceased any particular enemy, to your knowledge?'

'I know no more than I have already told you.'

For a moment there was silence. Then suddenly Sherry Carfax jumped to her feet with a sharp exclamation.

'What are we doing, just talking — talking like this?' She pointed at Doctor Morelle. 'Can't you see something's happened to Hugh? The Baron's secretary had been staying at Stormhaven Towers. Now we find him dead here — in Hugh's flat! And Hugh is missing! Isn't it obvious there must be some connection between the murder and Hugh? I know something's happened to him! I know it!'

She crossed to Doctor Morelle, her face anguished.

'You must do something!' she cried. '*You must find out what's happened to Hugh!*'

'Calm yourself,' Doctor Morelle murmured. 'Rest assured everything possible will be done —'

'Oh! . . . Oh, good gracious!'

The Doctor swung impatiently upon Miss Frayle, who had uttered the sudden, quiet exclamation. The other two turned to look at her.

'My *dear* Miss Frayle!' remarked Doctor Morelle icily. 'In what profound depths are you floundering? Or is it merely that you have discovered the presence of a mouse?'

For once, however, Miss Frayle was heedless of his sarcasm. Her attention was focused intently upon the floor, where a draught from the open door was gently blowing one or two of the many papers scattered about the disordered room. Her eyes remained fixed on a silver-framed photograph which had just been revealed, its glass upwards and broken, underneath some fluttering pages.

Ignoring the Doctor's and the others' scrutiny, she advanced slowly towards the photograph, paused to stare down at it, then with a sudden movement picked it up.

Her eyes were now saucer-like behind her spectacles as she regarded it as if mesmerized. A moment, and then slowly she glanced up at Doctor Morelle.

'Doctor!' she breathed. 'It *is* him! That man I told you about in the mews this evening . . . *the man with his face covered in blood*!'

8

The Unpredictable Doctor Morelle

'What do you mean?'

Sherry Carfax flung out the question, her voice hitting an agitated note as she crossed quickly to Miss Frayle. She took the photograph.

'This is Hugh!' She stared at Miss Frayle. 'What do you mean — the man in the mews?'

'Oh, dear — oh, dear,' gulped Miss Frayle in distress. 'Then it was him — Sir Hugh Albany!'

Doctor Morelle was at her side.

'Are you quite sure, Miss Frayle?' he demanded sharply. 'We cannot afford to make an error in a matter as vital as this.'

'Positive,' Miss Frayle told him firmly.

For the benefit of Sherry Carfax and the Baron, who had turned his gaze on her intently, she recapitulated the story of her encounter in the Mayfair mews.

Quickly and with, for her, remarkably little digression, she described her meeting with the young man and his subsequent disappearance upon her return to the mews with the brandy. Sherry Carfax's face had grown ashen with anxiety and Miss Frayle gave her a sympathetic look as she ended her story.

'But what's happened to Hugh now?' Sherry Carfax cried. 'He couldn't just have vanished into thin air!'

'What time elapsed between your leaving the injured man and your return, Miss Frayle?' Doctor Morelle asked.

'Well, it — it's rather difficult for me to remember exactly.'

Beneath the agonized gaze of the other girl whom she longed desperately to help, and the keen dissecting stare from Doctor Morelle, Miss Frayle began to fluster.

'Approximately?' the Doctor rapped at her impatiently.

'The — the place I got the brandy from,' Miss Frayle stammered, 'was round the corner —'

'Did your errand take you five minutes, five hours or five days?' exclaimed Doctor

Morelle through his teeth.

'Oh, I couldn't have been more than ten minutes at the very most,' Miss Frayle said unhappily. 'I was quick as could be —'

The telephone cut across her words with dramatic suddenness and impulsively Sherry Carfax rushed to answer it. Doctor Morelle, however, moving without apparent haste, reached it first.

'I think it would be better if I spoke,' he observed quietly and lifted the receiver. The others watching him heard him say:

'This *is* Sir Hugh Albany's flat . . . Who is that?'

The others saw him pause and flick the ash off his cigarette. No sign was to be read in his sharply etched features except for a slight narrowing of his eyes.

'Who is it?' Sherry Carfax queried in a low voice.

But he ignored her as he spoke into the telephone again.

'At what time was this? . . . Thank you. I will be there as quickly as possible, Doctor Bennett.' And he replaced the receiver.

'Doctor Bennett?' queried Sherry Carfax.

'What did he say?' Baron Xavier cut in.

Doctor Morelle stood for a moment in thought without apparently hearing the questions the others threw at him. Then he turned to the girl.

'Sir Hugh Albany has been found. He is at present in the care of Doctor Bennett.'

'What's happened to him? Is he badly hurt? I must see him!'

'Calm yourself,' Doctor Morelle said quietly. 'I can express no personal opinion as to the extent of his injuries for the obvious reason that I have not examined him. According to Doctor Bennett, however, he is suffering from the effects of a bullet-wound in the head. As to what *happened* to him — ' He considered the question judiciously before proceeding:

'The details at present are largely a matter of conjecture. However . . . ' He cleared his throat and continued. 'However, I think it can safely be assumed he was murderously attacked and, moreover, the attempt on his life and the murder of your secretary' — with a glance at Baron

Xavier — 'have some bearing upon each other, possibly even actuated by the same motive —'

'Doctor Morelle!'

Sherry Carfax's voice as she faced him rose forcefully, her eyes blazing. 'This may be a matter of academic interest to you, but *I* don't give a brass button who tried to kill Hugh or why!'

'My dear Miss Carfax —'

But his protest was unceremoniously brushed aside.

'All I'm concerned with,' Sherry Carfax continued, her voice shrill, almost hysterical, 'is that Hugh's been hurt and is in the hands of some doctor I've never heard of! Will you be good enough to tell me where he is so that I can go to him at once?'

Miss Frayle's eyes were wide and her mouth a large O as she listened to Sherry Carfax's attack on the Doctor. Secretly applauding her courage, at the same time she had the uneasy feeling the earth must open and swallow her up for daring to confront the formidable Doctor while he was in the very act, so to speak, of propounding a theory.

Her surprise was to heighten to utter amazement, however, the next moment. Not a muscle of Doctor Morelle's lean, saturnine countenance had stirred during Sherry Carfax's outburst. Perhaps his basilisk stare probed a little deeper beyond her own indignant face, that was all. Then, the corners of his thin mouth twitching faintly, he inclined his head.

'I stand rebuked,' he murmured gently. 'If you will permit me first to telephone the police in order to advise them of the situation here, we will then proceed immediately to Doctor Bennett.'

It was physically impossible for Miss Frayle's gaze or mouth to grow any wider. But as Doctor Morelle turned back to the telephone and dialled, she was experiencing the utmost difficulty in crediting her senses. Could she have heard him aright? Or had the evening's events proved too much for her with the result her imagination was now playing her light-headed tricks? The infallible, the omniscient, Doctor Morelle admitting himself to be in the wrong — and to a slip of a girl, at that! Wonders would never cease!

Miss Frayle kept a diary, and already was consumed with impatience to jot down her account of what had occurred during the last few hours. But now, capping the evening's succession of dramatic events, here was the most exciting moment of all! Here was something to which only the brightest red ink would do justice — she would find it impossible to describe the Doctor's mild acceptance of Sherry Carfax's rebuke in words alone sufficiently colourful. In fact, she decided there and then, all she felt she would be able to note would be simply:

'*He has a heart after all!*'

More than that would be beyond her powers of description.

9

Sufficient for the Day

Although it was now well past midnight, the lights were gleaming from the ground-floor windows of Doctor Bennett's house as he opened the door to them.

'How is he, Doctor Bennett?' asked Sherry Carfax in a low, tense voice. 'Can I see him?'

Bennett made no immediate reply. Closing the door behind them, and followed by Sherry Carfax, Miss Frayle and Baron Xavier, with Doctor Morelle darkly watchful in the background, he led the way into his consulting-room.

'Sir Hugh is in a nursing-home round the corner,' he said to the girl quietly. 'I think you might ask the nurse on duty if you could see him. But of course you won't be able to speak to him.'

'I'll take you round there if you like,' the Baron put in quickly, and Sherry

Carfax gave him a grateful look. She turned to Bennett.

'How did all this happen?'

'That's something I'm afraid I can't explain.' The other threw an oblique glance at Doctor Morelle. 'The whole business is mysterious, to say the least. Matter of fact, I was wondering if I should have 'phoned the police. Had you not answered my 'phone call, Doctor Morelle, I intended doing so.'

Doctor Morelle inclined his head slightly and Miss Frayle gave him a long look. Composed and impassive, he regarded Doctor Bennett from behind the veil of smoke from his inevitable cigarette. The other was speaking to the girl again.

'He's had a bad time, Miss Carfax, and at present is still unconscious —'

Sherry Carfax uttered a little moan and Miss Frayle moved towards her sympathetically. 'How did it happen?' the girl cried. 'How — why should this have happened to him?'

Doctor Bennett's expression was kindly. 'All I can tell you,' he said gently, 'is that my housekeeper found him at about half past ten this evening, lying in the basement area.'

'What length of time had he been there?' Doctor Morelle interposed.

'That I can't say. I dined out this evening and then went on to see a patient. I returned about ten, noticed nothing unusual and was working in my consulting-room when the housekeeper came in and told me the news. Between us we got him up here. He was unconscious, of course. I 'phoned the nursing-home and they took care of him right away.'

'You say the nature of his injury is compatible with that inflicted by a revolver-bullet?' It was Doctor Morelle again who put the question.

The other nodded. 'Sir Hugh's leg was lacerated and he was badly bruised, no doubt through falling down the basement steps, but the head injury appeared to me to be a bullet-wound.'

'I see . . . '

Miss Frayle noticed that Sherry Carfax was looking paler and she made a movement to attract Doctor Morelle's attention. He interpreted her glance and observed to Bennett:

'Perhaps Miss Carfax might go along to the nursing-home now?'

Doctor Bennett nodded, and at once Baron Xavier moved to the girl's side. At the door she turned.

'Are — are you coming, Doctor Morelle?'

He shook his head. 'It is unnecessary at the moment. Sir Hugh is in most capable hands. I may, perhaps, visit him tomorrow.' He turned to Bennett. 'I would like a brief word with you.'

'Of course.'

'I'll wait for Miss Carfax,' the Baron said, 'and see her safely home.' And he took her arm. They went out, Bennett following them, into the hall.

Eyebrows raised quizzically, Doctor Morelle suddenly swung round on Miss Frayle.

'Well, Miss Frayle . . . ?' he fired at her.

She jumped like a startled deer, her spectacles sliding down her nose. At that moment her thoughts and sympathies were with Sherry Carfax, and the

Doctor's unexpected query cut into her sentimental ruminations with the keenness of a knife.

'Oh . . . ' she exclaimed involuntarily. 'Well — what, Doctor Morelle?' she said hesitantly, adjusting her spectacles and gazing up at him. He sighed.

'And is that all you have to offer?' he asked. 'Merely the faint echo of my own question? Come, come! Is it possible you have reached no conclusions in this remarkable affair — no theory to advance? After all, you were, one might say, first on the scene, both insofar as Sir Hugh Albany is concerned and Baron Xavier's secretary.'

'I — I suppose I ought really to have some ideas,' she agreed nervously. 'And — and yet,' she concluded lamely, 'I can't think of anything.'

Doctor Morelle's finely chiselled nose rose higher as he observed: 'Perhaps after all that may prove fortunate for all concerned, my dear Miss Frayle!' He turned to Bennet, who had just come back to the consulting-room and was gazing first at Doctor Morelle then at

Miss Frayle. 'Your patient might have lain unconscious and undiscovered some considerable time?'

The other nodded slowly. 'If he fell into the area after dusk, he might certainly have stayed there all night.'

'You obtained his telephone number from papers on him, no doubt?'

'Yes. His address was in his notebook.'

Doctor Morelle nodded, and there was a little pause while he surveyed the tip of his cigarette in silence. Then: 'That would appear to be about all we can do tonight,' and moved towards the door. Miss Frayle followed him.

'I shall be in touch with the nursing-home during the night, of course,' Bennet told him as they reached the front door, 'and if there are any developments, I'll let you know.'

'Thank you, Doctor Bennett,' Miss Frayle smiled at him. 'I do hope Sir Hugh will be all right. Poor Miss Carfax — I don't know what she'll do if he . . . ' She left the possibility unsaid and her voice trailed into silence. The other murmured something sympathetically and then said

95

to Doctor Morelle:

'Hope you'll get a taxi all right.'

'If we fail to, the distance is not too great for us to walk. And possibly the cool night air will prove beneficial to Miss Frayle!' He cast her a sardonic smile. 'I fear the evening has been a somewhat hectic one for her.'

Miss Frayle offered no comment as they walked away.

They paused on a corner and the Doctor glanced up and down for signs of a taxi, Miss Frayle observing brightly: 'Well, Doctor Morelle, and now where?'

He favoured her with one of his more ironic stares and, hastily stifling a yawn, murmured:

'Where else but home?'

'You didn't really mean what you told Doctor Bennett?'

'Why not?'

'You're going to drop the case when you've only just begun on it?' she protested.

'I am unaware I made any reference to that effect,' he replied acidly. 'I merely propose not to lose any sleep over it. In any event, there is at the present juncture little more I can do. The police will by now have finished their work at the flat. Sir Hugh is in safe hands. The Baron will undoubtedly be escorting Miss Carfax safely home.' He smiled thinly and queried: 'What else should *I* be doing other than retiring to bed?'

'I — I — well, I thought you might want to go back to the flat and — and have a look round.'

He regarded her pityingly.

'If you can indicate what precisely might be achieved by my so doing, I shall be intrigued to learn it. Personally, all that would result would be loss of sleep and the possibility of a consequent headache in the morning.'

He relapsed into silence and Miss Frayle, suitably crestfallen, had nothing further to say as they made their way towards Harley Street.

But if she said nothing she was thinking hard. After such an exciting evening, it seemed to her extremely tame to be going home as if nothing out of the ordinary had happened. Her mind ran quickly over the events since she had left her hair-dresser only a few hours ago. First, the strange encounter with the man in the mews who now turned out to be Sir Hugh Albany. Then her meeting with Sherry Carfax, their arrival at the flat and the discovery of Baron Xavier's secretary, murdered.

Doctor Morelle's voice broke into her thoughts.

'I confess certain aspects of the case interest me,' he murmured musingly, and she glanced up at him with interest. He went on: 'An inquiry into the activities of Sir Hugh Albany, for instance, might be informative —'

'Sir Hugh . . . ?' Miss Frayle exclaimed, her eyes widening.

'In regard to his association with Baron Xavier,' the Doctor went on, still half to himself.

'Sherry Carfax seemed surprised about that secretary staying at Sir Hugh's house,' Miss Frayle put in, determined not to appear altogether in the dark, although in fact she had not the slightest idea what strange, dark theories were running through the Doctor's mind.

He glanced at her, the corners of his mouth quirking with amusement.

'I am intrigued to note, my dear Miss Frayle,' he remarked, 'that our minds pursue a similar course.'

'Great minds think alike, Doctor!'

Studiously ignoring her bright comment he murmured:

'If Stefan Zusky habitually used Albany's house in Sussex as his secret headquarters while in this country, as Xavier suggested, what errand brought him to Albany's flat — to the Baron Xavier's somewhat apparent surprise —?'

'Oh, dear . . . '

He turned at Miss Frayle's sudden interruption, to find her contorting her face in agony.

'Now what has occurred to you?' he queried. 'For only the most painful effort at concentration could produce the curious grimace you are wearing at the moment!'

'I've just thought of something,' she said with repressed excitement.

'I stand amazed!' Doctor Morelle

replied caustically. And then added: 'If, nevertheless, you would give some expression to your cogitations and come to the point immediately, you would tax my not entirely unlimited patience less. What incident *have* you suddenly recalled to mind?'

But Miss Frayle was muttering doubtfully to herself: 'Oh, I don't know . . . perhaps it's too silly after all.'

The Doctor glared at her and spoke through his teeth, obviously suffering under a certain strain.

'My dear Miss Frayle, if you cannot give coherent voice to whatever curious thought-process may be threading itself through the extraordinary phenomena you are pleased to refer to as your mind, kindly remain silent!'

'Well, actually, I — I was thinking of the man in the mews,' Miss Frayle said unabashed. 'The one I told you about.'

'Are you referring to Albany?'

'Oh, no. I mean the other one — the man who saw me into a taxi after Sir Hugh had disappeared.'

She paused for a moment thoughtfully.

'What about him?' Doctor Morelle snapped impatiently.

'You see . . . he was at Lady Tonbridge's party tonight — I've just remembered about him. I recognized him when he was talking to Sherry Carfax, and later I asked her who he was. She seemed to be frightened of him —'

'His name, his *name*!' Doctor Morelle groaned.

'I've forgotten it,' Miss Frayle admitted meekly. 'She did tell me, but it's gone now. She went on hurriedly as if to avert the storm she feared might burst upon her from the Doctor. 'I remember she said he was a friend of Sir Hugh's — or he pretended to be — but really he had some kind of hold over him —'

'What fantastic rigmarole and farradiddle are you trying to tell me?' exploded Doctor Morelle. 'Are you trying to suggest that this friend of Albany's — who isn't his friend — whose name you cannot remember —?'

'I just thought' — Miss Frayle managed to get in edgeways — 'it was rather odd this man being in the mews the same time

Sir Hugh was there, and then at Lady Tonbridge's afterwards. I don't suppose there's anything in it really,' she went on dubiously. 'Or do you think it's funny, too?'

Doctor Morelle's saturnine features glowered at her through a cloud of cigarette-smoke.

'No words, even from my somewhat extensive vocabulary, could possibly describe what I think!' Drawing a deep breath, he went on: 'However, under the circumstances, that is of little moment — if I *could* find words with which to express myself, they would be wasted upon you!'

And turning, he stalked ahead, his sword-stick tapping sharply on the pavement, looking, Miss Frayle decided, for all the world like some dark and gaunt bird of prey heading for its crag-hidden eyrie. She caught up with him and, for the rest of the way to the house in Harley Street, remained miserably silent.

10

The Purple Lake

Charles Gresham was not particularly clever, though possessed of a foxish cunning. Partly because of this he was to be reckoned dangerous. A clever man knows when to draw the line, even though his objective remains unattained. Gresham never knew when he was beaten — until he had got what he wanted or until a stronger character than his own halted him.

Completely without scruples, wholly devoid of conscience, acknowledging no obligations, his thin veneer of superficial charm covered an entirely ruthless brutality. He should have been a social outcast. Under any other conditions but those accepted and condoned by the circles in which he moved, he must long since have been expelled. In fact he was not only tolerated, he enjoyed a certain popularity.

He could entertain, knew a good horse, a good cigar, a good wine and made it apparent that he came of a 'good' family.

It was enough for the less discerning.

And Mrs. Latimer was by no means an undiscerning woman. While she, too, was dangerous, she was also clever, much cleverer than Gresham could ever hope to be. Tonight, as she looked at him, it was apparent something out of the ordinary had happened. He stood by the fireplace with a large whisky-and-soda in his hand, his evening clothes too perfectly cut, and looking slightly too well-groomed. But Mrs. Latimer knew something had gone wrong. His hard, rather staring eyes had a glassy glitter, a vein swelled thickly across his forehead.

She said tersely: 'What's happened?'

Gresham took a drink from his glass and, without replying, stared down at what was left, slowly swirling it round and round. Then suddenly he lifted the glass again, drained it at a gulp and strolled, his air elaborately casual, across to the corner table and poured himself more whisky. Reaching for the soda, he said:

'You didn't go to the reception.'

'I've been waiting for you. I never put one foot in front of the other without knowing where I'm going.' She paused, eyeing him carefully. 'I'd like to know just what has happened. I'd like to know now, before you get drunk on my whisky.'

He gave a short laugh.

'I shan't get drunk,' he said. 'I could drink a barrel tonight and, believe me, it wouldn't have the slightest effect.'

He gulped thirstily from the refilled glass, lowered it and stared at her truculently.

'Did you — kill him?' Cleo Latimer said in a low voice.

'I don't know . . . As a matter of fact I don't think I did. I fired and saw him stagger. It was one of the most enjoyable things I've —'

'Don't gloat!' Her voice was like a whiplash. 'Give me the facts. Then go off and gloat by yourself.'

'I waited for him,' Gresham replied sullenly, 'and then let him have it. But he couldn't have been as near as I thought — the light was bad, I suppose, and my aim —' He broke off with a shrug. 'Anyway, he staggered and fell, then pulled himself up and started to run, half-stumbling —'

'Where was this?'

'In the mews where I told you I'd wait for him. I went after him and pulled the trigger again, but the blasted thing jammed. While I was trying to get it to work, he'd got away up the mews. Then I heard someone coming along from the other end and I dodged back and waited. Albany must have collapsed and this damn' woman found him —'

'Woman?'

'Yes. A half-witted young girl.'

'So far, you'd bungled it nicely!' she cut in bitterly. 'What did you do then? Go and help her?'

His eyes flamed at her biting sarcasm. 'I stayed where I was out of sight,' he said, shifting from one foot to the other. 'She went off to get help and he must have crawled somewhere and hidden — it was much darker by then. Anyway, I couldn't spot the swine —'

'And so you left him to get away?'

The utter contempt in her voice stung him into a smouldering fury.

'What the hell else could I do?' he snarled. 'I told you he'd crawled somewhere in the dark — and then that girl came back anyway, and I just had to pack it up.'

She spread out her slim, white hands and said mockingly: 'I wonder you didn't break down and cry on the girl's shoulder, and tell her your troubles —!'

'Cut it out, Cleo!' he broke in. And now his eyes were dangerous. 'I've been through enough tonight.' The woman's face hardened, its beauty masked for a moment by a deadly rapaciousness. Then she said softly:

'All right, Charles. What next?'

Slightly mollified by her change of tone — Cleo Latimer knew well enough how to use her voice to persuade, cajole, threaten or placate, as occasion demanded — he said:

'As I say, this girl, all gaga — wore horn-rims, she did — came back. She'd got a glass of brandy. I managed to bluff her. Told her she'd been the victim of a trick and pushed her off in a taxi. When she'd gone, I went back to the mews again. But still no sign of the blighter. Of course by now he'd had time enough to get away altogether.' He took a deep gulp from his glass and over the rim his protruberant eyes stared at her.

She drew thoughtfully at the cigarette in the long holder clenched between her perfect teeth. He went on:

'So I went on to my flat to change and arrived at Lady Tonbridge's reception. You weren't there. But Sherry Carfax had turned up and was fussing like hell about where her precious Hugh had got to. I didn't enlighten her one little bit!' He paused and then observed, theatrically laconic: 'Someone else was there, too . . .'

'Who?'

'The damn'-fool girl I'd met in the mews!'

'*What!*'

The other's lips drew back in a humourless smile. He said:

'Made you jump, eh?'

'Did she recognize you?'

Gresham took a long drink reflectively.

'I'm not sure if she did, or not.' He shrugged indifferently. 'Not that it matters. As I say, she looked a complete half-wit. But as a point of interest, I did ask about her. Her name's Frayle. She's a sort of secretary or assistant to some doctor. Doctor Morrow or Merrill — some name like that.'

'Not Doctor Morelle, by any chance?' Cleo Latimer inquired softly.

'Believe that was the name,' he said casually. 'Tall, saturnine-looking chap.'

There was a little silence. Then Mrs. Latimer observed, through a cloud of cigarette-smoke:

'I think you're going to need another drink, Charles. I've never met Doctor Morelle, but I know a bit about him.'

'So what?' the other demanded indifferently.

'Only that he happens to be something of a criminologist. He's assisted Scotland Yard many times, and if this secretary of his tells him about tonight's business — which she's almost bound to do — it's not inconceivable that he might put in a little snooping.'

Gresham stared at her for a moment, scowling slightly. Then he blurted out:

'I should worry if he does! He couldn't pin a thing on me. Not a thing.'

'I hope you're right, Charles.'

He glared at her, then grinned wolfishly. 'What's on your mind, Cleo? Trying to scare me?'

She shook her head.

'I'm merely suggesting,' she offered, almost gently, 'it was a trifle unfortunate that the one person you had to bump into this evening turns out to be Doctor Morelle's secretary.'

'Oh, to hell with your Doctor Morelle!' he retorted. 'I tell you he's got nothing on me.' And, dismissing the idea, he went on: 'Anyway, I hung around at Lady Tonbridge's, just in case Hugh did turn up. But there was no sign of him. Sherry told me she'd phoned his flat once or twice, and got no reply. It seemed to me a good idea if I drifted along there and had a look round —'

'In God's name what for?' she exclaimed, her voice rising.

Her sudden interruption brought his

eyes up sharply, and once again he gave her that protruberant stare. Negligently, he put his hand into his inside pocket and produced a folded piece of paper. With an elaborate air of casualness, he extended it to her.

'I forgot to mention this,' he said.

She eyed him carefully and took the piece of paper.

'It's a telegram,' he went on, still with studied nonchalance. 'I picked it up in the mews. It must have fallen out of Albany's pocket.'

She read aloud:

'*IMPERATIVE SEE X STOP IF ANYTHING HAPPENS SEE PURPLE LAKE STOP WILL BE AT YOUR FLAT TONIGHT PLEASE INFORM STOP ZUSKY*'

Cleo Latimer's expression was like a mask as she took her eyes from the telegram.

'*That* is why I went along to Albany's flat,' Gresham said.

11

Worth a Million

Mrs. Latimer tapped the telegram and said:

'Don't you think you'd better tell me, Charles, exactly what's happened?'

Gresham answered her with a half-sneering smile.

'Not yet, Cleo. First you and I are going to exchange confidences. You see, although I'm not as cautious as you, there are times when *I*, too, like to know where I'm going —'

'What are you trying to say?'

The other paused and then went on coolly. 'I want to know all the details of your scheme about Baron Xavier. I don't want to be kept in the dark any longer.'

'You're too stupid, Charles,' Mrs. Latimer said slowly, 'and I'm not going to trust my secret with you. If you weren't a fool you wouldn't be taking the attitude you're taking now. I know what I'm doing and I'm handing out the orders. It's your job to obey them.'

Gresham made a movement of protest, but she cut him short.

'You and I have worked together for a long time, and so far you've never suffered as a result. In fact, it's been pretty easy going for you — you haven't even had to think.' Her lip curled and he scowled at the implied doubt in her tone that he was, in fact, capable of contributing much thinking to their partnership. She went on:

'All you have to do is what I've told you, and leave the rest to me.' She turned from him, her teeth clenched hard on her cigarette-holder. 'If you're not satisfied with the set-up,' she threw at him over her shoulder, 'you know just what you can do about that. I believe I'm quite capable of handling this alone.'

She faced him again. He met her long, level stare with a shifty glance. He knew there was no doubt she meant what she said. There was no need for her to rave at him or bluster. Her voice, her whole attitude, was one of complete self-assurance. Instinctively he cowered beneath the domination of her personality and the knowledge that she held the whip-hand and could make him jump through the hoop whenever she wanted.

Angrily he burst out: 'But damn it, Cleo, I've got to know what we're doing! You can't expect me to work in the dark. All I know is, you've got some kind of set-up planned for Xavier. But what's on the end of it?'

Her eyes, that had been a smoky greenish-grey, were now a brilliant blue as she answered him coolly.

'Not less than a million pounds, Charles,' she murmured.

He choked and his protuberant eyes literally goggled at her. For a moment he found difficulty in speaking. Then at last he gulped and said, his voice shaking with suppressed excitement:

'A million, Cleo? D'you really mean that?'

'I'm not in the habit of making jokes in the wrong places,' was her answer. There was a sudden warmth about her personality that had not been there before. It was as if the prospect of the prize she contemplated had thawed some of her coolness. Her eyes dilated and sparkled.

'It's the last trick, Charles,' she told him softly. 'The last trick of the game. I'll win it . . . and then we'll finish.' She paused and then continued: 'A million to share between us. Do you want to stay with me, Charles? Or do you want to get out?'

He began to speak, but she interrupted him: 'If you're going to stay, don't forget it's on my terms. You'll do what I say without question. You'll obey my instructions because there'll be a reason for it. Understand? Either that, or play the hand out on your own and get out of here now. Make up your mind.'

The other gave her that wolfish, mirthless grin and raised his glass to her.

'Whatever you say, Cleo,' he responded hoarsely. 'I'm with you all the way.' She noticed his hand trembled violently so that the whisky slopped over the glass, and she smiled to herself. It was a smile without a vestige of humour in it.

Gresham put down his drink and passed his handkerchief over his forehead that was suddenly glistening. She indicated the telegram she was still holding:

'So you went to his flat? What did you find?'

The other cleared his throat and there was a firmness in his tone as he answered: 'To say the least of it, that telegram is pretty oddly worded. 'X', of course, obviously refers to Xavier.

But that bit about '*If anything happens see Purple Lake*' — what the hell was all that about? And then who was this chap, Zusky, who was going to be at Albany's flat tonight?'

Cleo Latimer made no comment and the other went on:

'It was the reference to the Purple Lake that rang a bell,' he said. 'I remembered a picture Albany had at the flat. It was a small picture. Oil-painting of a lake with some trees round it, in the evening. And the shadows on the water made it look a sort of purple colour.'

'That was very smart of you to

remember it, Charles,' Mrs. Latimer murmured.

'Oh, I'm not dumb all the time,' he responded, and there was an edge to his voice.

'You were saying about this picture,' she reminded him.

'I wondered what was so important about it that made it necessary for this Zusky to mention it in the telegram. Of course the most obvious suggestion was that the picture covered up a wall-safe. If that was the case, I thought it would be interesting to see what that wall-safe contained.'

'And so you thought you'd like to poke your nose into something which you knew nothing about and which might land you into a jam?'

He glared at her. 'Why do you have to put it that way, Cleo? You know as well as I do that if Albany talks, we're sunk. Supposing I could have got something on him, it might have been useful to us both. That telegram looked like a godsend to me, and I was damn' well going to make the most of it.'

'How did you get into the flat?'

'Fire-escape.'

'All sounds very melodramatic!'

'Sneer if you like,' he retorted. 'I didn't want anyone to know I'd been near there tonight — considering what's happened to Albany.'

'And you're sure no one did see you there?'

'I'm positive,' he said.

'Supposing this man Zusky had arrived while you were there?' she asked him quietly.

He paused a moment before replying. 'That was a risk I had to run.' Then he said: 'Anyway, he didn't arrive.'

'Didn't he?' Her question was put quietly, almost negligently, and he shot her a puzzled look.

'I told you,' he snarled. 'No one saw me at Albany's flat tonight.'

She made no commen and he went on: 'The picture of the Purple Lake was there, all right, and I took it down.'

'Well?'

'There was nothing behind it.'

'So?' she said, eyeing him narrowly.

'I was convinced that picture pointed to something,' he went on grimly. 'Why else should it have been mentioned in that telegram —'

'You already said that,' she reminded him.

'Cut it out, Cleo!' he rasped. 'That funny stuff won't help us.'

'It doesn't look as if your snooping round Albany's flat has helped us much, either,' she rapped back at him. Then added wearily: 'Anyway, what did you do next?'

'I went through the sitting-room with a fine tooth-comb, but I didn't hit on a thing. Then I tried his bedroom, but I didn't turn up anything there, either.'

'You must have left the place in a fine old mess by the time you'd finished,' she mocked him.

He shrugged. 'I didn't worry about that. I had to work fast —'

He broke off suddenly to stare at her. Cleo Latimer's lovely face was deathly pale and deep shadows had appeared under her eyes.

'Cleo! What's the matter?' he said.

'I — I'll be all right in a minute.' She spoke in a painful gasp and sank into a chair. He crossed to her anxiously.

'Here, take a drink,' he said, holding out his glass. But she waved it aside.

'Don't — don't fuss!' she murmured.

He stood there indecisively watching her. He noticed with relief that the colour was slowly coming back to her face.

'Feeling better?' he said.

She nodded. The shadows that had been under her eyes were disappearing with her pallor.

'Just — just an attack of faintness,' she said.

'My God, you scared me,' he growled. 'Thought you were going to pass out on me.'

She gave him a stiff little smile. 'Don't overdo the anxiety stuff, Charles.'

As he began a vigorous protest, she went on: 'Give me a cigarette.'

She took one from his case and fitted it into her holder, and he lit it for her. 'So the Purple Lake didn't get you anywhere?' she queried. 'What happened next?'

He hesitated. 'Well . . . I left.'

'By the fire-escape?'

He nodded. 'No one saw me.'

'You seem so sure about that. How do you know?'

'I took damn' good care —'

She laughed shortly. 'All right, all right! I don't suppose you were seen.'

She paused a moment and then asked suddenly: 'By the way, where's that gun?'

He took the small black automatic from his pocket.

'I'd better get rid of it,' he said.

'Give it me.' She extended her hand.

Reluctantly he let her take it and she slipped it into the rosewood secretaire. She leaned against it for a moment and then picked up the telegram again.

'Did you notice where this was sent from?'

'Haywards Heath,' Gresham answered promptly, and then broke off with an exclamation: 'Albany's got a place down there! Stormhaven Towers.'

Mrs. Latimer nodded.

'You mean — you mean that's where this chap's been staying?' the other asked.

'It seems obvious. Albany's a great friend of Xavier. It looks as if Zusky's been staying down there.'

'I thought the place had been shut up for the last year or two.'

'That was the impression Albany gave me, too,' she said. 'Perhaps that was the impression he intended to give us.'

Gresham glanced at her sharply. Her face was enigmatic.

'What is all this?' he burst out. 'Xavier and Albany — and now this fellow, Zusky! What *is* your game? How do these three tie up with that million quid? Xavier can't have that amount of money. He's just another refugee who was lucky to get out with the clothes he stood up in. Surely you haven't got any damn'-fool idea that he —'

'I've already told you not to ask questions.' She froze him into silence. 'Don't let me have to keep on telling you. I find it a little boring.'

He eyed her from beneath brows drawn together in puzzlement. Then he shrugged.

'Have it your own way,' he muttered.

'For half a million, I'm happy to let you do the talking.'

'I'm worried about Albany,' she said thoughtfully. 'Thanks to you, he may still be able to throw a spanner in the works.'

'I can still take care of him,' Gresham burst out. 'It was just bad luck this evening —'

'I know, I know,' she told him. 'But I can't risk your being unlucky again.'

'What are you going to do about it?' he demanded truculently.

'Find out what's happened to him. I'll call round at his flat in the morning.'

'Isn't that a bit risky? The police'll be there and —'

'Shut up,' she snapped. 'When I want your advice, I'll ask for it — and heaven help me from ever having to do that!'

He began to mutter something, but she went on firmly:

'I'm not to know anything about what happened last night. I wasn't even at Lady Tonbridge's, so I don't even know he didn't turn up there. I shall be paying him a call in the ordinary way. If the police *are* there, I ought to be able to bluff them into telling me if he's dead or alive. If he's alive, I'll dig out of them where he is.'

She drew at her cigarette and slowly blew a cloud of smoke ceilingwards. He looked at her with covert admiration.

'You've got a nerve all right, Cleo,' he exclaimed thickly. 'You're a woman in a million.'

'*With* a million,' she corrected him softly. 'Very soon.'

12

Detective-Inspector Hood

Detective-Inspector Hood drew at his old briar, which bubbled noisily, and slowly expelled a great cloud of somewhat acrid smoke as he eyed the individual before him.

It was the morning following the discovery of the body in the bathroom and Hood had taken over the job of solving the mystery. The late Stefan Zusky, upon whom the police-surgeon had delivered his pronouncement, had been removed. The police photographers and fingerprint experts had completed their work and the Inspector, aided by a stenographer with his notebook, was now engaged upon eliciting what information he could from the porter of the flats.

The detective made a sturdy, alert figure as he clamped his teeth over his pipe-stem. Apart from its bizarre aspects which indicated that this was no ordinary murder, his interest in its investigation was not inconsiderably heightened when he learned that Doctor Morelle had already made an appearance at the scene of the crime.

Inspector Hood and Doctor Morelle were old friends[1] and, while he deplored the Doctor's arbitrarily condescending and superior attitude, at the same time he was forced to admit a profound respect for his deductive gifts. And, intermingled with this admiration, there was a sneaking, if inexplicable, warm-heartedness towards him which the detective found difficult to comprehend. The occasions upon which Doctor Morelle's heart ever appeared to attain a temperature higher than that of an iceberg were rare indeed.

---

[1] See the Case-books *Meet Doctor Morelle and Meet Doctor Morelle Again* (John Long) for descriptions of several investigations jointly conducted by the Doctor and Inspector Hood.

The man upon whom Detective-Inspector Hood now bent his gaze shifted uneasily and rubbed his hands nervously down the sides of his trousers.

'Your name's Arthur Burton?' Hood queried. 'And you've been employed as porter at these flats for twelve years?'

'That's right.'

'You live here?'

'That's right. On the ground floor.'

'Anything happen last night which you thought sounded suspicious?'

'Nothing at all, Inspector. It was a terrible shock to me when the police come and said they wanted to get into the flat.'

Hood eyed him contemplatively.

'Doesn't it strike you as a bit odd,' he grunted, 'that someone could come up here last night, fire off a gun and you not hear it?'

The other looked troubled. For a long moment he hesitated. Then he said:

'I dunno how to answer that question and that's a fact. All I can say is I never heard no guns let off up here at any time. This flat's on the sixth floor and the one underneath is unoccupied at the moment — tenant's away — and I should think it would be possible to fire a gun and nobody hear it. But I dunno.'

'Anyway, *you* didn't hear anything? About ten o'clock, it would be.'

'If I had, I'd have remembered. Me and my missus went to the pictures. But we was back a bit before ten. We had a cup of tea before we went to bed. Oh — I went down to the boiler-house just to make sure everything was okay. I made up the boiler for the night.'

'How long were you in the boiler-house?'

'Five or ten minutes, I'd say.'

'And you didn't see or hear anyone come in or go out?'

'No, I didn't. As soon as I'd finished in the boiler-house, I went off to bed like I said. Next thing I knew was the police arriving. That'd be about half past twelve.'

Hood's pipe bubbled somewhat alarmingly. He asked:

'What do you know about this Sir Hugh Albany?'

'Dunno as I know much about him,'

the porter answered promptly. 'I'm the porter here. He's a tenant.' He added: 'Makes a bit o' difference.'

The Inspector gave the other a gentle smile.

'How long's he had the flat?'

'Before I come here,' was the reply.

'Was he the sort who had many visitors?'

'I suppose you might say he was,' the other said judiciously. 'People used to come and go, like. He used to be quite lively one time. Lots of parties and things going on. But of course he's a bit quieter now.'

'Why 'of course'?'

'Well . . . there's his fiancée,' the porter explained. 'Miss Carfax. Been going pretty steady for some time, they have, and I expect that's made him a bit quieter. Preparing for when they was properly spliced, you might say.'

'You saw the dead man before he was taken away?' Hood asked.

The other nodded silently.

'Recognize him at all?'

Burton shook his head. 'Never seen

him before,' he declared emphatically.

'Sure?'

'Sure as I can be of anything, and that's a fact. I'm upset about this wot's happened — and perhaps I'm not quite so quick on the uptake as I might be — but of one thing I'm certain, and that is I never see that chap before. Unless he looked very different-like when he was alive.'

'All right, Burton. That's about the lot for now. You'd better carry on as usual. I'll let you know if there's anything else I want to ask you.'

As the porter quitted the sitting-room, a policeman came in.

'Doctor Morelle has just arrived, sir. Miss Frayle is with him.' Inspector Hood moved into the hall.

'I'd heard you'd interested yourself in this business, Doctor,' he greeted Doctor Morelle. 'How d'you do, Miss Frayle.'

Miss Frayle blushed a little with pleasure at the specially nice smile the Inspector bestowed on her.

'How d'you do, Inspector Hood,' she said and added, with a little sigh: 'I wish we didn't always seem to be meeting in circumstances so gloomy.'

Doctor Morelle glanced at her and his thin lips tightened.

'Before Miss Frayle launches upon a sea of empty superficialities, Inspector,' he observed icily, 'might I inquire if there have been any further developments in the case you are investigating?'

'Nothing very remarkable,' the other answered, leading the way into the disordered sitting-room. 'Been trying to get a line on Sir Hugh Albany's friends and acquaintances. Trouble is, his type know so many people.'

'Do I detect the inference that you consider the attack upon Albany and the murder of the Baron's secretary as being linked together?'

'It's a possibility,' Hood replied slowly. 'On the other hand, even if there is no connection, it is still a likely assumption that whoever bumped off Zusky did know Albany.'

'You mean because the poor man was murdered in Sir Hugh's flat?' Miss Frayle put in.

Hood nodded. 'That's the idea,' he said. He paused, then went on: 'Seems Sir Hugh Albany's in a pretty bad way. I 'phoned the nursing-home, but there doesn't seem to be much possibility of my being able to get a statement from him yet.'

'His condition may be described as dangerous,' Doctor Morelle said, lighting an inevitable Le Sphinx. Through the cloud of cigarette-smoke his narrowed eyes moved round the room. 'There's a suspicion that, as a result of the bullet-wound, a fragment of the skull is pressing on the left frontal lobe,' he went on.

'Won't that mean an operation?' Hood asked.

The Doctor brought his gaze to bear upon the other with a faint smile.

'I note,' he observed, 'your perception is not merely confined to police investigation, but extends into the realms of medicine.'

Inspector Hood grinned at him good-humouredly.

'Oh yes,' he replied, 'we flat-footed

bloodhounds do pick up a bit of knowledge now and again, apart from spotting the slip the criminal makes. Especially,' he added, 'when we're lucky enough to come into contact with certain eminent minds from whom a dull-witted cop cannot help picking up a few crumbs of wisdom.' And he winked at Miss Frayle.

She gave him a quick, delighted smile and turned to see how Doctor Morelle had taken Hood's somewhat heavy-handed shaft. To her amazement, instead of the cold, supercilious expression she expected to see on his saturnine features, his eyes were twinkling with amusement and he was actually chuckling.

Good gracious me! she thought. He's *laughing* . . . Then she glanced at him more sharply, with a little worried frown. Could it be, she asked herself, that he's sickening for something? Her conjectures in this direction, however, were interrupted by his reply to the detective.

'You flatter me, my dear Inspector,' he said simply. Then: 'In point of fact, Owen is performing the operation this morning.'

'Sir David Owen,' Miss Frayle supplied, and added enthusiastically, 'He's a wonderful surgeon —'

She broke off as Doctor Morelle rasped irascibly:

'The Inspector has already intimated that he relies upon somewhat loftier intelligences for his scraps of wisdom than your gratuitous garrulities would signify.'

Suitably crushed, Miss Frayle subsided.

'Well, let's hope he pulls through, anyhow,' Hood grunted. 'If he doesn't, our unknown friend may have *two* murders hanging over him.'

'Still harping upon the connection between the two crimes?' Doctor Morelle murmured jibingly.

'I'm not stating it as a fact,' the other retorted. 'Just my personal opinion at the moment. 'I admit I haven't a definite clue pointing that way, but it seems to me to tie up. As I said before, this chap Zusky getting knocked out here in Albany's flat within three or four hours of Albany himself being attacked in the mews . . . '

He paused, and eyed Doctor Morelle expectantly.

To Miss Frayle it seemed as if his remarks had been made rather in the hope that they would invite the Doctor to offer some information of which the Inspector was so far unaware.

Doctor Morelle, however, merely smiled enigmatically and tapped the ash off his cigarette.

'It would appear,' he observed, 'that whatever other pearls of wisdom you may have gleaned from our association, my ratiocinative methods have not impressed you sufficiently to apply them yourself.'

He cleared his throat with a little cough, giving Miss Frayle a moment in which to steal a glance at Inspector Hood, who was watching him attentively. This time, however, Hood did not give her one of his surreptitious winks.

His eyes remained fixed on the tall, dark, brooding figure before him, and Miss Frayle realized, as she had occasion to do before, that however much the Doctor's pomposity and posturings may have secretly amused him, the other's respect for his deductive gifts was in no way diminished.

'As you are no doubt by now aware,' Doctor Morelle was announcing, '*I* do not permit myself to form an opinion until I have actual data to go on. I cannot agree that the facts as we know them at present are sufficient to serve as anything more than a basic theory.'

He drew thoughtfully at his Le Sphinx, expelling a long spiral of cigarette-smoke ceilingwards before he continued:

'What indeed are the established facts regarding this case that have so far been collated?' he murmured, his tone rising on a question mark. 'And might not this be an appropriate moment for us to examine them?'

13

Doctor Morelle Theorizes

'At approximately seven thirty last night,' Doctor Morelle began, 'Sir Hugh Albany was shot and wounded in the head. Three hours later, Doctor Bennett's house-keeper found him in an unconscious condition lying in the basement area of Doctor Bennett's house. Doctor Bennett has declared that when he returned home last night, in the region of ten o'clock, he failed to notice Albany's presence, from which it may be assumed that he had fallen into the area between ten and ten thirty p.m. What happened to him in the time which elapsed between his being attacked in the mews and his discovery by the housekeeper? That is the question we are unable to answer definitely.'

The Doctor paused to draw at his Le Sphinx.

'However, I can advance a theory,' he

went on. 'Which is, that despite his having been shot, he was able to conceal himself from his assailant. No doubt the approaching darkness aided him in this. Having thus eluded his would-be murderer, Albany lapsed into unconsciousness. Some time later, he gained consciousness sufficiently to permit him to make his way to Doctor Bennett's house.'

Inspector Hood's black pipe-bowl bubbled furiously and he expelled a cloud of acrid smoke which caused the Doctor's nostrils to twitch, while Miss Frayle gave a little cough.

'I agree, Doctor,' Hood observed. 'What you say fits in pretty neatly. Although other alternatives could be suggested, any of 'em equally possible.'

Doctor Morelle nodded. He said:

'The alternatives appear to be so numerous that we ought not to reach any conclusions at this stage in our investigations.' He paused and cleared his throat. 'However, one factor is perfectly evident.'

'What's that, Doctor?'

Inspector Hood and Miss Frayle put

the question almost in unison, and Doctor Morelle bestowed upon them both one of his frostily superior smiles.

'It is this,' he said. 'That Sir Hugh Albany is, wittingly or otherwise, the possessor of information which an individual, or individuals, are desperately anxious to obtain from him. Incidentally,' he continued. 'I noticed when I arrived that you had been questioning the porter here. Did he vouchsafe any information?'

'Nothing that added up to much,' Hood answered.

'At what hour did Albany leave here yesterday?'

'The porter saw him when he went out just before lunch. He didn't see him return and I think we can safely assume he didn't, in fact, come back.'

Doctor Morelle inclined his head in agreement while the other continued:

'We take it the flat was empty until nine forty last night, when whoever it was got in and went through the place like a whirlwind.'

Miss Frayle stared at Hood with respectful admiration.

'Why, Inspector!' she exclaimed with a little laugh, 'I do believe you've stolen a march on Doctor Morelle, fixing the time the murderer was here.' And she turned brightly to the Doctor.

Doctor Morelle regarded her with pitying condescension as he replied:

'On the contrary, Inspector Hood is twenty minutes wrong in his estimate.'

'What!' the other grunted indignantly. 'How d'you mean, I'm twenty minutes out?'

For answer, the Doctor crossed to the writing-desk which had been wrenched open. From beside it he picked up a small travelling clock. The glass was broken and the hands pointed to ten o'clock.

He held the clock for Miss Frayle to see.

'I can't believe,' he sighed elaborately, 'that it requires any great effort to note that this clock has clearly been brushed off this writing-desk by the intruder hastily searching for his objective. The clock was obviously working before the mishap. It may therefore be taken for granted that the Inspector is basing his estimate of the time at which the intruder arrived upon the moment at which this stopped.'

Miss Frayle blinked in bewilderment as she gazed first at the clock then at Inspector Hood, then back to the clock and finally at Doctor Morelle.

'But — but — he said the time was twenty to ten,' she stammered. 'That says ten o'clock.'

'Precisely,' Doctor Morelle said drily, and shot a piercingly triumphant glance at Hood. But the detective appeared not in the least nonplussed. On the contrary, he seemed to be hugging himself as if he, in fact, held a card up his sleeve with which to trump the Doctor's assertion. Inspector Hood would not have been human if the anticipation of scoring off Doctor Morelle was not something to be savoured with relish.

He unclamped his teeth from his pipe and waved it about in emphasis as he said, deliberately:

'It's evident enough that Sir Hugh Albany had something — information or whatever you like — that somebody else wanted. This somebody else was prepared to commit murder to obtain that information and, in fact, nearly succeeded in killing Albany in the process. But, having half-murdered him, they still couldn't find what they wanted, so they set out to look for it in his flat.'

He paused and began to pace slowly and heavily up and down.

'They broke in here by way of the fire-escape which opens into the bath-room. Not a particularly difficult way of getting in. Now, then . . . The bathroom leads to the bedroom, doesn't it?'

Doctor Morelle did not think it necessary to furnish the obvious reply. Miss Frayle, however, obliged by answering with a grave:

'Yes.'

'Surely then,' Hood declared, 'anyone breaking in with the idea of searching the place would start looking in the room he first entered — the bedroom! Apart from the fact,' he added, 'that the bedroom would be quite a likely hiding-place for whatever he was seeking. And so I reached the logical deduction that the intruder searched the bedroom before the sitting-room. Furthermore, as we've seen, he couldn't have searched it more thoroughly. And that took time. Say, twenty minutes. Still not finding what he wanted, he came in here, starting on that writing-desk first. And it was *then* that he knocked the clock off, stopping it at ten p.m. — *twenty minutes after he broke in!*'

Inspector Hood halted his pacing, drew noisily at his pipe, and waited for Doctor Morelle's response.

'I really don't think that the time element is of much importance at this juncture,' the Doctor commented, in a tone that loftily dismissed the other's argument.

'Oh!' Miss Frayle put in, more in sorrow than in condemnation. 'Aren't you being rather mean to Inspector Hood? I think he's worked out the time business very clearly — you might at least acknowledge that.'

'I would if it were correct,' was the prompt reply, at which Inspector Hood frowned, somewhat puzzled. Both he and

Miss Frayle stared at Doctor Morelle, who had turned his back on them and was gazing apparently aimlessly around the room.

Reminding Miss Frayle of a dark, angular cat, he picked his way carefully over splinters of glass from a number of pictures which had been wrenched from the walls and wantonly thrown to the floor. One picture stood out sharply among the disorder of the room, if only for the fact that it, alone, appeared to have been regarded with any care, for it had been propped on the writing-desk, its glass intact.

It was a small oil-painting in a carved, gilt frame, depicting a miniature lake with a background of trees which were reflected in its mirror-like surface. An evening mist hung on the water and the artist had caught the sunset colouring with almost uncanny realism. Added to which a faintly sinister quality hovered over the scene, to which the curious purple light which the dark trees threw across the lake contributed.

Doctor Morelle glanced from the

picture to the spot clearly marked above the desk where it had hung. Its hook still remained there. His eyes travelled round the patches on the walls where the other pictures had been and where in each case the hooks had been impatiently wrenched out. Through a cloud of cigarette-smoke he surveyed the picture of the lake again.

'Nice little painting, that,' Inspector Hood remarked affably. It was evident that, still very pleased with his triumph regarding the time of the intruder's entrance into the flat, and unshaken by the Doctor's refusal to accept his calculations, he felt he could afford to be expansive. 'I was admiring it myself, just now.'

For a moment, Doctor Morelle made no reply.

Still careful to avoid the bits of broken glass, he stepped back, regarding the small oil-painting with his head slightly on one side. Then he turned and moved across to the door, which was immediately opposite the writing-desk.

'Extremely intriguing,' he murmured. And then, with elaborate casualness, queried: 'You say you examined the picture, Inspector?'

Inspector Hood smiled broadly.

'Can't say I've got quite the same interest in art that you have, Doctor,' he replied. 'Or the same knowledge, I expect. It just appealed to me, that's all. You seem to admire it yourself, too.'

The Doctor regarded him, and the corners of his thin mouth were quirked in secret amusement.

'Indeed, it possesses some quite significant qualities,' he said. 'In fact I might go further —'

Doctor Morelle, however, was not to be permitted to expand further upon the inner significance he had perceived in the picture of the lake. At least, not for the time being. A sudden ring at the door-bell caused him to break off and, together with Inspector Hood and Miss Frayle, he glanced in the direction of the ring.

'Who could that be?' Miss Frayle queried, her eyes round behind her horn-rims.

Her question was answered to the extent that the newcomer was a woman, for they could hear her speaking to the policeman who had opened the door to her. Almost unconsciously Miss Frayle registered that it was an attractive voice, with warm tones and a certain huskiness which added to its appeal. It may be true that she did, in fact, experience a sense of foreboding even upon only hearing the newcomer. At any rate, that was to be her claim later, though it was rejected by Doctor Morelle with his typical wholehearted contempt for her intuitive attributes.

'There's a lady wishes to see you, sir,' the policeman came in and announced. 'Says she's a friend of Sir Hugh Albany. Mrs. Latimer.'

Hood's eyebrows shot up and he glanced sharply at Doctor Morelle. His pipe was bubbling furiously as he grunted:

'Friend of Albany's, eh! Sounds as if she might be able to put us on to something, Doctor. So, if you don't mind, I suggest we postpone our art discussion.' And he turned to the policeman. 'All right. Show Mrs. Latimer in.'

14

Doctor Morelle Meets Mrs. Latimer

Cleo Latimer possessed that commendable quality of stillness and repose. Perhaps the observer less dazzled by her attractiveness might on occasion find it difficult to decide whether the repose also contained an element of watchfulness — but few, even of the discerning minority, bothered to conjecture on the almost predatory expression which might sometimes mar Mrs. Latimer's striking beauty. She was striking without being spectacular. The dress she wore was simply cut, though the line was exquisite enough for Miss Frayle, taking one look at it, promptly to experience a forlorn frustration.

On the threshold she made a curiously dominating picture as she stood there, the policeman hovering in the background, Miss Frayle frankly goggling,

Doctor Morelle saturnine, still and poised, and Hood eyeing her appreciatively. She paused for just the right moment or two before, her large, lustrous eyes wide, she came forward and rested her gaze questioningly on Inspector Hood.

'Will someone explain what has happened, please?'

A faint fragrance, a memory rather than a definite perfume, stirred with her, and Miss Frayle's sense of frustration deepened as she experienced a longing to go out and buy things madly. She threw a glance at Doctor Morelle and at once felt an unreasonable but definite dislike for this tall, exquisite woman who seemed only to move into a room to command it.

Miss Frayle admitted to herself that her dislike was quite unreasonable and unfounded. But as she saw Doctor Morelle standing back in the shadows, watching the newcomer, the dislike became most definite, too definite to be ignored. True, the Doctor's expression remained inscrutable, yet Miss Frayle thought she could sense a silent appreciation that she found vastly irritating.

It was Hood who answered Cleo Latimer's question.

'I am Detective-Inspector Hood of Scotland Yard — ah — Mrs. Latimer. I am here to investigate — um — certain circumstances. I should be most glad if you can help us. This is Doctor Morelle — and Miss Frayle, Doctor Morelle's secretary.'

Mrs. Latimer gave Miss Frayle a friendly smile, inclined her head to Doctor Morelle.

'I've heard of you, Doctor Morelle, of course. And now would you mind explaining to me what has happened. I called to see Sir Hugh Albany and find —'

She broke off and glanced around her with an expression of utter bewilderment.

'I'm sorry to have to tell you that Sir Hugh met with an accident last night,' Inspector Hood said quietly. 'He was the victim of an attack — '

'Oh, but how awful!' Mrs. Latimer's eyes were wide, dark with apprehension.

'Is he badly hurt? Where is he? Is he here?'

'He is not here now.'

It was Doctor Morelle who spoke from his shadowy corner. 'He is in the care of Doctor Bennett and Sir David Owen. The latter is performing an operation this morning. In fact I expect to hear the result of it soon.' And he drew at his cigarette.

'He was attacked last night at some time between seven and eight,' Hood began, but she interrupted him.

'But — but — this is terrible! Have you caught whoever did this ghastly thing?'

'Not yet,' Inspector Hood said, somewhat gloomily. 'But we will, never fear. Meantime — er — perhaps you could help us a little?'

'I shall be very glad to, of course. But I hardly see how.' She made a little gesture of helplessness. 'I'm so completely confused by this. Sir Hugh was with me yesterday afternoon. He had tea with me —' She faltered, her eyes widening, and looked at them with dismay. 'Why, he must have been attacked soon after he left me!'

'What time did he leave?' Hood asked quickly.

'Latish. We were chatting and didn't notice how the time was passing. Then he said he must hurry as he had an appointment before he went on to Lady Tonbridge's reception. That would be about half past six, I should think.'

'Do you know with whom he had the appointment?'

'I'm afraid I don't.' Cleo Latimer looked from one to the other, then glanced round the room. She said quickly: 'But why is his flat in this state? Has there been a burglary?'

'There has been a murder.'

It was Doctor Morelle again who spoke. From the shadows his voice came, cold and impersonal. Mrs. Latimer was suddenly very still. Her beautifully poised head lifted the merest trifle, showing the lovely line of her throat. Her features had the clear pallor of alabaster.

Inspector Hood cast a quick look at the Doctor. Then Mrs. Latimer said in a thin, strained voice:

'You — you said — murder?' She shivered, and went on: 'I don't understand. This is a terrible shock. I wonder if I could sit down.'

Hood got a chair quickly and she sank into it. Doctor Morelle moved away from the shadows, closer to her. In his calm, passionless voice he asked:

'Are you a close friend of Sir Hugh Albany?'

'We have known each other for some time. Yes, I think I could say I am a fairly close friend. We meet often, we have many mutual friends. Why do you ask?'

'In the hope that you may be able to help us. You will appreciate that Sir Hugh is not in a position to give us any information.'

'Please, Doctor Morelle!' Her voice was sharp with anxiety.

'I had no wish to cause you unnecessary pain,' he murmured and, as Inspector Hood gave a little cough, turned to him. 'Accept my apologies, Inspector,' he said urbanely. 'I may perhaps have assumed too much upon myself in informing Mrs. Latimer —'

'Oh, that's all right, Doctor,' Hood said quickly, but giving him a rather puzzled look. 'I intended telling Mrs. Latimer myself what had happened.'

Cleo Latimer said slowly: 'Was — was it in here? In this flat?'

Hood nodded. 'At ten o'clock last night Sir Hugh Albany was found unconscious in the basement area of Doctor Bennett's house. And about the same time, that is to say, just before ten o'clock, this flat was entered by someone who for some reason made a thorough search through it. Nothing of value has been taken, so far as we can ascertain at present. It would appear the intruder was surprised by someone else while in the middle of his search. Either in panic, or deliberately, the intruder shot this other person dead.'

Mrs. Latimer listened to the Inspector with fixed attention, her wide, softly brilliant eyes fixed on his face, her lips faintly parted. She seemed scarcely to breathe as she asked:

'And have you not been able to discover who they are?' Her voice was very low. 'The first intruder — and the other who was shot?'

'The man who was shot has been identified as Baron Xavier's private secretary. Man named Zusky. Stefan Zusky.'

'And the man who shot him?'

Miss Frayle, watching her, thought she was showing signs of strain, the strain of shock. Her lips were pale and there were dark, violet shadows under her eyes.

'That will be merely a matter of time,' Doctor Morelle answered her. Then he added: 'Were you by any chance acquainted with Zusky?'

She shook her head.

'Why do you think I might be?'

Her eyes narrowed a little and a curious spasm, as of pain, crossed her face. Miss Frayle, her eyes wide and rounded behind her spectacles, saw the slender gloved hand press against her heart.

'It seemed a not unreasonable question,' Doctor Morelle murmured. 'You are a friend of Albany's. This man was found dead in Albany's flat. It occurred to me you might have met him.'

'No,' Mrs. Latimer said with a little gasp, and fainted.

It was quiet and slow, the way she went. She swayed in the chair and slid a little to the side before anyone quite realized that anything was wrong. As she fell forward and dropped to the floor in a limp heap, Doctor Morelle was beside her. He carried her towards a big settee.

Miss Frayle, like Hood, was utterly taken aback.

'Oh, dear! Oh, dear me!' she exclaimed.

Doctor Morelle cast her a glance of intolerant annoyance.

'Kindly desist from clucking like a hen, Miss Frayle!' he snapped. 'Open that hand-bag,' indicating Mrs. Latimer's hand-bag which had fallen to the floor. 'I have no doubt you will find therein a box containing small ampules.'

'Yes, Doctor Morelle,' Miss Frayle stammered. She picked up the plain dark square hand-bag, dropped it again, adjusted her spectacles, recovered the hand-bag, and fumbled in it agitatedly.

Inspector Hood drew at his pipe so

that it bubbled like a cauldron and watched Doctor Morelle, who was closely examining Mrs. Latimer's still features, his long, slender fingers laid lightly on her wrist.

'She was more shocked than we thought, Doctor,' he muttered. 'I thought she looked a bit pale.'

'Undoubtedly she was shocked.' The Doctor's reply was somewhat enigmatic. 'Pray do cease fumbling so inadequately, Miss Frayle —'

'Here they are,' Miss Frayle exclaimed excitedly. 'Are these what you want?'

She passed a small gold box containing a few minute ampules, less than an inch long and hardly thicker than a match, encased in small sachets. Doctor Morelle broke one and held it beneath Mrs. Latimer's nostrils.

Slowly a faint colour stole into her pale cheeks, she gave a little quivering sigh. The slim gloved hand made a little fluttering movement, crept up and clasped Doctor Morelle's.

'Oh, Doctor.' Miss Frayle cried excitedly, 'how clever of you! However did you guess those things would be in her hand-bag?'

Doctor Morelle gave her a withering look and then turned his attention to Cleo Latimer. Her dark eyelashes fluttered, then her eyes opened.

'You are quite all right now,' Doctor Morelle said gently. 'You have had these attacks before, have you not?'

'Yes.' Her voice was hardly more than a breath. 'Not — quite so suddenly . . .'

Her gloved hand still clasped his. Her cheeks still had their clear pallor, but beneath there was a returning glow. A mistiness which had suffused her eyes gradually cleared. She looked extraordinarily beautiful as she lay there, her face like a flower against the dark soft fur of her coat.

Miss Frayle subjected her to a gaze that was slightly narrow. Inspector Hood was thinking abstractedly that Doctor Morelle and Mrs. Latimer looked rather well together. Both possessed fine, distinctive features, if perhaps a little arrogant.

With sudden brightness, Miss Frayle

said: 'Here's your hand-bag, Mrs. Latimer. You dropped it and I had to open it . . . '

'Thank you.' Life had come back to the other's voice. She smiled up at Doctor Morelle, then her glance swept down to her own hand, still clasping his. As she drew her hand away she gave him one quick, upward, appealing glance.

'I'm so sorry to have been such a nuisance,' she said. 'I don't often behave so badly.'

'Nasty shock for you, running into this so unexpectedly,' Inspector Hood put in. 'Not to be wondered at if it knocked you all of a heap. You'd better rest a bit.'

The telephone rang sharply as he spoke. Miss Frayle went across to it and spoke into the receiver, her eyes still fixed on Mrs. Latimer.

'Yes, Doctor Morelle is here,' she said. Habitually Miss Frayle's voice was soft and rather pretty. Even Doctor Morelle was once known to declare that it would be quite attractive if only she used it to utter a few words of sense occasionally. But now, unaccountably, the softness seemed to have vanished; her tone had quite an edge to it.

'Hold the line, please. I'll tell the Doctor.'

She handed Doctor Morelle the receiver without looking at him and said stonily: 'Doctor Bennett's house. Sir David Owen to speak to you.'

15

Miss Frayle has an Intuition

Doctor Morelle gave her a quizzical glance, one eyebrow uplifted. Then he turned his attention to the telephone. After a minute or two he said: 'There has been no statement of any kind? . . . Miss Carfax's name? . . . ' There was a long pause as he continued to listen before he observed: 'I see. It is difficult to say if it will help very much. What do you consider his chances are? . . . Quite so. Thank you, Sir David. I shall be back at Harley Street within the next half-hour . . . Yes, she may come along if she wishes. Good-bye.'

He replaced the receiver, stood for a moment in thought, his long, slender fingers caressing his chin. Hood watched him, waiting for him to speak, and Miss Frayle, her voice still sharp, asked: 'How is he, Doctor?'

'Too early to say that he is out of danger,' was the almost absent-minded answer.

'He wasn't able to say anything?' Miss Frayle queried. 'I mean about who attacked him, or anything like that?'

'My dear Miss Frayle — ' the Doctor began, then broke the sentence off short. More gently he said, simply: 'He was unable to give any information. He had not recovered consciousness before the operation. At present he remains unconscious.'

'Hmm . . . ' Inspector Hood grunted, and chewed on his pipestem, his expression registering a certain disappointment. He turned to regard Mrs. Latimer.

She seemed to have quite recovered. As Doctor Morelle finished speaking, she gave a sigh and said quickly: 'He'll be all right, then, Doctor Morelle? Sir Hugh, I mean?'

'Sir David appeared to be fairly satisfied, but would vouchsafe nothing specific at this juncture. But,' and his tone seemed to grow more gentle, 'how are you feeling now?'

'Much better, thanks to your promptness,' she smiled at him. 'You discovered the little cachets I carry. I don't know that they're really very much use.'

'Are you subject to these attacks frequently?'

'They seem to have been increasing lately. Nothing to worry about, of course. It's just that — sometimes — everything seems to swim in front of me.'

'Any pain?'

'A little stabbing pain occasionally.' She lifted her hand to her heart. 'But I haven't been to a doctor since I was in Vienna. I suppose I should, really.'

'It would be advisable,' Doctor Morelle nodded. 'It does not do to let these affections progress without advice.'

'Well, Doctor,' Hood broke in suddenly, 'what are you going to do? Stay on here and have a look round? Personally, I'm off to have a chat with this Baron Xavier chap. Made an appointment earlier. D'you know him, Mrs. Latimer?'

'Yes,' she answered readily. 'He is a great friend of Sir Hugh Albany.'

'So he is, so he is,' Hood said.

There was a little thud and Mrs. Latimer uttered a little exclamation as her bag dropped to the floor. Both Doctor Morelle and Hood moved to pick it up. The Doctor reached it first and handed it to her. He turned to the Inspector.

'Perhaps you wouldn't mind if I returned here later?' he asked smoothly. 'I might like to view the scene again.'

The other nodded affably. 'Any time you like, Doctor. I'll leave word with the man on duty.' He turned to Mrs. Latimer. 'We can get in touch with you if by any chance we should want to.'

She gave him her address and telephone number. 'I shall be only too glad to help in any way — ' She broke off and drew in a sudden, sharp breath. Again her hand made that quick little pressing movement to her heart. After a moment: 'I think I'll go — I — I have been rather upset by — all this.'

She moved to the door. Hood hesitated, looking at Doctor Morelle. But the Doctor appeared to be sunk in thought and Hood said quickly: 'Sure you're fit enough, Mrs. Latimer? I'll get one of my chaps to find you a taxi — '

'Please don't bother,' she begged him quickly, flashing him a brilliant smile. 'The air will do me good. Good-bye . . . Good-bye, Doctor Morelle. Thank you so much for your kindness.'

Doctor Morelle looked up with a slight start.

'Forgive me,' he said. 'I was somewhat preoccupied. Good morning.'

Hood saw her to the door. Mrs. Latimer was gone. There remained only the memory of her from the faint fragrance which hung on the air. Hood returned, crossed to the chair where his hat and coat lay and picked them up. 'Very attractive woman, eh, Doctor?' he said.

'She certainly possesses a grace and feminine pulchritude not often encountered.'

Miss Frayle distinctly sniffed. While she was not altogether certain of the exact definition of Doctor Morelle's observation — a position in which she frequently found herself — she was in no doubt whatever this time of his meaning and profound agreement with Inspector Hood.

'Anyone can make the best of themselves when they've got the time and the money to do it,' she declared, still that sharp note in her voice. 'That fur coat didn't come with a packet of tea! I thought it was rather ridiculous to see the way you two men fussed about when she fainted. It was quite an ordinary thing to do, in the circumstances.'

And Miss Frayle sniffed again. Louder.

'Really, my dear Miss Frayle,' Doctor Morelle said mildly. 'Poor Mrs. Latimer appears to have aroused a certain antagonism in you.'

Hood lifted his hand to his mouth to hide an irrepressible grin as Miss Frayle retorted: 'Poor Mrs. Latimer, indeed! Personally, I think you ought to have arrested her, Inspector Hood!'

Hood's grin faded and his eyes widened. Doctor Morelle stared inscrutably at her. Her face had grown quite pink, her eyes sparkled behind her horn-rimmed spectacles. He said levelly:

'That is an interesting statement, Miss

Frayle. Do you suggest that Inspector Hood should have arrested Mrs. Latimer because she happened to be a friend of Albany and he partook of tea with her yesterday afternoon, or because — '

'I don't know about that,' Miss Frayle interrupted him darkly. 'I just don't trust her, that's all. What did she call here for this morning?'

'Presumably to see Albany,' the Doctor replied. 'Can you suggest any other reason?'

'I can suggest plenty of reasons why she *shouldn't* call on Sir Hugh Albany,' Miss Frayle said with increasing vehemence. 'If she's such a friend of his she must know that he and Sherry Carfax are going to be married. So what's her idea? Tea with him alone in the afternoon, then calling here for him again in the morning!'

Miss Frayle became quite breathless and agitated and ended up stoutly: 'I don't like it at all, and I don't — well — I don't trust her!'

The Doctor said, with unaccustomed mildness: 'You still have offered no real reason why Mrs. Latimer should have been arrested — other than a most unaccountable personal antagonism. Incidentally, how do you reach your deduction Sir Hugh Albany and Mrs. Latimer had tea *alone* yesterday afternoon? I shall be more than interested to follow your reasoning.'

But Miss Frayle merely contrived to look deep. With as near a snort as she could ever approach, she exclaimed: 'Huh! It doesn't need reasoning.'

Hood stared at her over his bubbling pipe, while Doctor Morelle's eyebrows lifted.

'Indeed, Miss Frayle? Tell us more, I pray. Perhaps you have reached other startling conclusions about Mrs. Latimer? Perhaps you even *know* something which may be of material help to us in the elucidation of this mystery? You habitually make, I believe, a fairly exhaustive study of the society papers — '

'Oh, I've seen her in those,' Miss Frayle responded quickly, aided by another sniff. 'At races and parties and things. She gets around all right.'

Doctor Morelle winced.

'A particularly loathsome expression!' he snapped. Then his tone, resuming its unusual mild quality, continued: 'And is that all you have to tell us from your personal knowledge?'

'I've got intuition as well,' Miss Frayle said defiantly. 'And I'm willing to bet we haven't seen the last of Mrs. Latimer. I bet she comes to you for a — a consultation pretty soon!'

'How soon, do you suppose?' Doctor Morelle asked with bland seriousness.

Inspector Hood was openly grinning now and clearly enjoying himself. But the grin was wiped from his face at the withering glare Miss Frayle gave him from behind her spectacles, which had slipped in her indignation and were now balanced precariously on the end of her nose. With an impatient movement she pushed them back.

'You're both teasing me because I don't like her,' she snapped. 'Well, you'll see.'

Doctor Morelle turned to Hood. 'And do you think we had grounds for arresting the lady?'

'Not yet!' was the chuckled reply. Then the Inspector said briskly: 'Well, I must be off. I'll keep in touch with you, Doctor.' And to Miss Frayle: 'Cheer up! You may put her behind bars yet, if you persevere!'

'You'll see,' was all Miss Frayle could think of in answer to him as he bustled out.

In one respect, at least, Miss Frayle's intuition was perfectly correct. They had left the building in company with Hood but, refusing a lift from him in the police-car, were walking towards St. James's Street. Suddenly Miss Frayle gripped Doctor Morelle's arm.

'There! What did I say!' she exulted. 'There she is on the corner — waiting for you!'

Sure enough, there was the tall, slender figure of Mrs. Latimer and, as they approached, she began to walk towards them. Doctor Morelle flicked a swift, cold glance at Miss Frayle, opened his mouth as if he were about to speak, then closed it with a snap. His eyes were narrowed and cold. He listened gravely as Mrs. Latimer spoke.

'Are you returning to Harley Street now, Doctor Morelle?'

'We are.'

She looked directly into his eyes, her own softly brilliant and appealing.

'Would you be kind enough to let me come with you? I intended to ask you when you suggested I should get medical advice. Please, Doctor.'

He considered her for a moment, while Miss Frayle darted looks at his face, then at the other's, then back to his.

'I think I can spare you a little time, Mrs. Latimer.'

A faint exclamation sounded beside him. Miss Frayle gave a cough and said dryly:

'Here's a taxi coming. Perhaps we'd better take it.'

Miss Frayle maintained a stony silence and frozen profile all the way to Harley Street. Whatever triumph she might have felt at the vindication of her intuition, she seemed to be getting very little satisfaction out of it. Doctor Morelle appeared sunk in thought and Mrs. Latimer lay back against the cushions of the taxi, her eyes closed.

When they were in the consulting-room, Doctor Morelle motioned to Miss Frayle to remain.

'Sit down, Mrs. Latimer,' he murmured. 'Have you come to seek my professional advice? Or — ' and his narrow gaze seemed to bore into her wide eyes as if to drag out her innermost secrets that lay behind them — 'is it to explain why you lied when you said you did not know Stefan Zusky, had never even heard of him?'

16

Cleo Latimer Plays for Sympathy

Doctor Morelle spoke coolly and without any hint of accusation in his tone. It was simply a blunt statement of fact. Miss Frayle frankly gasped and Mrs. Latimer uttered a little choking cry. Her face had gone ashen, and about her lips was that blue, pinched look which Miss Frayle had noticed when she had fainted before. She looked as if she were going to faint now. She swayed, her hand pressed against her heart, her eyes fixed on the Doctor.

Then, slowly, she sank back into the chair. She was fighting for breath, fighting for control, and desperately fighting the faintness which, it seemed, threatened to overwhelm her.

As Doctor Morelle approached her she motioned him away.

'I'm all right, Doctor. Just — give me a minute.' Though her lips were trembling she smiled at him. After a moment she said faintly: 'That was — quite brilliant of you, Doctor Morelle. I did not think I had been obvious. It is quite true. I have come to you for two reasons. To ask your professional advice. And the other because — because I *did* lie. It was — incredibly stupid of me.'

'Perhaps — dangerous,' Morelle murmured. 'Miss Frayle — when you have been good enough to emerge from your trance-like condition, would you procure a glass of water?'

'Yes, Doctor.'

Gone was the sharpness from her voice. She spoke with warm respect, gazed at Doctor Morelle with the awe a child gives a conjuror who has just produced six white rabbits from a hat.

Cleo Latimer took the glass from her with a grateful smile and sipped the water.

After a moment she said: 'Was it such a dreadful thing to do, after all, Doctor? I was frightened — that was why I denied knowing Zusky. It was all so sudden. I had called at the flat this morning simply to see Hugh. And then to be confronted with the news that he was gravely injured, and someone had been murdered in his very flat! My first thought was — was — to avoid getting mixed up in such a horrible business at all costs. A very selfish reaction, I know. But, you see, I didn't know this Zusky, really. I had met him, that was all. About two years ago, in the South of France. It seemed I could serve no purpose by admitting I had known him and, as a result — well — getting dragged into the case as a witness. Was it so wrong of me to think like that?'

'It is not permissible to obstruct justice,' Doctor Morelle replied. 'Not only is it impermissible, it is extremely dangerous. A wrong construction might so easily be placed on your action.'

'How did you know I lied?'

'You were shocked when you heard a man had been murdered in the flat last night. You were obviously, to me, even more shocked when you knew his name. You concealed your shock well, but not well enough. It was sufficient to set up a train of thought in my mind. Your fainting attack followed. That did not altogether surprise me. I suspected you were subject to them very soon after you arrived.'

He paused for a moment. She made no reply to his scrutiny and he went on:

'Subsequently, you admitted you are acquainted with Baron Xavier, inferring that the acquaintanceship had sprung from your friendship with Albany. He is a close friend of the Baron. It was perfectly clear, therefore, that you must surely have been aware, at least, of the existence of Zusky, since he was not only Baron Xavier's secretary, but in the nature of being a close friend.'

'You make me seem so very stupid,' Cleo Latimer sighed. 'I suppose it was just as clear to the Scotland Yard detective that I wasn't telling the truth?'

Doctor Morelle gave a wintry smile.

'Inspector Hood did not attain his present position from lack of cerebral activity, my dear Mrs. Latimer.'

The other's fine eyes widened a little, while Miss Frayle said, a trifle unnecessarily:

'Doctor Morelle means he's no fool.'

'Thank you, Miss Frayle!' the Doctor mocked her softly.

'It's more than I can say for myself,' Mrs. Latimer said ruefully. She looked at the Doctor with disarming frankness. 'Can you advise me what to do? Should I go to Scotland Yard and tell them?'

Again Doctor Morelle smiled, though this time with more than a little grimness.

'Have no fear but that Inspector Hood will himself call upon you if he wants to learn anything further from you. Though no doubt,' he added judiciously, 'he will be satisfied if you explain to him your motive in — ah — deceiving him.'

Miss Frayle stared at him round-eyed.

To say she was astonished at his gentleness with Mrs. Latimer after her admitted deliberate deception — an admission he had forced from her — was putting it mildly. She was completely flabbergasted. She had expected a crisp order from him to telephone the police, at least, while the possibility of seeing the beautiful Mrs. Latimer taken off in handcuffs had occurred to her ever-colourful imagination. Miss Frayle felt her heart wouldn't have been broken, exactly, at the sight of such a dramatic exit.

Instead, here was Doctor Morelle chatting away to her mildly as if to a patient with an anxiety-complex, or in real need of sympathetic attention. Miss Frayle's eyes as she looked at Mrs. Latimer had a basilisk-like glare behind her spectacles.

'I — I told you,' the other was saying, 'it was because I was scared of getting involved in a horrible murder.'

She leaned forward, clasping her gloved hands lightly.

'But perhaps you don't quite understand, Doctor,' she went on. 'Let me explain. You've heard of actresses who've reached a certain degree of fame having to fight to keep their position? The same thing often applies to a woman like myself. After all, I'm well-known, and before long the newspapers are going to get hold of this story. There will be an inquest and all the rest of it. Headlines. Photographs. It all flashed through my mind even as you asked me if I knew him. I'd be dragged into all that horrible publicity. The sort of publicity anyone like myself can do very well without! Questions would be asked in court, questions that I would have to answer. My — my friendship with Hugh.'

Her hands tightened.

'Oh, you don't understand!' she exclaimed passionately. 'The mud people are ready to fling! The innuendoes that will be whispered! I'm a woman alone, Doctor. Defenceless. I didn't want to be the cause of breaking things up between Sherry Carfax and Hugh. Don't you see? And that's only one thing might happen if I'm called as a witness. It would ruin their happiness. It would ruin me socially.' She faced him defiantly. 'Of course I lied! And now you know why!'

And the lovely, poised, incomparable Cleo Latimer suddenly burst into a fit of weeping.

Doctor Morelle frowned and snapped a finger and thumb with evident impatience. To him a woman's tears were no more than a disturbance of the lachrymal ducts induced by emotional crises or hysteria, and to be avoided at all costs. He shrugged and turned away, with a faint glance of contempt for Miss Frayle, who was fluttering round the weeping figure with words of comfort.

The soft heart and gentle nature of Miss Frayle were easily imposed upon. Although she instinctively disliked Mrs. Latimer, the sight of her tears moved her to quick sympathy.

Doctor Morelle turned his back on the spectacle and stalked across to a cabinet, before which he stood for a moment in contemplation. Then, opening a drawer, he selected a small box from which he shook a couple of white tablets.

When he returned to her side, Cleo Latimer seemed to have recovered her composure somewhat. She gave him a wan smile.

'Please forgive me, Doctor,' she said, her voice husky with emotion. 'I'm afraid I am being nothing but a bore to you. Suppose I'm — well — rather frightened.'

'I fully appreciate that. Take these tablets and remain quiet for a quarter of an hour or so. Miss Frayle, kindly conduct Mrs. Latimer to the waiting-room and see that she is comfortable.' He turned to the other again. 'You will be quite undisturbed there.'

'You are being most kind, Doctor Morelle.'

He inclined his head coldly, regarded her with inscrutable eyes as, accompanied by an attentive Miss Frayle, she went from the room. Then, as they were crossing the hall, he called in his peculiarly carrying voice:

'Be good enough not to waste time, Miss Frayle! I wish to make a number of important notes on this case.'

When Miss Frayle returned to the study, he was standing in an attitude of profound concentration. As she sat waiting, notebook and pencil ready, he lifted a quizzical eyebrow.

'Is Mrs. Latimer comfortable?'

'Yes, Doctor.'

Miss Frayle blinked at him, hesitated, then said: 'Is she really ill? Or is it put on?'

His glance was sardonic.

'I fancy she is too clever a woman to attempt to deceive me. After all, Miss Frayle, I am not without — um — some

— ah — practice in the matter of discerning the difference between real and assumed indisposition!'

Suitably squashed, Miss Frayle subsided.

Doctor Morelle went on relentlessly, his gaze bleakly on her. 'What extraordinary convuluted thought-process has led you to the suspicion that Mrs. Latimer might be feigning illness? Why should she?'

'To gain your sympathy, of course,' Miss Frayle said. She fluttered a little. 'That's what she's been trying to do ever since she first set eyes on you.'

'You flatter me!' he returned sardonically, adding sententiously, 'it is seldom necessary for a beautiful woman to attempt to evoke sympathy.'

Miss Frayle thinned her mouth, looked at a vague point beyond his shoulder, and made no comment. Her expression alone spoke volumes of disapproval.

After a moment she asked with forced brightness: 'However . . . I thought you were impatiently waiting to make some notes on this murder case?'

17

Miss Frayle takes Notes

In every case in which he was involved, it was the practice of Doctor Morelle to keep a journal in which Miss Frayle meticulously entered every detail, no matter how seemingly trivial, of facts and events which had a bearing upon that particular episode.

Accordingly the next fifteen minutes were devoted by Doctor Morelle to a brilliant summarizing of the case as it had so far developed. No aspect was missed, no circumstance, however slight, left unexamined. Although she had assisted him on a great number of similar occasions, Miss Frayle never ceased to be impressed by these summaries in which were carefully collated his theories and definite deductions, and his reasons for arriving at them.

After reviewing the general facts of the

attack on Albany and the murder of Stefan Zusky, the Doctor proceeded in his clear, precise voice:

'There can be little doubt that the two incidents are linked and, in effect, may be investigated as one. It is evident from the manner in which the flat was ransacked that the motive was not one of ordinary robbery or housebreaking. Various valuable items were left, although they had been handled by the intruder. There were, I observed, a number of ornamental pieces in the sitting-room which an ordinary thief would have pilfered. While, in the bedroom, a platinum dress-watch and other valuable items were merely moved or thrown to one side. This leads inevitably to the conclusion that the intruder was searching for a particular object.

'Detective-Inspector Hood's theory that the intruder broke into the flat at about 9.40 and immediately began searching the bedroom is completely false — '

Miss Frayle gave a gasp at this revelation. Doctor Morelle bestowed upon her a self-satisfied smirk and then went on.

'By arriving at this inaccurate deduction, Hood missed the most important clue which has yet presented itself. I refer to the oil-painting in the sitting-room called the Purple Lake. The picture is of some artistic merit, though not sufficient to deserve close attention. Nevertheless, it is sufficiently interesting *in relation* to the case to cause one or two inquiries to be made. For example, how long it has been in Albany's possession, who was the artist and so on.

'It is quite apparent,' continued the Doctor tirelessly, and without hesitation or pause, 'that the intruder was already aware of the significance of the Purple Lake. He broke into the flat at approximately ten o'clock and went straight to the picture. But evidently it availed him nothing in his search. In other words, he possessed the key, but did not know how to employ it.'

As if suddenly aware that Miss Frayle, while taking down every word with truly remarkable speed and efficiency, was at the same time sending him beseeching looks, the Doctor now condescended to halt for a moment.

'I trust the rapidity of my dictation is not preventing you from taking notes correctly?' he inquired ominously.

'Oh no. But you're not giving reasons for your conclusions,' she complained.

'In my innocence I imagined they were sufficiently obvious even to your intelligence, my dear Miss Frayle. Must I dot every 'i' and cross every 't' throughout? Surely after this long time you can follow my train of thought sufficiently well to realize what happened at Albany's flat?'

He bent his mesmeric gaze upon her so that she experienced what she imagined must be the sensations felt by a rabbit encountering a cobra.

'I — I haven't the faintest idea,' she managed to blurt out. 'In fact,' she confessed, 'while I've been taking this down I've been wondering if — well — if you could be mistaken.'

There is only one possible way of describing his reaction to her not entirely discreetly chosen words: he lunged at her like an angry beast of prey about to descend upon its chosen victim.

'Mistaken!'

For a moment she feared his rage would choke him. 'Are you really suggesting,' he contrived to enunciate with withering clarity of diction, 'that *I* could be making a mistake, Miss Frayle? Or can it be you have completely taken leave of your senses?'

'N-n-no, Doctor,' Miss Frayle gulped. 'I — I mean — for the sake of the record — you — you — '

But he cut her words short with a scornful gesture, and his lip curled with enraged offence.

In strained, rapid tones he rapped:

'It should have been obvious to anyone the flat had been ransacked and the desperate search had taken place *subsequent to the removal of the picture of the Purple Lake from the wall*. It was then that the clock was stopped by being precipitated to the floor.'

He drew at his Le Sphinx as if to steady frayed nerves, glaring the while at Miss Frayle's downcast head. After a moment he continued:

'The picture was in no way tampered

with. The hook from which it was suspended remained intact in the wall. The wire supporting it was also intact, the picture itself undamaged. It had obviously been taken down with the care usually bestowed upon any picture that is lifted down from the wall in the ordinary way.'

Miss Frayle nodded to herself as if the import of his words had sunk home. Whereupon he glowered at her with increased ferocity, then realizing she was unconscious of his continued wrath, he went on:

'Several other pictures were then removed, however, as if the intruder was still expecting to discover, perhaps, a wall-safe behind them. In each case, however, these had been torn down without care. Their hooks wrenched out, supporting wires broken, the pictures thrown down carelessly. From this may be deduced the fact that the intruder went to the first picture immediately, and not until he had removed it did he realize he had *failed* to understand the significance of the Purple Lake.'

Doctor Morelle paused, this time with

dramatic emphasis.

'Thereafter,' he declared through a cloud of cigarette-smoke, 'he began to search, becoming progressively more destructive as his search proved unavailing. Is that now clear enough, Miss Frayle?'

There was a short silence. Then:

'How do you know the search did prove unavailing?' Miss Frayle asked quickly and with extreme temerity.

'Continue with your shorthand,' Doctor Morelle snapped peremptorily. Miss Frayle ducked down her head and he dictated:

'I have not conclusive knowledge, but I incline to the theory that the search was unsuccessful. For the rest of the flat was ransacked as if the searcher were extending his quest in the destructive desperation of despair.'

The Doctor drew at his Le Sphinx and added, through a cloud of cigarette-smoke: 'From this may also be deduced that if it were Albany's assailant who later entered the flat, that person did not come into possession of the clue to the secret for which he searched there until *after* his attack on Albany. Otherwise, obviously being of a desperate character, he would have compelled his victim, either by trickery or force, to reveal the secret before attempting to eliminate him from the scene.'

Miss Frayle drew a quick breath and asked:

'In that case, what was the motive, then, for the attack on Sir Hugh?'

'Fear or revenge. Not gain. Not at the time of the attack, that is. Circumstances have since changed, admittedly, and gain may be an added factor. From which we may assume that a further attempt on Albany's life *may* be made unless we take proper precautions. That is, if the assailant concerned already knows Albany's whereabouts.'

Her pencil flying over the pages of her notebook, Miss Frayle was looking thoughtful and a little anxious. She knew little about Sir Hugh Albany, except what she had occasionally read about him in the glossy weeklies. She had never even met him except for her encounter with him as he lay unconscious in the mews.

But she knew and liked Sherry Carfax, a nice, charming, unspoiled girl, genuinely in love with him. Added to which, she rather doted on the picture she had built up in her mind about the romance between these two.

Already, she reflected, quite a lot of people knew where Albany was. Doctor Bennett, for instance, and the staff at the nursing-home. The police knew where he was. Baron Xavier knew. Mrs. Latimer. Possibly, too, the criminal might have seen him carried into Doctor Bennett's house. And then, perversely, Miss Frayle's mind returned to Cleo Latimer.

There, she recognized, was a clever woman. Clever enough to realize and admit the mistake she had made when she had lied about knowing Zusky. Clever enough to give a pretty reasonable excuse for that lie. And a convincing one. Even Miss Frayle, despite her antipathy towards Mrs. Latimer, felt inclined to believe that excuse.

Mechanically following Doctor Morelle's dictation, Miss Frayle permitted herself to ponder upon Mrs. Latimer. She had, without saying so in so many words, at least hinted at a love-affair between her and Sir Hugh Albany.

Miss Frayle's imagination waxed even more romantic. If there *had* been a love-affair between them, then Cleo Latimer would, obviously, be jealous of Sherry Carfax. And, thought Miss Frayle, her mind unconsciously running on the lines of a somewhat highly coloured romance she had recently been reading, do all in her power to stop the marriage. Even, perhaps, to the extent of instigating the attack on Sir Hugh Albany!

Miss Frayle's eyes popped at that thought. Became so flustered she almost dropped her pencil. Why, she could just imagine Mrs. Latimer hiring some desperado, saying to him: 'Go and beat up the brute who has cast my love aside — he wants to marry another!' In that case, why had she turned up at the flat to call?

Obviously, Miss Frayle decided, to discover how the land lay. To find out what she could. Yes, Miss Frayle thought excitedly, it was not impossible. It could fit into the sort of scheme a woman like

Mrs. Latimer might evolve. She lived not far from where Sir Hugh had been found. Then, Miss Frayle's thoughts rushed on, there was that man she had offered the brandy to. Who had helped her into a taxi and whom she had seen later at Lady Tonbridge's party.

Where did he figure in all this?

Sherry Carfax had said he was a friend of Sir Hugh. What was he doing in those mews at that time? She must remember to ask Sherry Carfax about him again. It was odd — and she frowned momentarily to herself so that Doctor Morelle imagined she was experiencing difficulty with one of her hieroglyphics — that she'd forgotten him until now. Forgotten all about him. Perhaps he was in league with Mrs. Latimer? Perhaps it was *he* she'd asked to attack Sir Hugh?

And then Miss Frayle's carefully fabricated and rather exciting melodramatic little romance fell to earth with a decided bump.

It suddenly struck her with irresistible logic that obviously Mrs. Latimer had been badly shocked when she had learned at Albany's flat someone had been murdered there. Yes, Miss Frayle had to admit, she had been so shocked she had deliberately lied in order to avoid the possibility of being called as a witness. And what was more, Miss Frayle recalled, her spirits ebbing to zero, Mrs. Latimer herself had pointed out that by being involved, she might well cause a rift in the lute between Sherry Carfax and Sir Hugh.

Then did she call at the flat just to find out what was happening? Miss Frayle reflected. She didn't trust the woman. She didn't trust her an inch. Look at the way she had made eyes at the Doctor! Look at the way she'd inveigled herself into his house and was trying to gain his sympathy!

Suddenly something clicked in Miss Frayle's mind so that she gave a half-muttered exclamation.

It was so sudden, so startling, that her purely mechanical notations of Doctor Morelle's dictation ceased abruptly. She sat up, her mouth open and her pencil poised over the notebook, as the Doctor was in the act of winding up his summary of the case as it stood.

He was still dictating when Miss Frayle moved quickly out of her chair and swiftly crossed to the door.

Doctor Morelle broke off with an expression of outraged amazement. Never before had Miss Frayle left him, so to speak, in mid-sentence, engaged as she was in the midst of a task demanding his utmost concentration!

'Miss Frayle!' he rapped. 'Are you quite insane today?'

She turned to him quickly, raising her finger to her lips. Reaching for the door-handle, she turned it and flung the door wide.

On the threshold Cleo Latimer smiled at her.

18

Two Women Meet

Cleo Latimer said with unruffled equanimity: 'Thank you, Miss Frayle. I was just about to come in.'

Her coolness was astonishing. But in Miss Frayle's mind there was no shadow of doubt she had been standing there on the other side of that door listening to every word Doctor Morelle had been dictating.

'I feel so much better now, Doctor.' Mrs. Latimer turned to Doctor Morelle. 'I came in to thank you. I hope I'm not interrupting you?'

It was seldom that Miss Frayle became angry. Her nature was genuinely too gentle and her long association with the Doctor had taught her the uselessness of losing one's temper. But now she was extremely annoyed, to say the least. Her worst suspicions were confirmed.

Her cheeks were quite pink and behind her horn-rimmed spectacles her blue eyes glinted.

'Really, Mrs. Latimer!' she burst out. 'I must say I consider it quite — '

But Doctor Morelle interrupted her smoothly.

'My dear Mrs. Latimer, I am gratified to have been of some service,' he said quickly. 'I trust the rest has been beneficial, and you found the tablets a useful restorative. You have had a very trying morning. I — ah — I advise you to take things more easily for a while.'

'I will, Doctor. Thank you so much for your kindness.' Cleo Latimer fired a veritable broadside of charm at him, then turned to Miss Frayle, still smiling.

Miss Frayle was stupefied at the Doctor's attitude. Couldn't he see the woman was making a perfect fool of him? Couldn't he *realize* she had been behaving like a cheap eavesdropper? She made no reply to the other's: 'And thank you too, Miss Frayle. You have been most kind and sympathetic.'

Miss Frayle responded with a stony stare.

'Er — Mrs. Latimer,' Doctor Morelle murmured, 'I think perhaps I should give you a word of — ah — warning. You must not neglect obtaining medical advice as soon as you conveniently can. These attacks, you know — '

'Perhaps I could come and see you again,' she said quickly.

'I could advise you of a specialist to consult,' he nodded. 'Shall we make an appointment now?'

'Not now,' was the reply in somewhat hurried tones. 'I — I will telephone you later.'

At that moment the door-bell rang. The Doctor's gaze narrowed as Mrs. Latimer's hand moved in that quick, pressing gesture to her heart.

In a stifled voice Miss Frayle murmured: 'Excuse me,' in much the same way as she might have said: 'You make me sick!' and went to answer the door.

As they followed her, Mrs. Latimer said, low-voiced, to Doctor Morelle:

'What d'you think I'd better do about my — my foolish mistake of this morning? Shall I get in touch with

Inspector Hood?'

'That is a matter upon which I can scarcely advise you. Of course, you realize it will be my duty to inform the Inspector if I should happen to see him before you do.'

'I see. Thanks.' Mrs. Latimer's voice seemed just a shade harder than its usual soft tone.

It was Sherry Carfax who stood at the front door. She looked pale and anxious, and there were tired shadows under her eyes. But she brightened as she saw Miss Frayle. 'You are expecting me, aren't you?'

Then her eyes went beyond Miss Frayle to Mrs. Latimer. Her voice trailed off. Her expression hardened. For a brief moment the two women stared at each other. Doctor Morelle stood apart, his eyes veiled but watchful as a hawk.

Sherry Carfax's expression was candid enough. There was in her eyes a look of angry affront. Mrs. Latimer, on the other hand, appeared somewhat nonplussed. She had stopped uncertainly as she saw the other standing there. She looked faintly puzzled. Perhaps something more. Perhaps even a shade alarmed. But it was only momentary. A flickering of expression across that lovely face. It might almost have been a trick of light. A moment later she was walking forward, a faint, almost mocking, smile on her beautiful mouth.

'Hullo, Sherry,' she said. 'I'm so terribly sorry to hear about poor Hugh. How is he now?'

Sherry Carfax drew in a quick breath. Miss Frayle watched her with a fluttering feeling of sympathy. Then in a quick, brittle voice came the reply:

'I don't think you and I have anything to say to each other, Cleo. I see you're leaving.' And she stepped on one side to let the other pass.

Without batting an eyelid, Mrs. Latimer went out.

Miss Frayle drew Sherry inside and closed the door. The girl saw Doctor Morelle, and said in a quick, bitter voice:

'What was she doing here? What does she want?'

The Doctor's thin mouth tightened, his

eyes were like chips of ice.

'That,' he retorted coldly, 'is a question I do not feel disposed to answer.'

'I'm sorry!' the other said quickly. 'I'd no business to speak like that. I'm pretty well all in!'

She dropped into a chair. 'I only came in for a minute. I've come straight from the nursing-home. All they tell me is that Hugh's going on as well as can be expected. Sir David's cautious. Says the operation was successful so far as that part of it's concerned, but he won't say definitely that Hugh's out of danger.'

'No surgeon would, under the circumstances.' Doctor Morelle's tone was somewhat milder. 'He will not be satisfied until Albany has recovered consciousness. Did he give any indication when that might be? Tonight, at some time, I imagine.'

'He thought so. Perhaps.'

'And doubtless advised you to go home and rest?'

She smiled wanly.

'Just that,' she nodded. 'I was on my way, but thought I'd come and see you.'

And then she flashed out, 'Not that I'd have done so if I'd known that woman was here!'

'If it will in any way lessen the strain on your nerves,' Doctor Morelle observed, 'permit me to inform you that Mrs. Latimer is not a regular patient of mine. While I was with the police this morning investigating the events at the flat, Mrs. Latimer called. Ostensibly for a friendly chat with Albany. Apparently she was unaware of what had happened. She was unfortunately taken ill while she was there and returned with us for some treatment.'

Unexpectedly he smiled. It was a somewhat enigmatic quirking at the corners of his mouth, but he smiled. Which, for Doctor Morelle, was something.

'That, my dear Miss Carfax, is the sum total of my acquaintance with Mrs. Latimer.'

Sherry was frowning.

'She called on Hugh? This morning? Why should she have done that?'

Suddenly she went to him impulsively,

laying her hand on his sleeve.

'I'm frightened,' she said in a low voice. 'I'm frightened of that woman, Doctor Morelle! There's something — something sinister about her.'

She hesitated, then burst out:

'Somehow or other she's got Hugh in her power — blackmailing him, or something — she and her precious friend. I know Hugh was going to tell them yesterday afternoon he was finished with them both. That he wanted no more to do with them. With Cleo Latimer or Charles Gresham — '

Miss Frayle gave a sudden, sharp crowing noise, not unlike that of a robust hen, and her spectacles slid agitatedly down her nose. The Doctor cast her a freezing glance, but for once Miss Frayle remained unfrozen.

'That's the name I've been trying to remember!' she gulped excitedly. 'Charles Gresham! The man who spoke to you at the reception last night, Sherry. He was the man I spoke to in the mews after I'd found Sir Hugh!'

Miss Frayle gulped again, pushed her

spectacles back with an impatient movement and, as they promptly slid down her nose again, turned to Doctor Morelle and demanded dramatically:

'Don't you see how it all fits in?'

19

Sherry Carfax takes Orders

Doctor Morelle frowned.

'It would be more impressive if you would learn to arrange your ponderings before uttering them. And could you not refrain from jigging about so excitedly merely because you have recollected some item which should have been impressed upon your memory from the beginning?'

And, turning on his heel, he marched into the consulting-room, followed by Miss Frayle and Sherry Carfax.

'But this is important, Doctor,' Miss Frayle squeaked, trotting after him eagerly. 'I'm sure now that Charles Gresham — '

'I haven't the least doubt it was important,' was the icy response. 'It may be regarded as a foregone conclusion, my dear Miss Frayle, that anything which has once vanished from that ephemeral miasma which you fondly refer to as your mind has at some time been of considerable moment. It is important data only which you forget. Whether it remains important when it is recalled to you by extraneous circumstances remains to be seen. Proceed.'

Sherry Carfax threw a glance of sympathy at Miss Frayle as the Doctor fired his heavy broadside. But Miss Frayle was either too accustomed to it or too excited to notice. She ignored Doctor Morelle and turned to Sherry.

With a certain amount of histrionics which caused the Doctor more than once to cast his eyes ceilingwards, Miss Frayle recounted to Sherry the circumstances of her discovering Albany in the mews, followed by her encounter with Gresham there, and then seeing him again at Lady Tonbridge's party.

'I didn't think very much about it when I saw you talking to him,' Miss Frayle finished. 'You see, I didn't know then the unconscious man was Sir Hugh — '

The other had jumped to her feet.

'Yes, that's it!' she exclaimed in a low, tense voice, and Doctor Morelle turned his gaze on her. She went on: 'Hugh went to see him and Cleo Latimer yesterday afternoon to break off with them for ever. They quarrelled. Gresham went after him and — and shot him.'

'Have you any reason to suggest why he should do such a thing?' the Doctor interposed. 'It was a not inconsiderable risk for him to take.'

'He hates Hugh!' the girl flashed back at him. 'He's a rotter, Doctor Morelle. Dangerous! And he didn't take such a risk. It was getting dark. The mews would be quite deserted at that time. I know — I know he and Cleo Latimer fixed it between them!'

For a moment she stood silent, her hands clenched.

She was very pale now, and her eyes were blazing. There was a moment's silence while Doctor Morelle and Miss Frayle watched her. Then she said, in a low, breathless voice:

'I'm going to see this Gresham man now. I'm going to get the truth out of him if it's the last thing I do!'

'You will do nothing of the kind.'

It was the Doctor's voice which stopped her in her tracks.

Sherry Carfax turned. She was not accustomed to receiving orders, and there was no mistaking the peremptory command in Doctor Morelle's tone. As she was about to make some reply, he raised his hand and brushed her answer aside before it reached her lips.

'You will do nothing of the kind,' he reiterated firmly. 'You will be good enough to remember there is more at stake than some enmity between Albany and this other individual. This is a case of some seriousness, Miss Carfax. A case, in fact, of murder!'

She flinched at that and he seemed to tower above her, his narrowed, glittering eyes fixed on hers, his keen, saturnine face grim and set. He looked formidable, the apotheosis of avenging justice.

'A man has been shot dead in cold blood,' he continued levelly. 'Whether or not Gresham is implicated in that murder is a matter for investigation. Proof must be forthcoming. Proof which must be available before he may be confronted with any accusation. It is for this proof that the police and I have been searching. I will not have a case in which I have interested myself jeopardized by the hysterical interference of a young woman in — ah — love. I will not have the course of justice endangered by any wayward impulse such as the one upon which you contemplate acting. I trust that I make myself perfectly clear!'

There was a long pause.

Miss Frayle, her round eyes switching from the girl to the Doctor and back again, waited for Sherry Carfax's answer.

'I'm sorry,' she said at last. 'You're right, of course. I'm afraid I was thinking of Hugh and myself, not of — the man who was murdered.'

'I think we understand each other,' he said. 'Now,' he went on coolly, flicking the ash off his Le Sphinx, 'what can you tell me of Albany's association with Gresham and the woman Cleo Latimer? For example, how long have they been acquainted?'

She looked at him for a moment before making a reply.

'About a year, I think,' she said slowly. 'Mrs. Latimer was abroad until about a year ago. America, I believe.' Then she added: 'She's always been rather' — she shrugged — 'well — mysterious.'

'You suggested that Gresham was a confederate. That was the description you used, a description implying a rather more than ordinary association. What exactly were you wishing to infer regarding their relationship?'

She answered him frankly:

'Nothing that I can state with any definite proof. It's just that they're . . . well . . . shady. People — well-known people — have been friendly with them, then suddenly dropped them. No reason has ever been given. But there's been talk. Hints of parties where people have lost a lot of money. One man — I can't remember his name — was nearly ruined, I believe. And Gresham was implicated in some way. It was something to do with gambling but I know nothing of the details. But I do know this' — she looked steadily at him as she continued — 'a lot of people are definitely scared of those two. It's as if almost . . . ' She hesitated a second, then said flatly: 'It's as if they're a pair of blackmailers!'

Miss Frayle gave a gasp and looked quickly at the Doctor.

He drew at his cigarette and then, as if speaking to himself:

'And in his association with them, Albany might have obtained evidence of that.'

'And,' Miss Frayle put in excitedly, unable to restrain her excitement any longer, 'Gresham attacked him to try and get the evidence back!'

Doctor Morelle cast an oblique glance at her, but, her voice rising higher and higher, she was not to be daunted as she continued: 'And then — then he searched the flat! That's it in a nutshell, Doctor, isn't it?' She turned to him eagerly. 'While he was searching the flat, Zusky caught him and so Gresham shot him — !'

She caught his look, her voice fell, tailed off into an incoherent murmur.

The Doctor's eyes were half-closed.

Upon his fine, chiselled countenance rested an expression of long-suffering anguish patiently borne.

'A most remarkable performance, Miss Frayle,' he observed, scathingly. He opened his eyes, and now they were glittering balefully. 'Perhaps I should retire and leave the investigation in your hands?'

'Oh, no, Doctor,' Miss Frayle breathed. 'I — I was only summarizing from data you have provided by questioning Miss Carfax — '

'A most generous admission.' The Doctor's sarcasm was heavy enough to invite comparison with a sack of potatoes. 'Most generous. And now, having treated us with this illuminating deduction, perhaps you will recall for our benefit the time of Zusky's murder?'

Miss Frayle pondered for a moment.

'Umm . . . ' she mumbled, struggling to answer his query. 'Ah, yes! You fixed it at between ten and eleven o'clock.'

He nodded, and asked in a voice that dripped honey:

'And at what time,' his voice beginning

to turn sour now, 'at what time did you recognize this Gresham individual last night?'

'About ten o'clock.'

Her jaw dropped and she slowly subsided.

'Oh,' she said, blankly. 'Oh, dear! He couldn't have done it, could he? He must have been at the party at the time the poor man was shot.'

'Precisely,' Doctor Morelle nodded, and his voice had an edge like a razor. 'Precisely, my *dear* Miss Frayle!'

'I think,' Sherry Carfax put in gently, 'Miss Frayle was only trying to be helpful, Doctor.'

'That is one of my misfortunes.' He turned to her, smiling mirthlessly. 'Miss Frayle has a faculty for attempting to be helpful at the most inopportune of moments.'

'And anyway, it mightn't alter the fact,' the girl went on, thoughtfully, 'that Gresham probably was the one who searched Hugh's flat. He could easily have done that after his attack on Hugh, and before going on to Lady Tonbridge's.

He would know there would be no one there to interrupt his search.' She paused and asked him: 'Are you — are you going to see Gresham?'

'Eventually. Not immediately, however. Do you know his address?'

She nodded quietly.

'Be kind enough to write it down for me, will you?'

A considerably deflated Miss Frayle handed the other a pencil.

While Sherry Carfax wrote, Miss Frayle glanced nervously at the Doctor. He appeared sunk in thought.

Her own brow became corrugated as she realized that something elusive was running through her mind, something too ephemeral to be described as a concrete idea. A hint which, if she could only grasp it and give it coherent expression, might restore her to favour with Doctor Morelle.

If only she could, figuratively speaking, lay her hand on the vague notion that bothered her.

'Miss Carfax,' the Doctor said suddenly, 'are you cognizant of a picture in the flat?

A picture named the Purple Lake?'

The girl looked puzzled.

'Why — yes,' she answered. 'I know it. Hugh is rather sentimental about it. His father painted it years ago — '

'Dud — Doctor Morelle!' Miss Frayle suddenly began to stutter. The idea that had been chasing round her head was losing its tenuousness, becoming more definite. She was almost afraid to speak lest she lost it again, and yet she had to. She had to risk being turned to stone by the Doctor's basilisk glare.

'Mum-may I ask a question?' she at last managed to blurt out.

He regarded her as she stood there blinking at him, and when he answered his voice was unexpectedly mild.

'I trust it will be a sensible one.'

'It's only this . . . ' She hesitated, then took the plunge. 'If Charles Gresham did search the flat, why did he go to that picture first? You remember, you deduced that whoever searched the flat went straight to the picture and took it down? You know, didn't begin tearing the flat up until afterwards . . . '

She gulped, frightened by her own temerity, and gazed wide-eyed at him.

And then, slowly, a sudden sense of delightful relaxation came to her. He was favouring her with a smile. A frosty smile, true, but to her it was as welcome as a radiant burst of sunshine. She had at least reinstated herself in his eyes. He had gathered the drift of what she was trying to say.

'Precisely what I am wondering myself,' he agreed. 'But,' he went on, cryptically, 'I think we shall have to look further than Gresham.' He turned back to the other. 'How long has the picture been in the flat, Miss Carfax?'

Thoroughly mystified, she answered:

'I haven't the least idea. It's been there ever since I can remember. I seem to remember Hugh telling me his father had brought it up from Stormhaven Towers years ago.'

'Are you acquainted with the subject of the picture?'

She looked puzzled and he explained.

'The circumstances in which it was painted. *Where*, for instance, it was painted.'

'I'm afraid I'm not. But Hugh would know, I expect.'

His eyes narrowed, Doctor Morelle stared at her. Then he turned to Miss Frayle.

'Telephone Baron Xavier at his hotel.'

'Yes, Doctor.' Miss Frayle promptly reached for the telephone.

'Ask him to give me an appointment as soon as possible.'

'Yes, Doctor.'

'That is to say,' he added, 'immediately.'

'Yes, Doctor Morelle.'

The Doctor turned back to the girl.

'Do you know Xavier well?' he asked.

'Not awfully well. He's an old friend of Hugh. They were at school together — Baron Xavier was educated over here, you know. I've only met him on two or three occasions.'

'And Stefan Zusky?'

'I'd heard his name, that was all. I gathered he was the Baron's secretary and a close friend, but I never met him.'

While they were talking, Miss Frayle got through to Xavier's suite at his hotel. Her voice was bright and crisp: 'This is

Doctor Morelle's secretary here . . . '

'Well, how nice, Miss Frayle!' a man's cheery tones cut in. 'How are you?'

'Who's that?' she queried with a puzzled expression. The voice was somehow vaguely familiar.

'I'm the chap you were kind enough to dance with last night. Remember?'

'You . . . ? Good gracious! I never realized — ! I mean, you never told me . . . '

Miss Frayle stuttered in her surprise. It was the nice, dark-haired young man who had recognized her at the party. And she had, she recalled, while they were dancing, pointed out to him the man she now knew to be Gresham.

'You never asked me,' he was saying, his voice tinged with amusement as it came over the wire. 'And you gave me the impression that somehow you wouldn't have been very interested if I'd volunteered the information!'

Miss Frayle remembered with a blush that she had indeed lost interest in him from the moment she spotted the man she had met in the mews, and had rushed off, hardly waiting to thank him for the dance.

'This is a rotten business, isn't it?' he said, more gravely. 'Has Doctor Morelle discovered anything yet?'

'That is not for me to say at the moment,' Miss Frayle responded primly. 'But what are you . . . ? I mean — that is — '

'Oh, I'm only Baron Xavier's secretary,' at which Miss Frayle's spectacles slid down her nose in surprise. 'Is there anything I can do for you?' he went on helpfully.

She pulled herself together to say: 'Doctor Morelle wishes to come round and see him, please. As soon as possible.'

There was a slight pause and then he said:

'Inspector Hood's here at the moment, interviewing him, but I suppose it'll be all right.' And he added: 'Will you be coming, too, Miss Frayle?'

She blushed and murmured: 'I don't know. I hope so.' And he was sounding more cheerful again.

'I shall want to hear all about it from

you. Anyway, I'll leave word for them to bring Doctor Morelle up as soon as he arrives. I hope to see you with him.'

And he rang off.

Miss Frayle replaced the receiver and told Doctor Morelle that Inspector Hood was having an interview with Baron Xavier. The Doctor, after thanking her with his customary sardonic courtesy, dashed her hopes to the ground by adding:

'I shall not require you to accompany me. I would prefer that you escorted Miss Carfax to her home.'

'Oh, that's not necessary,' Sherry protested. 'I'm perfectly all right — '

'Nevertheless,' he insisted, 'that is what I prefer. It is essential you obtain rest and remove from your mind any question of seeing this Gresham individual. Your place will be by Albany as soon as he is recovered.'

He turned to Miss Frayle. 'You will return here when you are assured that Miss Carfax is comfortably settled. You will receive further instructions from me later.'

'Very well, Doctor,' she replied woodenly. He eyed her for a moment, then turned again to the other.

'Have I your assurance that you will not attempt to communicate with Gresham?'

Sherry shrugged. 'As you wish, Doctor.'

Miss Frayle realized how much she must long to find Gresham and drag the truth from him, but no doubt she saw the wisdom of Doctor Morelle's advice in not interfering in a matter with which he and the police were dealing.

20

A Frightened Man

It had been a morning of shocks for Cleo Latimer, culminating in that awkward little meeting with Sherry Carfax.

But she walked along Harley Street with the graceful serenity of a woman conscious of her beauty, with no greater anxiety on her mind than might be occasioned by the prospect of having to select a piece of jewellery in Bond Street.

Her face was a mask for a mind which was seething. The news of Zusky's murder and Doctor Morelle's manner of presenting that news to her had been the greatest shock. She was a woman with a zest for danger, had lived all her life dangerously, but had a strong distaste for being unprepared.

Cleo Latimer was ready to take risks — big risks — so long as she had the opportunity of weighing them up first.

During a career which, to say the least, had more shade than light on it, she had matched wits with many adversaries, and before long had learned to despise them. Not that she had ever made the mistake of underrating an opponent. It was simply that she possessed a peculiar insight which enabled her quickly to sum anyone up with accuracy. For example, while her respect for Doctor Morelle was high, her acumen in no way allowed her to underrate Miss Frayle.

What was causing her certain annoyance at the moment was the stupid blunder she had made in denying any acquaintance with Zusky. It gave her no satisfaction to tell herself she had committed the error in a moment of shock when she had not been able to think with her customary speed and lucidity.

At least, however, she congratulated herself she had been quick enough to amend the mistake by admitting it frankly. Though again, her respect for Doctor Morelle had been enhanced by his prompt perception of the lie and his studied attack. Nevertheless, she was satisfied that she had, with some adroitness, turned it to good account by her explanation. She felt assured her explanation had been convincing.

Cleo Latimer was keenly aware that Doctor Morelle was a man to watch with extreme care and who, unless she was always smart enough to turn every circumstance to her own advantage, might succeed in trapping her. Such reflections did not dismay, but merely stimulated, her.

Another factor which had sent her estimation of Doctor Morelle soaring, was the masterly summary which she had contrived to overhear him dictating to Miss Frayle. In particular she had been impressed by his deduction pointing to the significance of the picture called the Purple Lake.

Intuitively, too, Mrs. Latimer was very aware of Miss Frayle's mistrust of her. It was a factor she had not failed to take into consideration. If, for the time being, she shelved the potential danger from that quarter, it would not be forgotten, nor ever ignored, until she was satisfied that

Miss Frayle was rendered harmless. Because of her perception of Miss Frayle's mistrust, she had not been taken unawares when the door had suddenly opened while she deliberately eavesdropped on the Doctor's dictating. And she was convinced that, despite whatever suspicions Miss Frayle might cherish, she had, at any rate, successfully deceived Doctor Morelle.

In fact, the whole consequence of the morning was that Cleo Latimer was fully alert to danger, without being apprehensive.

Before reaching Oxford Street, she turned into a side-entrance of a big store. She went direct to a telephone-box and there rang up Charles Gresham. His voice, hoarse and whisky-roughened, sounded over the wire.

'It's Cleo. I want to see — '

'I've been trying to get you the whole morning!' He was nervy and irritable. 'Where've you been? Have you seen the morning papers?'

'No. But I can guess what you're worried about.'

'Do you know Zusky's been found

dead at Hugh's — ?'

'Don't be a damned fool!' she interrupted him quickly, her voice sharp with the hard, clear quality of a diamond.

He broke off, muttering.

'Hell, I'm worried,' he went on after a moment. 'What's it all in aid of?' Then he asked: 'Where have you been, anyway?'

She told him quietly: 'I shall be home in ten minutes or so. Come and see me. We can talk.'

'D'you know anything — ?' he started to ask her.

But she replaced the receiver without replying.

She had been in her flat ten minutes when she heard the taxi outside, and a moment later a ring at the bell.

It was Gresham.

'Couldn't find a blasted taxi . . .'

He followed her, cursing and muttering, obviously in a bad temper. None of it disturbed her. She merely smiled to herself. She knew well enough his ill-temper was inspired by fear. And the fact that he was afraid left her unruffled. She nodded to a chair.

'Sit down and relax.'

'I've got the damned jitters so badly!' He threw himself into a chair and lit a cigarette with an unsteady hand. 'What's this about Zusky?'

'He was murdered last night,' she said in a matter-of-fact voice. 'Shot dead. Didn't you do it?'

'Me!'

He sat up and stared at her, his protuberant eyes wide. They were bloodshot and had a hard, menacing glitter. 'I wouldn't do a damned silly thing like that!' he rasped. 'What object would I have in killing him? I didn't even know the man.'

'What time were you at the flat last night?'

'I went there before I went to Lady Tonbridge's party. After Albany vanished out of the mews, I wondered what the hell to do. I was a bit anxious. Didn't know what had happened to him, or where he might pop up. I went home, changed, then took a taxi to St. James's Street. I walked to the block where his flat is and went up the fire-escape.'

'I know all that,' she put in coldly. 'I'm

simply asking you what time it was.'

'Dunno,' he grunted. 'About half past eight. I know I left the place before nine, because of the telegram' — he tapped his pocket — 'that he dropped.'

'Give me the telegram,' she said.

He shook his head slowly. Smiled at her thinly.

'You don't want it. I might. You remember it said Zusky would be there at nine-thirty, so I got to hell out of it long before there was a chance of him turning up. Who shot him? Why?'

'You could have done,' she told him calmly.

His face grew dark. Then the colour receded and his mouth was thin and ugly looking.

'What are you getting at?'

He rose and stood close to her.

'Listen, Cleo,' he said. 'What the hell game is this you're trying to play?'

'I'm not playing at anything,' Cleo Latimer drawled. 'I'm simply saying what it looks like. What the police might think. What Doctor Morelle might think. You're in a spot, Charles.'

'*I'm* in a spot!' he choked. He tapped the ash off his cigarette with a savage movement.

'Where d'you get that '*I*' stuff? You're in this with me. Only last night you were practically threatening me if I didn't play along with you. Now *I'm* the one in a spot!'

'You're an awful damned fool.'

And Mrs. Latimer sighed expressively. 'I'm simply pointing out the danger of your position, I'm not thinking of our association. You've got to look at facts. *You* shot Hugh yesterday. *You* ransacked his flat. *I* didn't. In other words, it's you we've got to worry about for the moment, and not me.' She paused and drew at the cigarette in her long holder. He said nothing.

'I've been up to the flat this morning,' she continued. 'I've been with the police and Doctor Morelle, and I know which way things are pointing. They are pointing towards you, and it won't be very long before that secretary of Doctor Morelle's suddenly remembers *you* were the man she saw in the mews, and saw again later at last night's party. And she'll yap.'

The other made as if to speak, but she went on quickly.

'Get this, Charles. This Doctor Morelle is nobody's fool. He's a clever, dangerous man. It won't be long before they establish the fact it was you who tried to bump off Hugh and then broke into his flat.' And then added coldly, deliberately: 'Even if he doesn't recover from that bullet you pumped into him.'

He stared at her without speaking for a moment. He was obviously frightened now, and a very faint smile touched her lovely curved mouth.

Gresham swallowed hard. Then:

'Albany — is he going to — to — ?'

He broke off, unable to get the word out, and stared at her questioningly.

'I don't know. They're operating on him. He hasn't recovered consciousness yet. In any case, they'll hold you for that. If he dies . . . ' She shrugged.

Gresham dropped into his chair heavily. 'What a mess!' Then he leaned forward and said in a hoarse voice: 'But I didn't do it! Zusky, I mean. I didn't do it. I don't give a damn how clever the police are, or this Doctor Morelle — they can't make me do something I didn't do and I didn't kill Zusky. I don't know anything about it. I didn't do it, I tell you!'

'All right, all right, you didn't do it.'

For the first time Cleo Latimer showed signs of strain. 'For God's sake don't keep telling me,' she told him. 'I believe you. We've got to think.'

'You know damned well I didn't,' Gresham said again, hoarsely.

Then suddenly his glaring bloodshot eyes fastened on her and he struggled to his feet. A new expression had wiped the fear off his face.

'I didn't even know the man,' he said slowly, still staring at her fixedly. 'You haven't condescended to tell me anything about this million pound scheme, or what the set-up is where Xavier is concerned. But' — he ground the words through his teeth — '*you knew Zusky*! You said so. Did *you* shoot him, Cleo? Eh? Did you? It might have been a smart thing for you to do!'

21

Cleo Latimer makes a 'Phone Call

Gresham's viciously uttered words died away into a long silence. A silence that was broken only by a taxi hooting as it rattled past.

Gresham moved towards her slowly, his hands hanging loosely at his sides, while Mrs. Latimer regarded him with faint distaste and icy contempt.

He continued:

'You said you were going to Lady Tonbridge's party. That you'd meet me there. But you didn't turn up. Where were you? Bumping Zusky off and making it look as if I'd done it? You had your reasons for wanting him out of the way. If you could pin a murder on me, it would get me out of the way too, wouldn't it? And leave you with a clear million — '

'Shut your mouth, you fool!'

Her voice was a chilling whisper that

brought him up with a jerk.

She went on contemptuously: 'I've always thought you were a fool, but I didn't know you could be quite so stupid. Why quarrel with me when all I want to do is help you? I didn't know you were going to search the flat. I didn't know Zusky was going to be there until you showed me the telegram. If I wanted to get rid of you, d'you think I'd leave it to chance like that?'

He was eyeing her cautiously, but she saw her words had got home. His face sagged. She touched his arm.

'Listen! Now is the time to *use* your head, not lose it. There's only one thing to be done so far as you're concerned, and that's to get you out of the country. Quickly!'

He was listening intently to every word she had to say. She knew by his expression he was already beginning to appreciate the sense of what she said.

It was true, he was thinking, she knew nothing about the telegram until after he had shown it to her. And that had been after he had searched the flat, after Zusky had been killed. His suspicions ebbed, his own plight loomed ominously.

'Maybe you're right,' he started to mutter. 'Maybe I'd better clear out for a time . . . '

'You'll need money. How much can you draw?'

'A few hundred — '

'I've a couple of hundred you can have. You'd better try and get a seat on the next 'plane for Paris this afternoon. Wait there until you hear from me.' She was speaking rapidly now, her voice alert and incisive. 'I'll get in touch with you within the next two or three days. Don't try and communicate with me here — '

'Don't rush me,' he interrupted with sudden harshness. 'I've got to think it out. Give me a drink . . . '

She said, 'That's the last thing you want at the moment.'

He glared at her, the old suspicion creeping back into his face.

'Is this a double-cross?'

He gripped her arm. His bloodshot eyes strove to read her mind. 'Are you trying to brush me off?' he growled thickly.

She answered him calmly.

'If you don't believe me,' she shrugged, 'I can't make you. It's your spot, not mine.'

'For half a million you'd stop at nothing,' he muttered. 'And neither would I!' He thought for a moment, pulling nervously at his lower lip. Then: 'I'm going back to my rooms to pack. Give me that money.'

She went to a drawer, took out a flat packet of notes. After a quick glance at them, he thrust them in his pocket and nodded.

'Shall I see you later?' he asked.

'Not here,' she said. 'I'll be over in Paris any time within the next two or three days. With your share.'

He gave her a long, hard stare.

'For your sake, I hope so,' he said hoarsely. 'Because if this *is* a double-cross, Cleo, I won't rest until I've got you!'

And he raised his strong hands in a significant, gripping gesture.

She went to the window and watched

him disappear round the corner, looking for a taxi as he went. Then she turned, unsmiling, to the telephone and dialled a number.

After a moment, Mrs. Latimer spoke quietly into the mouthpiece.

22

Richard Whitmore

Doctor Morelle was shown by a good-looking, dark-haired young man into the little panelled room, done in brown and gold, that was evidently used as an ante-room. There were a couple of big leather armchairs, and a Chippendale desk was placed near the window. A side-table with drinks stood near the door.

'I'm Baron Xavier's sort of social secretary. Whitmore's my name.'

Doctor Morelle inclined his head.

'Been trying to get hold of you for the last ten minutes,' the other went on. 'I'm afraid the Baron went out before I could remind him you were coming along. An Inspector Hood's been up here interviewing him, you know, and I think it — er — bothered him a bit.'

The Doctor frowned. He was unaccustomed to having an appointment upset.

'Have you any idea where Baron Xavier has gone?' he asked coldly. 'Is he likely to be long?'

Whitmore went over to the desk and glanced at a diary.

'He has a luncheon appointment. And I've an idea he said something earlier about going to see how Sir Hugh was getting on. But that was before the Inspector turned up. Ghastly business, all this, isn't it?' he continued cheerfully. 'Poor old Zusky.' His face grew grave.

'Were you well acquainted with the deceased?'

The other nodded. 'Of course, I've never had anything to do with any of the Baron's business connected with his own country. That was what Zusky took care of. But I met him often and knew vaguely what was going on. I suppose he was done in by somebody who took a dim view of the Baron and what he stood for.'

'You are of the opinion this murder is a political assassination, then?'

'Off-hand, I'd say it was,' Whitmore agreed. 'Baron Xavier isn't popular with the party now in power in his own

238

country, naturally. And that'd go for Zusky, too. Probably they were afraid over there the Baron might stage a come-back, or something.'

He paused, then went on thoughtfully:

'In all these political set-ups there's a power behind the figurehead. In this case, Baron Xavier's the figurehead, and Zusky the real power and adviser. Zusky's whole life had been devoted to politics and the rest. He was the Baron's father's adviser, too.'

'Was Albany concerned in any way with the activities you have just mentioned?'

Richard Whitmore grinned at the idea, and shook his head.

'He'd be even less interested than I was. And Lord knows, I steered clear of it! I'd say it was pure coincidence he got shot on the same night Zusky was murdered.'

'Why should anyone wish to attack Albany?'

The young man shrugged.

'Some chap maybe saw an opportunity for pinching a wallet. Perhaps he was drunk. Perhaps starving, desperate. Who knows?'

'That is a possibility,' Doctor Morelle murmured. 'Though it appears somewhat odd that Zusky should have been murdered in Albany's flat. Is that not stretching the arm of coincidence too far?' He added: 'Were you aware that Zusky had been staying at Albany's residence in Sussex?'

'Not until this morning. I knew he used to pop to and fro between London and the Continent, but I didn't know exactly where he stayed when over here. He and Baron Xavier kept that secret between them.'

Whitmore took a silver cigarette-box from the desk and offered it to Doctor Morelle. The Doctor explained that he smoked only his own Le Sphinx brand, specially made for him. The other smiled understandingly and flicked a lighter.

'Won't you have a drink? There's some rather good sherry. If you like it dry.'

Doctor Morelle accepted the invitation.

While the other moved to the side-table, the Doctor murmured: 'Was there any quarrel between the Baron and Zusky? Did they hold any divergent opinions in certain aspects of business or policy?'

The other appeared not to have heard the query as he bent over the drinks. A decanter clinked against a glass.

'I think you'll like this,' he said, crossing to the Doctor with a glass of pale, straw-coloured sherry.

Doctor Morelle took the glass. Then: 'Excellent.' He took another sip.

'I had the pleasure of meeting that nice secretary of yours, Miss Frayle, last night, Doctor.'

'Indeed?' Another appreciative sip of sherry. 'So,' he murmured over the glass, 'you found no time to become interested in the politics of Baron Xavier's country?'

'Bags of time,' Whitmore smiled, 'but no inclination. No politics for me. As I told you, I'm simply a sort of social secretary here. You know, fix luncheon engagements, see who's coming to dinner, see that they're not placed next to people they loathe, entertain elderly dowagers who bore everyone else to tears, keep off any undesirable types.'

He gave an amused laugh.

'I've got all the attributes,' he said. 'I

can talk for hours about nothing. Can be amusing to people even when I sometimes long to kick 'em where it would do most good! Still, it's a job. And I flatter myself I've made myself useful.'

'I'm sure,' Doctor Morelle nodded. 'How long have you occupied the position?' he asked casually.

'A couple of years. I was in Cannes and was introduced to Baron Xavier when he was down there for a brief stay. Zusky was with him then, I remember,' he added.

Doctor Morelle gazed reflectively at the glass in his hand, as he observed quietly:

'Would I be very far out if I hazarded a guess that, subsequent to your meeting with the Baron at Cannes, it was Stefan Zusky who suggested you should take your present post?'

The other glanced up sharply, his good-looking face alive with surprised admiration.

'That's damned quick of you!' he exclaimed. 'As a matter of fact you're dead right. Though I didn't know it until later. The Baron approached me with the idea, and I accepted. He told me later it was Zusky's suggestion. How did you know?'

'I did not *know*,' Doctor Morelle murmured; 'merely surmised. As I hinted at just now in a question which you chose not to answer, it suggested itself to me that the Baron and his secretary held political and perhaps other opinions which at times diverged. Zusky possibly resented interference from the Baron in political activities in which he, as the power behind the — ah — figurehead, was engaged. No doubt he was anxious for Baron Xavier to devote more time to social affairs. Apparently he had no — ah — social secretary before you. It appealed to me therefore, as a justifiable surmise, that Zusky might have suggested you for a post to be specially created.'

'Damned ingenious!' the other said, enthusiastically. He laughed, showing even white teeth. 'I should hate to be up against you if I were a murderer!'

'Then perhaps you would be good enough to inform me,' Doctor Morelle went on with quiet insistence, 'if you are aware of any personal quarrel between the Baron and Zusky?'

Richard Whitmore stared at him.

Then, after a little silence, his expression hardened and he spoke with quiet intensity.

'Are you suggesting that — that Baron Xavier himself has anything to do with this affair?' he demanded. 'Because if so, you're barking up the wrong tree . . .'

'I am suggesting nothing,' was the Doctor's retort.

His voice had the hard ring of steel. He continued: 'It is not my place to hint at any alternative that has not the support of evidence. It is evidence I seek. Evidence and motive. Permit me to impress upon you that it is not a social digression which has been committed. It is murder! A man's life has been taken, and it is only the interests of justice which have to be considered. Nothing else.'

The other mumbled uncomfortably: 'I'm sorry, Doctor. You see, I'm in an awkward position. I realize you've been asking me questions in the hope of throwing some light on the murder of Zusky. I've been only too anxious to help.

I liked old Stefan. I mean, he was quite a decent scout, except I — I — well — rather felt he liked power a bit too much. But you must see that I am in a tricky spot — '

Doctor Morelle uttered an impatient exclamation.

'Where murder is concerned,' he snapped, 'the position of all people who might be concerned in it, no matter how remotely, is difficult. It may remain difficult until the murderer stands revealed. By your reluctance to answer this question, of whether or no there was any personal rift between your employer and the deceased, you lead me to infer that there was a schism of some nature. I do not care to be led to infer without evidence.'

'But I don't know if there *was* anything!'

Richard Whitmore looked unhappy. Then he said slowly:

'You're quite right when you said their views weren't always the same on certain issues. I used to hear them having pretty acrid discussions on political matters, for instance, the pair of 'em talking pretty heatedly. But I never heard them quarrelling. In fact, the Baron thought the world of Zusky as a man. They were old, staunch friends. And anyway, Baron Xavier had been fed up with politics from the day it became clear that his country preferred a Republican Government to him!'

Doctor Morelle asked: 'You were not aware when Zusky last left his native country?'

'Not to the day. But then, I never knew for certain when he was there or here. Almost from the moment I started this job, I learned that it was better for me not to ask questions about Zusky's movements.'

'Did Baron Xavier and Zusky communicate with each other when the latter was abroad?'

'They may have done. I don't know.' The young man paused. Then he said, firmly: 'Doctor Morelle, don't you think you'd get more satisfactory answers if you asked Baron Xavier himself all this?'

The Doctor's smile was frosty.

'Your employer is not available at the moment,' he replied blandly. 'And the questions are ones to which I would have preferred an immediate answer. However, it seems I must wait.' He tapped the ash off his cigarette and surveyed the tip for a moment before asking: 'Are you aware if he left Lady Tonbridge's party last night for any length of time?'

'That's another answer for which you'll have to wait,' the other said. 'I just don't know. I'm sorry to seem unhelpful,' he apologized, his face clouded and troubled.'

'Then perhaps.' Doctor Morelle persisted icily, 'you can tell me if, in your capacity as his social secretary, you are aware if he received any personal messages yesterday?'

Young Whitmore frowned and studied his empty sherry glass, twiddling it about between finger and thumb.

After a moment he said thoughtfully:

'There were quite a lot of calls, but I dealt with all of 'em — ' He broke off and exclaimed: 'Sir Hugh rang up in the morning.'

'Albany?'

The other nodded.

'It was before lunch. He said he wanted to talk to the Baron.' He nodded towards the house-exchange telephone on the desk. 'I put him through to the private sitting-room.'

'You are not aware of the nature of the conversation?'

Whitmore answered promptly and huffily: 'Naturally not.'

'Of course not,' Doctor Morelle agreed amiably. 'You know Albany well?'

Richard Whitmore shrugged.

'You know how it is. I've known him for years. We meet and chat and then go our ways.' He grinned pleasantly. 'The old social round.'

One of the telephones on the desk began to ring. The young man glanced at the Doctor with a murmured excuse.

He crossed to the desk and sat on the edge of it, one leg swinging, as he picked up the receiver and spoke into it.

23

What the Butler Saw

Whitmore said: 'Hullo?' He turned to look at the Doctor with the blank, unseeing stare of one listening to a conversation on the telephone.

In a formal tone he said: 'I regret Baron Xavier is not available at the moment. This is his secretary. Yes. Yes.'

Doctor Morelle observed Whitmore's reflection in a mirror. The young man nodded in answer to something the caller was saying. After a moment he said into the telephone: 'I will tell him. Good-bye.'

He replaced the receiver, sat for a moment on the desk in abstracted thought, then slid off and returned to Doctor Morelle.

'Sorry for the interruption,' he said, with a casual smile. 'How about another glass of sherry?'

'Thank you, no. I must not take up

more of your valuable time.'

The other laughed and made a deprecating gesture. 'As you can see at the present moment, it's not all that valuable!'

As he took up his hat and stick, Doctor Morelle asked: 'Are you acquainted with any of Baron Xavier's personal friends?'

'Some of them, anyway.'

'Do you know a man called Gresham? Charles Gresham.'

'Gresham?' He thought for a moment. 'Oh, yes. I've met him once or twice, and probably Baron Xavier has, too. But Gresham's by no means a personal friend — he's got a rather rum reputation, by all accounts. A friend of Sir Hugh Albany, isn't he . . . ?'

'And a Mrs. Latimer — '

'Ah, the beautiful Mrs. Latimer!' The other's face lit up. 'Now there's a very attractive woman.'

'Would Mrs. Latimer be an acquaintance of yours?'

'Oh, I'm small fry for Cleo Latimer!' the other answered, with an easy laugh. 'It's my boss she's interested in. You know her, then, Doctor?'

'A mere slight acquaintance,' Doctor Morelle murmured. 'It is an acquaintance, however, I would like to foster. But I fear I, too, am considered somewhat small fry.'

He blew a cloud of cigarette-smoke ceilingwards. Then moved towards the door.

'Thank you for your assistance.'

'Glad to do anything I can to help,' Whitmore assured him, accompanying him to the door. 'Remember me to Miss Frayle, Doctor. And I hope you haven't got any wrong ideas about this business.'

Doctor Morelle regarded him for a moment.

'I invariably avoid getting wrong ideas,' he murmured.

He was thoughtful as he made his way through the busy hotel foyer and stood poised on the steps outside.

A top-hatted commissionaire produced a taxi with a flourish, almost as if he had taken it out of his magnificent hat, and the Doctor gave the driver Lady Tonbridge's address.

Lady Tonbridge was out.

Her housekeeper, mesmerized by Doctor Morelle's charm, was prepared to answer any questions he wished to ask.

'I merely wish to ascertain at what time Baron Xavier left the reception last night.'

The woman said she didn't know, but could find out, and rang for the butler.

The butler was explicit.

'The Baron left finally at about half past eleven, Doctor.'

'Why do you say he left 'finally'?'

'Well, the Baron had been out once or twice before during the reception. Once with you, Doctor, if you will remember?'

Doctor Morelle nodded.

'That was at about eleven o'clock. He was worried about Sir Hugh Albany and Miss Carfax. At what other time did he go out?'

The other looked doubtful. He coughed and loosened his collar.

'Well, as a matter of fact, Doctor,' his voice dropping to a confidential tone, 'Mr. Whitmore — the Baron's secretary — asked me to be discreet about this. It was at the height of the party, so to speak — about nine thirty or so — when he came to me and said the Baron would be slipping out for a quarter of an hour or so unobserved.'

'Mr. Whitmore approached you about this?'

The butler nodded.

'That's right. He said the Baron was hot and tired and wanted a breath of fresh air and a little stroll. I left the small garden-door at the back open for him.'

'Did you observe him go out?'

'Oh, yes, Doctor. I saw him all right. He went out by way of the conservatory and I stayed in the vicinity to keep an eye on the door. It wasn't very light in the conservatory, but I saw Baron Xavier pop out.'

'How long was he gone, do you know?'

'Matter of minutes, that's all.'

Doctor Morelle's eyebrows shot up.

'Minutes?' he queried softly. 'How many minutes? Twenty? Twenty-five?'

'Oh, no, nothing like that,' the butler answered. 'Five or ten minutes, maybe. Certainly not more than ten. Because I remember being a bit surprised at seeing him in the ballroom when I thought he was still outside. Mr. Whitmore had given me the impression he was going for a bit of a stroll round the houses. But I suppose he changed his mind.'

'I see.'

'Will that be all, Doctor?' the butler asked.

Doctor Morelle told him that was all.

He took a taxi back to Harley Street. As he sat with his eyes closed, his saturnine features wreathed in cigarette-smoke, he grimly contemplated the undeniable fact that it was impossible for anyone to get from Belgrave Square to Jermyn Street and from Jermyn Street back to Belgrave Square within the space of ten minutes.

24

Gresham Changes his Mind

Charles Gresham was frightened. He was at any time a dangerous man, but now that he was frightened he was doubly dangerous.

He had been surprised and uneasy when he had read of the murder of Stefan Zusky. After what Cleo Latimer had now told him, his uneasiness had deepened to definite apprehension.

He returned to his flat, jumpily nervous and in a foul temper. Gresham trusted no-one. The prospect of having to bolt to Paris, not knowing what was happening or what was going to happen, not even being sure if he were going to get his half-share of the stupendous coup Cleo Latimer had promised, maddened him. He had nothing on Cleo, no hold on her at all. He did not even know by what means she was going to bring off the coup. He simply knew she was playing for a million-pound stake.

A million pounds.

It was a tantalizingly tremendous sum. For all his suspicions and apprehensions, Gresham never doubted the authenticity of the million-pound stake for one moment. He knew Cleo Latimer well enough to realize she was not a woman who indulged in pipe-dreams. If she said there was a million to be picked up, that was good enough for him. He knew her to be a hard realist, despite the aura of glamour that surrounded her.

Gresham was enduring the strain of a violent inner struggle at the thought of half a million almost within his grasp. Half a million. The sum, when he wrote it down — as he had scribbled it several times — made him sweat. Desperately he desired to stay and see the game played out to the end — and that he got his share. On the other hand, if his remaining in London would jeopardize the outcome, if it would handicap Cleo's plan — and she had said it would — his only sensible action was to clear out. Not only that. By remaining behind, he was placing himself in danger. Cleo had made that clear to him.

It would be relatively easy for him to get away at this stage.

Gresham was a man who had often found it not inconvenient to be able to slip quickly and quietly out of the country for various reasons. Even if he were to miss a seat on the afternoon 'plane to Paris, it would be a simple matter for him to charter an air-taxi.

His Mayfair flat was little more than a *pied à terre*. It comprised two small rooms on the ground floor of an old house converted to service flats. Gresham dispensed with the service as he did with personal servants. He trusted no-one.

By the time he had returned to his flat, his uncertainty had given place to a savage temper. When he thrust his key into the lock of the door and it jammed, he wrenched it furiously, his face suffused, and, cursing witheringly, at last got the door open. He slammed it behind him so violently that the lock broke and the door bounced open again. He glared at it, then, with another shrivelling flow of curses, pushed it shut and shot the small bolt under the lock.

His flat was compact. At the end of the tiny hall was a kitchenette. One room led from another, the bedroom from the sitting-room, the bathroom from the bedroom. He flung his hat on a chair in the sitting-room, went straight through to his bedroom and began packing. Throwing open a couple of pigskin bags, he began pushing clothes into them. His nervous, almost panicky haste began to unnerve him. He suddenly realized he was packing articles without thought or reason.

He straightened up, panting, wiping his brow with his handkerchief.

'I need a drink, that's what,' he muttered aloud. 'What the hell am I getting in a flap about? They've nothing on me!'

He uttered a short laugh and returned to the sitting-room. From a cocktail cabinet he took a bottle of whisky and poured half a tumbler, adding a fraction of soda. He drank it down in three or four long swallows, mixed himself another of the same strength, then flopped into a chair, staring at the glass he was holding.

The drink began to have its effect. It quieted and steadied him. He sat thinking things over, taking an occasional gulp from his glass. When it was empty, he rose and filled it mechanically and dropped back into the chair again.

He scowled as he began to turn over more calmly the facts of his position. Cleo had told him there was a million involved, and had promised him a half-share. If he was in partnership with her, he had a right to know what the game was. When they worked together before on his schemes, she had always known all about it. People always worked better together when they knew the lay-out. Why was she so suddenly secretive about this particular scheme of hers? Was she playing him for a mug? Was she simply trying to frighten him off? He uttered a queer, thick, growling in his throat. Yesterday he had shot Albany down in cold blood. He had experienced quite a satisfaction in doing it. He had always hated Albany . . . He hadn't found the swine's diary (his thoughts took a new line). All he had got had been that telegram Albany had dropped.

Gresham slowly and carefully pulled the telegram from his pocket, spread it on his knee and scowled at it. How the devil did it tie up with a million? And what had Albany got to do with it? What was the Purple Lake? A picture on the wall in Albany's flat, that was all.

If the blighter *had* died, he suddenly thought, he, Charles Gresham, would have been guilty of his murder. He stirred uncomfortably in his chair. Somehow he fancied Albany wasn't going to hand in his checks. Cleo hadn't sounded urgent enough. She'd have been much more excited if he had been definitely going to croak. If Albany recovered, he could accuse him, Gresham, of having tried to murder him. But again he felt confident Albany would prefer to keep his mouth shut.

Then there was the murder of Stefan Zusky.

A fresh idea occurred to him. Surely if

he ran for it now, mightn't the police think he was concerned in that? They might even try and pin it on him. The police could establish that he had been in Albany's flat the night that chap had been done in there.

And there was that Doctor Morelle fellow and his assistant. The girl, Miss Frayle. She had seen him in the mews after he'd shot Albany. She had evidently spotted him at the reception, too. Without a shadow of doubt she would have tipped off Doctor Morelle.

The more he brooded over it, the more it seemed apparent that to run away now was about the worst thing he could do. At the moment, no one had a thing on him at all. And at least he had a perfectly clear conscience so far as the Zusky fellow was concerned.

'What the hell!' he growled. He stood up somewhat unsteadily and poured himself another drink.

It was plain as a pikestaff.

Running away would get him *into* danger, not out of it. And it was Cleo Latimer who had urged him to take that very course of action. To beat it. She had even given him money to get away.

His face grew malevolent. His fingers curled around the heavy, cut-glass tumbler, whitened with the strength of his grip.

Cleo Latimer had seared the life out of him in order to get him out of the way! She knew well enough they hadn't got a thing on him. She knew he hadn't killed Zusky. Maybe it was Cleo herself! He thought round that for a moment. He didn't know what her set-up was, so maybe she had some good reason for getting Zusky out of the way. But if he did a bunk, and the police found out he'd been up in that flat!

Gresham drew a long, long breath. So that was it. Cleo was trying to give him the brush-off. To double-cross him. Half a million wasn't enough for her, she wanted the lot.

He drained his glass purposefully, his eyes narrowed and vicious. His impulse was to get back to Cleo and call her bluff. Then he pulled himself together. Though he was by no means drunk, he wasn't exactly sober. Not sober enough, he told himself, to meet her as an enemy. And that was the way she appeared to him now.

Yet there was still the million.

How could he keep himself in the clear and yet contrive to make at least some of it stick to his fingers?

He stared at his empty glass automatically, rose again to fill it, then paused. A thought came to him. He pondered over it for several minutes, frowning with the effort of concentration. Then he grinned thinly and without humour. Resolutely he put his empty glass down beside the whisky decanter.

From his desk he took the second half of the London Telephone Directory, flipped through the pages. He stopped at the one he wanted and ran his finger carefully down the columns until he found the name he was looking for.

He reached for the telephone.

25

'Phone Call for Miss Frayle

Miss Frayle was in a buoyant mood.

She had dutifully taken Sherry Carfax home, according to Doctor Morelle's instructions, and Sherry had insisted on her lunching with her. The lunch had been preceded by cocktails, and it was partly the effects of these unaccustomed intoxicants — Miss Frayle had daringly knocked back two drinks — which accounted for her effervescence. There was a decided lilt in her walk as she turned up Park Lane, back towards Harley Street. She had managed to persuade Sherry to rest for the afternoon and, of course, repeat her promise that she would make no attempt to contact Charles Gresham.

Sherry had laughed.

'I promise. You've done me such a lot of good, Miss Frayle. It was kind of you to come along. I feel I can leave everything safely in your hands — yours and Doctor Morelle's. All I'm going to do is rest until I can go along to Hugh again.'

There had been a message from Doctor Bennett awaiting Sherry Carfax. It said that Albany was sleeping normally and that Sir David Owen was visiting him again at six that evening.

Miss Frayle had enjoyed herself tremendously. She had got quite a kick out of having a quiet little lunch with Sherry. Even more than that, she was delighted that the girl was so obviously genuinely deeply in love with Albany. She had wallowed in an hour spent in chatter and talk which would have driven Doctor Morelle to distraction, but which made a wonderful change for her.

Yes, Miss Frayle told herself, she felt fine.

Given a couple of clues, she felt, and she could solve the Zusky murder case in no time at all! Her mind seemed so singularly clear and keen.

She had been disappointed that Doctor Morelle had not allowed her to accompany him to Baron Xavier's hotel. But that disappointment had now been amply compensated. And this afternoon she was determined she would certainly pop along with him when he went to see Charles Gresham. She had no doubt that the Doctor would see Gresham directly after he had finished with the Baron. In fact, she reflected, in all probability Doctor Morelle was even now awaiting her at Harley Street.

In that Miss Frayle was disappointed.

The Doctor was not at Harley Street and had evidently not returned. Miss Frayle gave a gay little shrug and seated herself at her desk. In a moment she was immersed in Doctor Morelle's summary of the case up to date.

Presently she leaned back in her chair. Her horn-rimmed spectacles slipped to the end of her straight little nose, she stared down at her neatly typed notes.

The key to the whole case, she reflected, seemed to lie in the picture of the Purple Lake, if only one could recognize the clue. That, and the motive for Stefan Zusky's murder. Then, of course, what was the reason for the man being in Albany's flat? And why had Albany been attacked?

If only she could find the answer to those questions, she would have solved the case. She thought it was rather neat, the way she had brought it down to such simple terms. She decided to take each question, one by one, and examine it. Starting with the vitally important question: where was the clue in the picture of the Purple Lake?

Suddenly the telephone on her desk jangled and Miss Frayle started up as if she had been shot. To her intense annoyance and mortification, she realized she must have dropped off into a doze while staring at the typewritten notes and attempting to puzzle hut the answers to the questions the notes prompted. It seemed her sparkling clarity of mind had been somewhat deceptive.

She answered the telephone with her usual briskness, arrived at only by a certain amount of effort.

'I want to talk to Doctor Morelle.'

It was a thick, hoarse voice speaking.

'It's important, tell him.'

'This is Doctor Morelle's secretary,' Miss Frayle answered, fighting against sleepiness. 'I'm afraid the Doctor is out at the moment. Who is it, please?'

'Is that Miss — er — Miss Frayle?'

'Yes. Who is that?'

'My name's Gresham.'

Miss Frayle's eyes popped wide open.

'Charles Gresham,' the voice went on. 'Tell him if he wants to hear something interesting about — about a case he's — er — investigating, I can put him wise.'

He gave an address which Miss Frayle scribbled down excitedly.

'You mean — the Zusky murder?' she gasped.

There was a slight pause. Then he gave a short laugh.

'Maybe.'

Followed the click of the receiver being replaced. Miss Frayle slowly replaced the telephone, staring at it goggle-eyed.

'Charles Gresham,' she breathed. 'Charles Gresham!'

He was the last person in the world she had expected to hear on the telephone.

The unexpectedness of his call left her completely nonplussed. The marvellous crystal clarity of mind which had given her such a comfortable feeling of superiority on her return from Sherry Carfax's lunch had vanished utterly. She was as beset with doubts and uncertainties as she had ever been at any time. She wished longingly for Doctor Morelle to walk in so she could give him the message immediately and let him act upon it.

Such was her immediate reaction. Indeed, she at once telephoned Baron Xavier's hotel. Her inquiry, however, got no further than the reception desk. Doctor Morelle, she was told, had left the hotel some little time.

And then, once she realized the Doctor was not instantly available, Miss Frayle began to think for herself again, exercising that faculty which had never been encouraged by Doctor Morelle — he not infrequently expressed the opinion that more often than not her efforts resulted in nothing but disaster.

Nevertheless the idea became fixed in Miss Frayle's mind she should not just be sitting about awaiting his return. She felt she should pursue some course of action, something definite, conclusive. And the most definite and conclusive action she could think of at the moment was to hurry off and see Charles Gresham herself.

The temerity of her idea shook her at first. Especially in view of the fact that Doctor Morelle had expressly, and in no uncertain terms, forbidden Sherry Carfax to go anywhere near Gresham.

But, Miss Frayle argued to herself, as she hastily straightened her spectacles and dabbed a powder-puff on her nose, that command had been directed particularly to Sherry. Not to her. And since Doctor Morelle had given his orders, the situation had changed not inconsiderably. Gresham himself had telephoned. He had offered important, perhaps vital, information.

If she delayed obtaining that information, he might change his mind. Anything might happen.

Upon which conclusion Miss Frayle flurried round like a miniature whirlwind. Gathering up hat and hand-bag, notebook and pencil, she paused long enough only to scribble a triumphant note which she left propped conspicuously against the telephone.

Have gone to see Charles Gresham.

She had a fleeting but shattering vision of Doctor Morelle's icy rage upon reading a message so scanty and even rebellious-sounding, and added:

He telephoned urgently. Said he had news about the case. Follow me immediately.

She added the address, rather liking the 'Follow me immediately' part. It had drama. It savoured somewhat of Doctor Morelle himself.

Her satisfactory feeling of resourcefulness, engendered by her decision to act on her own, was dampened slightly by her inability to find a taxi. One cruised past on the opposite side of the street as she slammed the front door after her. It was obviously driven by a graven image, however, for the figure at the wheel made not the slightest effort to turn his head as Miss Frayle uttered shrill cries and eagerly waved her arms. Majestically, the taxi sailed on.

Catching the amused glance of a passer-by, Miss Frayle hurried on, with the uncomfortable conviction that trying to get a taxi was like attempting to change the forces of nature. Only more humiliating. It was not until she reached Oxford Street that a taxi swerved to the kerb beside her, and to her amazement the cheerful-faced driver leaned confidentially towards her.

'Keb, miss?'

Ten minutes later she was pressing the bell of Charles Gresham's ground-floor flat.

She knew it was his flat by the visiting card bearing his name framed in a little brass bracket under the bell. She noticed the front door was open an inch as she waited for someone to answer her ring. While she waited, she reflected on the best line for her to take with Gresham.

Tell him that Doctor Morelle would be following her very soon? And that in the meantime she had come along to hear what he had to say?

If he proved difficult, she thought she might remind him of her meeting with him in the mews after she had discovered

Albany lying there wounded.

Reaching the conclusion he hadn't heard the first ring, she rang again. She heard the echo of the bell through the partially opened door. Several more moments passed. Still no answer.

Miss Frayle frowned, considering the open door. She pushed it gently with her gloved hand, and it swung slightly wider. He could not be far away, she reflected. It could not have been much more than half an hour at the most since he had telephoned her. Probably he had slipped out for a minute, purposely leaving the door ajar. No doubt gone to get some cigarettes. Since he had telephoned, he would certainly be expecting Doctor Morelle.

She wondered what his reaction would be when he found it was only her. She rang again. No reply.

Miss Frayle's frown deepened.

As was her custom in a situation where she found herself considering her next course of action, Miss Frayle asked herself what Doctor Morelle would do in identical circumstances.

The answer to this one was easy.

She had no doubt whatever that he would merely walk straight in. And at the same time take the opportunity to have a good look round. When his presence was discovered, he would blandly apologize and say he considered his action better than hanging around a half-open door.

Summing up her courage, Miss Frayle walked in.

26

Miss Frayle Plays Detective

Her heart was fluttering, and Miss Frayle felt pretty much as she imagined a fly must feel when buzzing around a web. The only difference being that in her case she knew the web was there and the fly didn't. She stood uncertainly in the little hall, not quite sure what to do next. Behind her the door bumped to, then banged open again and remained ajar.

The hall was unremarkable, with pale grey wallpaper, hung with a couple of incomprehensible modern pictures. Miss Frayle saw the tiny kitchenette at the end. A door opened into the sitting-room. Through the door, on the far side of the room, she could glimpse a door leading to another room. That was closed.

For some seconds she remained nervously hesitant without moving, not quite knowing what to do. It seemed silly just to stand there waiting. She had an uncomfortable feeling he might after all be in. Perhaps in that further room with the door shut. In which case he might not have heard the bell.

She gave a little cough and called out: 'Mr. Gresham.'

Her voice fell emptily. She tried again.

'Mr. Gresham. It's me — or should it be 'I'?' she muttered to herself: 'I never *can* remember. It's Miss Frayle.'

For some inexplicable reason, calling out his name increased her nervousness.

She wasn't actually frightened. It was simply that the sound of his name echoing in the little hall made her suddenly acutely aware of the fact that Charles Gresham wasn't exactly an easy proposition to handle. He had, she had little doubt, done his best to kill Sir Hugh Albany. Apart from the definite possibility that he was mixed up one way or another in the murder of Stefan Zusky.

Still, it *was* broad daylight. She *was* within shouting distance of people passing by in the street. She drew a deep breath and reassured herself. All the same, she was forced to admit, it wasn't at all turning out the way she had visualized it.

In her imagination, she had pictured herself calling on Charles Gresham. He would open the door, ask her in, and she would keep him with a few questions until Doctor Morelle arrived. But it hadn't gone at all like that. It was somewhat disconcerting, to say the least of it. The quietness of the flat, its obvious emptiness.

A sudden panic engulfed her and she turned to escape. Then she felt extremely foolish and paused. It seemed rather ridiculous to enter the flat and leave it again without even looking round. She had a swift image of the Doctor, his sardonic laughter if he learned of the way in which she had acted. Here was a golden chance to take a quick look round, and she was passing it by from sheer silly nerves.

Miss Frayle squared her shoulders and marched boldly into the sitting-room.

She stood in the middle of the room and stared about her. Though she did not quite know what she should be looking for, she was nevertheless acutely conscious she ought to be on the look-out for something.

The room had that impersonal quality of not being much lived in. It was decorated with the same pale grey paper as the hall. Plainly furnished with fat square modern chairs and chesterfield, it had a cocktail cabinet in a corner, open, with a whisky decanter on the flap. It had about an inch of whisky in it. A heavy cut-glass tumbler lay on the rug and Miss Frayle stared at it without picking it up. It had evidently been empty when it fell, for she noticed the rug was dry.

As she turned from her contemplation of the glass, a scrap of paper tucked between the cushion and the side of a chair caught her eye. She pulled the scrap out. It was a telegram. It was addressed to Albany, at his Jermyn Street address.

Miss Frayle read: *IMPERATIVE SEE X STOP IF ANYTHING HAPPENS SEE PURPLE LAKE STOP WILL BE AT YOUR FLAT TONIGHT STOP PLEASE INFORM*. The telegram was signed 'ZUSKY'.

Miss Frayle goggled at it. Then, with a sudden resolute movement, slipped it into her hand-bag. She looked around her with nervous furtiveness as she did so. If Charles Gresham were to step in at that moment, she hadn't an excuse in the world.

She clipped her hand-bag shut, went back to the open door of the sitting-room and called again.

'Mr. Gresham! Mr. Gresham!'

Silence.

Miss Frayle began to wonder if in some obscure way this was a plot. A plot to get her here. But what for, if no one was awaiting her arrival? She glanced at her wrist-watch. It was now three-quarters of an hour ago since Gresham had telephoned asking Doctor Morelle to come along as quickly as possible because he had information for him.

She wondered disappointedly if he had changed his mind and cleared out. At the thought, she looked into the hall to see if she could find any hats or coats there. There were none. She opened the front door wider and looked out to see if there was evidence of a porter whom she might question. Evidently, however, there was no one.

Miss Frayle began to experience a sense of oppression and disappointment. She was uncertain what to do. She couldn't just hang around outside. That would look so silly when Doctor Morelle arrived, if Gresham hadn't turned up by then. And she couldn't go back to Harley Street for fear of meeting the Doctor on his way after reading the note she had left for him.

She returned to the sitting-room and stood there looking timidly around her, frowning indecisively.

'This is all very silly.'

And, squaring her shoulders again, she marched decidedly across to the closed door leading to the other room which, so far, she had not explored.

The room was empty.

Miss Frayle glanced round and saw it was in a considerable state of disorder. Rather smaller than the sitting-room, in one corner was a double divan bed, littered with clothes and some pigskin luggage. A dressing-table stood by the window, and there were a couple of large, built-in cupboards, one of which was open. A trail of clothes led from it to the bed. Whoever had been packing had gathered up armsful of garments, shedding some of them on their way to the bed. A heavy blue silk dressing-gown, without a cord, draped from the end of the bed to the floor, where it had been flung carelessly.

Even for Miss Frayle, it required little powers of deduction to see that someone, presumably Gresham, had been in the midst of packing to go away. And from the disordered way things had been pulled out of drawers and cupboards, and pushed into the suit-cases on the bed, the packing had been performed in no slight haste.

Miss Frayle advanced gingerly into the room.

Another door was open, leading into the bathroom. She threw a glance at it, then confined her attention to the bedroom. As before, she had no very clear idea of what it was she was looking for. She was vaguely conscious of the telegram she had picked up and which was now in her bag, wondering dimly if she might spot something which would tie up with it. Some clue which might perhaps have a bearing on that other clue. The clue of the picture called the Purple Lake.

She crossed to the dressing-table under the window. There was nothing of particular interest that Miss Frayle could see. Some brushes, bottles of hair-lotion, a racing almanac, a large ashtray.

Miss Frayle turned away from the dressing-table. She glanced at the open cupboard. One or two suits hung in it. Some pairs of shoes lay in a row on the rail at the bottom. She shrugged helplessly, turned slowly, taking in the rest of the room. She had to admit to herself she didn't know what to look for, what next move to make.

She had a vision of Doctor Morelle and how he would have taken command of the situation. Impassive, saturnine, his keen glance taking in every detail, he would have stood there. Magically, miraculously, he would have been able to describe in detail exactly what had recently transpired in the room. Even, Miss Frayle thought wryly, deduced just exactly where Gresham was at this moment and what he was doing.

Making up her mind at last, she decided the best thing after all she could do was to go out and wait around until either Gresham or the Doctor showed up.

She had reached the bedroom door when she saw the closed cupboard. More from a sense of thoroughness than from any particular curiosity, she crossed to it and opened the door.

So far as the immediate present was concerned, Miss Frayle's search was at an end.

In the shadowed recess of the cupboard, Charles Gresham lay back against the clothes, for all the world as if he were attempting to conceal himself. His protuberant blue eyes gazed up at her as she, in turn, stared back at him in utter stupefaction. Then, as she stepped backwards, her eyes still fixed on his, he moved slowly towards her.

He tottered out of the cupboard with a slow lurch, silently sagging forward so that he fell on hands and knees. Slowly he rolled over and lay face upwards, still staring at her with those pale blue eyes.

Miss Frayle looked down at him in freezing horror. For a moment, unable to move, she contrived to utter one strangled exclamation as Gresham continued to regard her with the meaningless stare of the dead. Tightly knotted around his neck was the blue cord of the blue silk dressing-gown. Over his temple a livid bruise.

Miss Frayle took in the spectacle like a fleeting, horrifying image flashed on a screen. Then she turned and blindly ran.

In her long association with Doctor Morelle, she had encountered not a few unpleasantnesses and had, on occasions, been horribly scared. She had never been alone like this, though, and seen anything as terrifying as the thing that had just toppled out of the cupboard to collapse before her. Certainly she had never been more frightened.

Gasping and choking, incoherent, half-sobbing with shock and terror, she fled wildly from the scene.

She gained the street just as a taxi drove away and its tall, lean passenger turned towards her. Miss Frayle goggled at that sardonic countenance which bore upon it a familiarly foreboding expression of impending storm.

Unable to speak, she cast a terrified glance over her shoulder, waved her arms feebly and uttered an incomprehensible gurgling sound.

Then Miss Frayle dropped in a neat, quiet faint at Doctor Morelle's feet.

27

The Unbolted Door

When Miss Frayle regained consciousness, she was lying on the big square chesterfield in the sitting-room.

She opened her eyes without even enjoying the doubtful pleasure of groaning: 'Where am I?' She knew at once where she was. The knowledge hit her with swift and horrid impact. She sat up, saw Doctor Morelle by the writing-desk. He was replacing the telephone receiver.

He threw her a saturnine glance.

'My *dear* Miss Frayle! I am happy to observe you have returned to such consciousness as you habitually achieve. I have just telephoned Inspector Hood. He will be here shortly.'

She gulped and swung her legs down from the sofa. She blushed as she realized what a fool she had made herself appear before his eyes. Why did she have to go and faint like that, she asked herself miserably, and Doctor Morelle having to pick her up and carry her into the house as if she were some stupid, frightened child? It was humiliating. Infuriating. Her glance had unwittingly travelled towards the door to the bedroom and she suddenly heard herself asking in a broken, husky whisper:

'You — you've seen . . . ? In there . . . ?'

'Why, otherwise, would I telephone for Inspector Hood?' he rapped. 'I do not require the assistance of Scotland Yard to revive you from yet another of your routine fainting fits!'

Miss Frayle saw he was in good form. She consoled herself, however, with the reflection that perhaps the sting of his words was delivered as a deliberate restorative. At all events those biting tones acted upon her like cold water dashed in her face.

'It's enough to make anyone faint,' she defended herself stoutly. 'To go into a strange man's flat and find him dead in a cupboard. And I didn't know he was dead at first. He moved — '

'Naturally. He had been wedged in the cupboard. Your opening the door dislodged the body. What were you doing in there? Why did you open the cupboard?'

'I was looking for clues.'

Doctor Morelle rolled his eyes to the ceiling.

'The orders I gave to Miss Carfax applied equally to you. I should have thought even your intelligence could have grasped that. What are you doing here at all?'

'Didn't you get my note?'

'Kindly do not reply to my questions with other questions . . . '

'But I left a note for you in the study,' she quavered.

'I have not been to Harley Street,' he said between his teeth. 'I have been extremely busy. Explain. Expound. But be brief.'

'I had lunch with Sherry,' she began, 'and then I — '

'Desist from embroidering!' he interrupted. 'Relevant facts only, if you please. I am patently aware of your return to Harley Street. You say you left me a note . . . '

'Charles Gresham telephoned to say he wanted to see you at once,' she replied, somewhat crossly. 'I wish you'd let me explain things my own way, Doctor. You only muddle me.'

The Doctor opened his mouth, then shut it again without speaking, as if words failed him. The impact of his bad temper was having a favourable effect upon her. The colour had returned to her cheeks, her eyes had lost their scared look and her voice was stronger. Perhaps it was that which restrained him.

'At all events,' he said, his voice controlled, 'I assume the murdered man in there is Charles Gresham.'

She nodded vigorously.

'He's the man I saw in the mews after I'd found Sir Hugh Albany, and the same man that I saw at Lady Tonbridge's. As I was trying to tell you, he telephoned, asking you to see him at once. I explained you were out — '

'How long ago did this telephone conversation transpire?'

'Less than an hour ago.'

'How long have you been here?'

'Fifteen to twenty minutes, perhaps. Nearer fifteen.'

'How long did it take you to get here from Harley Street?'

'About half an hour. I didn't decide to come right away after his telephone call. I thought about it a bit first. Then at first I couldn't get a taxi — '

'You arrived here, and then?' he interrupted her.

'I rang the bell when I arrived here, but no one answered. Then I thought it better to go in, so I did so. The front door of the flat was open, you see.'

'I saw. You entered? Did you touch anything?'

'No,' she answered promptly. 'I'm always so careful about that, Doctor — ' She broke off suddenly. 'Oh, but wait. I — I did find this, and picked it up and put it in my bag.'

She opened her bag and handed him the telegram she had found.

He glanced at it, nodded his head as if in silent agreement with some thought of his own, and put the telegram down on a table.

'It merely confirms the syllogism I used earlier today at the flat,' he observed. 'You will recall I averred the Purple Lake is the significant clue in the case.'

'The picture,' she nodded. 'It was so clever of you — '

'I remarked that the *Purple Lake* is the significant clue,' he returned with emphasis. 'Where did you find this telegram? Was it on the person of the deceased?'

'Oh, no! I c-couldn't have touched him!'

She shuddered at the thought. Then pointed. 'It was in that chair there. Tucked down between the side of the chair and the cushion.'

In a small, neat notebook, Doctor Morelle was making a copy of the telegram's message. He shut the notebook with a snap and glanced out of the window as a dark car drew up outside.

'Inspector Hood has wasted little time.'

A moment later the Inspector came in briskly, accompanied by a plain-clothes sergeant and a police-surgeon.

He threw a glance at Miss Frayle, then addressed the Doctor.

'I was coming along here to interview this chap anyway . . . Suppose you were, too?'

Doctor Morelle nodded.

'That had been my intention. Miss Frayle arrived here first and discovered him.'

'Let's have a look at him.'

Doctor Morelle led the way into the bedroom, leaving Miss Frayle in the sitting-room.

The police-surgeon bent over the body, where it lay as it had toppled out of the cupboard when Miss Frayle had opened the door.

'Death by strangulation. Not been dead very long, either.'

'How long?' Hood grunted, searching in his pocket for his inevitable pipe and filling it with black tobacco.

'Within the last hour.'

'What about that crack over his head? That bruise.' Inspector Hood jerked his pipe. 'Could that have killed him?'

'No. The blow just laid him out. He was strangled with the cord afterwards.'

'The murder was committed by a tall

man, who was not unknown to the deceased.'

It was Doctor Morelle who spoke. He went on quietly: 'I think if you look around, or possibly on the body, you will find that the key which he uses to enter the flat is bent, or faulty.'

Hood was staring at him with a serious face.

'Uh-huh?' He nodded. 'Go on.'

'May I use the telephone in the next room, please?' the Doctor asked politely. The Inspector eyed him narrowly. Then:

'Go ahead. I'll come too. While you're 'phoning, I'll ask Miss Frayle all about it.'

Doctor Morelle dialled and asked to be put through to Baron Xavier's suite.

'Richard Whitmore here, Baron Xavier's secretary.'

'Ah, would you be good enough to inform me if the Baron has returned yet?'

'Oh, hullo, Doctor,' Whitmore answered cheerfully. 'No, I'm afraid he hasn't yet. Can I get him to ring you as soon as he returns?'

'It is of insufficient importance. You did say, did you not, that Baron Xavier was acquainted with a person named Charles Gresham?'

'Gresham?' The other sounded vague. 'Gresham?' And then more brightly: 'Oh, Gresham! Sorry, the name didn't ring a bell for the moment. Yes — but only vaguely, you know. I think I told you, he's a rum sort of bird — not exactly — er — well, you know. Why?'

But Doctor Morelle merely answered smoothly: 'Thank you. I may call Baron Xavier later.'

He replaced the receiver thoughtfully, and turned to find Miss Frayle and Inspector Hood watching him as if he were a rabbit who'd just produced a *magician* out of a hat.

'You surely — do you mean to say Baron Xavier did it?' Miss Frayle gasped. 'Is *that* why you 'phoned to find out if he was there?'

Doctor Morelle gave her an enigmatic look.

'The number of suspects you have hit upon merely by jumping to conclusions is really quite remarkable, my dear Miss Frayle,' he observed. 'Before long I feel positive you will arrive at the actual person or persons responsible by the process of elimination!'

Hood chuckled.

'I thought Mrs. Latimer was your pet suspect, Miss Frayle?' he threw at her.

'Well, she was a friend of Gresham, wasn't she?' Miss Frayle flashed. Then blushed as the Scotland Yard man laughed.

'A logical conclusion for murdering him, Miss Frayle? No, this job was done by a man. Can't see Mrs. Latimer cracking someone over the head and then strangling him with a dressing-gown cord.'

He glanced at Doctor Morelle with puzzled admiration.

'You were right about the key, Doctor. It's bent and doesn't fit the lock properly. Lock's busted, anyway. That's why Miss Frayle found the door open when she arrived.'

Doctor Morelle nodded.

'I noticed deep scratches and indentations around the keyhole which, as you observed, is of the Yale type. The lock had been broken by the door being slammed from the inside. If it had been forced from the outside, the socket, taking the tongue of the lock, would have been out from the lintel of the door. Instead, it is forced inwards from the effect of the door being slammed violently against it. As Gresham's key doesn't fit it properly, one may assume that in a fit of impatience he slammed the door violently, thus breaking the lock which was already weakened.'

'Which would leave the door open for the murderer to creep in and — and — murder him,' Miss Frayle said.

'Excepting that Gresham bolted the door in order to keep it shut,' Doctor Morelle answered her dryly.

He led them to the front door and pointed up to the small brass bolt.

'Small pieces of dust and fluff have recently been dislodged, indicative of the fact that the bolt had hitherto not been used for some considerable time.'

Inspector Hood nodded his head in agreement.

'Very smart, Doctor. Gresham came in, slammed the door, bust the lock, then bolted it so as to keep it shut — '

He broke off with a sudden exclamation.

'In other words,' he said, '*Gresham must have known who the caller was — and let him in!* That's what you're driving at, Doctor, isn't it?'

28

The Suspects

Doctor Morelle smiled thinly at the burly Inspector's sudden undisguised animation. 'Precisely,' he murmured. 'Gresham heard the ring at the bell, whereupon he opened the door to his caller. If it were merely a message the caller had to give, Gresham would have taken it at the door. As it was, the visitor was admitted. He then attacked his victim suddenly. There is no evidence of a struggle. Gresham was struck down in all probability with a walking-stick. Then his murderer carried him into the bedroom. There he used the cord from the blue silk dressing-gown for the purpose of strangling his victim. It was swift and silent. Speed was the essence of his actions. I should estimate not more than five minutes elapsed between his entering and quitting the flat. He was forced to leave the front door open, the lock being broken. He was unable to bolt it from the outside.'

There was a little pause. Then Inspector Hood sighed.

'I can't help but agree with you,' he said. 'And unfortunately I don't want to. I've been working on the theory that our late friend, Charles Gresham, was the bird who bumped off Zusky. Everything pointed to it. At least, I thought so. But there's only one thing clear now. Gresham knew or suspected who did kill Zusky, that person knew he suspected him, so bumped Gresham off before he could talk.'

They returned to the sitting-room. The police-surgeon had bustled off, other plain-clothes men had arrived and were busy with photographic and fingerprint paraphernalia. Inspector Hood picked up the telegram which the Doctor had placed on the table.

'Miss Frayle informs me she found it tucked in the side of the armchair there,' Doctor Morelle told him.

The other glanced at him, then at Miss Frayle, then back at the piece of paper.

'If Gresham hadn't been murdered,' he said, 'I'd have said this just about tied up the evidence against him having killed Zusky. It's addressed to Sir Hugh Albany.'

He tapped the telegram with his pipe-stem.

'I've established enough evidence to satisfy myself, anyway,' he went on, 'that Gresham attempted to murder Albany yesterday. Gresham isn't altogether unknown to us, as I've found since checking up. Never pinned anything on him, but we've connected him with quite a few nasty businesses. Always managed to slither out. Bad lot all right. Off the record, I'd say quite a lot of people will breathe easier when they know he's had his.'

'He was a blackmailer!' Miss Frayle declared with sudden vehemence. 'Sherry always suspected that. And, don't forget, he was a friend of Mrs. Latimer.'

Inspector Hood regarded her indulgently.

'So was Albany,' he remarked.

'Not willingly, I'm sure,' Miss Frayle retorted. 'I think Gresham and — and that woman . . . ' She paused, then wound up darkly with: 'Got him into their toils.'

Hood gave a delighted yelp, which he hastily stifled on seeing Miss Frayle's indignant expression.

'You should spend your spare time in writing thrillers,' he told her. 'You have a nice turn of phrase.'

'But no spare time,' Miss Frayle said shortly, giving Doctor Morelle a look.

Inspector Hood was chewing at his gurgling pipe while he glanced at the telegram again.

'I'm told I'll be able to talk to Albany for a minute or two early this evening,' he grunted after a moment. 'I've no doubt he'll be able to confirm my theory that Gresham shot him. This telegram in Gresham's possession merely underlines the fact. He must have come by it after he'd knocked out Albany. It's clear Albany was acting as agent or intermediary between Zusky and Baron Xavier. I think we're safe enough assuming the 'X' in the telegram implies Xavier, eh, Doctor?'

'Undoubtedly.'

Hood quoted:

''If anything happens see Purple Lake.''

There was a pause while his pipe bubbled noisily.

'What the deuce that Purple Lake business is, frankly I don't know,' he exclaimed at last. 'But the implication is that Zusky suspected something might be going to happen to him.'

He turned, jabbing his pipe at Doctor Morelle who eyed him impassively.

'For the moment, let's skip motive. Let's enumerate the people who were aware this Stefan Zusky was going to be in the flat last night.'

'Proceed,' Doctor Morelle murmured, equably bland. 'This is most interesting, my dear Inspector.'

The other cocked a swift look at him, a shrewd look.

'You wouldn't by any chance be holding something up your sleeve, Doctor?' he suddenly demanded.

Doctor Morelle gave him a wintry smile.

'I have my own theories which, as you

302

know, I never express until I can confirm them with proof positive.'

'I've got a dim suspicion,' Hood said slowly, 'that you're working on different lines from me. However, let's hope we both arrive at the same place.'

He smiled broadly, winked at Miss Frayle, and went on:

'Gresham knew Zusky was going to be at the flat,' he grunted. 'Albany knew, since he received the telegram.'

'But he couldn't have had anything to do with it,' Miss Frayle objected. 'He was lying half-dead outside Doctor Bennett's house at the time Zusky was killed.'

'Inspector Hood is merely concerned with tabulating those people who were aware Zusky had a rendezvous at Albany's flat,' the Doctor told her.

Hood nodded.

'In any case, Miss Frayle,' he said, 'we don't know just what Albany was doing between your finding him in the mews and his arrival at Doctor Bennett's. Though we assume he was in a state of unconsciousness or semi-consciousness somewhere. Then, Baron Xavier knew

Zusky was going to be at the flat. I learned that in my interview with him this morning. Albany telephoned him yesterday, as soon as he got the telegram, and delivered the message.'

'He received the message personally from Albany?'

It was Doctor Morelle who put the question, his eyes slightly speculative.

'He was quite frank about it. He said Albany spoke to him on the 'phone. If you ask me, I think he's a bit too frank altogether.'

'Too frank?' Miss Frayle's gaze was round behind her horn-rims.

'His answers are too pat. Seems over-anxious to help.'

'Well, after all,' Miss Frayle objected, 'naturally he wants to do all he can to help catch the murderer. Wasn't Zusky his friend as well as his secretary? An old and trusted servant?'

'The best of friends fall out,' Hood murmured, puffing at his pipe. 'And the oldest servants sometimes get the bird.'

He paused with a heavy sigh.

'I never care for cases like this,' he went

on. 'People with big names are hard to handle. They hit the headlines at once, and if you've made a mistake — ' He broke off with an eloquent shrug. 'Give me a murder involving plain Mr. Brown or Mr. Smith.'

'What are your plans regarding Xavier?' Doctor Morelle asked.

Hood's pipe bubbled and spluttered.

'He'll be available when I want him. He's an intelligent man. He'll know I haven't been asking him questions just to pass the time. If he makes a move to leave his hotel — I'll nab him, and risk the consequences.'

The Doctor contemplated him gravely. 'I trust you will be — ah — kind enough to consult me before taking such a step,' he said.

'Have you finished with your list, Inspector?' Miss Frayle put in, sweetly. Perhaps just a little too sweetly, for the Inspector frowned as he turned to her.

'Because you have left Mrs. Latimer out!' Miss Frayle ended triumphantly.

Hood gave her a wide grin.

'Don't worry, Miss Frayle. I'm not

305

allowing that one's charms to deflect me. I've got an appointment to keep with her presently.'

Miss Frayle looked disappointed.

'You know she knew Zusky?'

'She 'phoned and admitted to me she had told a lie,' he answered. 'On the face of it, it was a natural one. She was afraid of getting mixed up in the case.'

He observed Miss Frayle's scornful expression.

'Oh, I know, I know, Miss Frayle,' he went on. 'But people who don't want to get mixed up in anything unpleasant often try to lie their way out of their responsibilities. Mrs. Cleo Latimer's got a pretty tough interview coming to her, believe me.'

He paused, his expression hardening. Then he continued:

'You're assuming she knew Zusky was going to be at the flat because she's an associate of Gresham?'

Miss Frayle nodded vigorously.

'Fair enough. I'll be going to work on that idea, anyway, when I see her. Meantime, I'm going back to the Yard to

306

pick up a dossier on Gresham. Maybe I'll get round to a few tips on your Mrs. Latimer, too.' He turned to Doctor Morelle. 'You doing anything special, Doctor? Like to come along, too?'

'I will accompany you, Inspector, if I may.'

The Doctor paused and said to Miss Frayle:

'You will return to Harley Street.'

'Yes, Doctor.'

'Communicate with Miss Carfax, with whom you appear to be on the friendliest terms, and ascertain if you can remain in her company until she visits Albany at the nursing-home. Then await me at Harley Street.'

'Supposing she asks me about Gresham? What do I tell her?'

'You may tell her precisely what has happened,' he replied. And added, with sardonic amusement:

'It may help to add to the brilliance of your conversational gifts, while no doubt affording you the opportunity of re-examining, sifting and finally solving the mystery for us, my *dear* Miss Frayle.'

29

The Sentimental Nurse

Cleo Latimer stepped out of the taxi with a purposeful air.

She had changed from the simple but extremely smart black dress she had worn in the morning. Beneath the expensive coat, which had given Miss Frayle a certain amount of heart-burn, she now wore a tweed coat and skirt. Maybe it was this which gave her an air of purpose. At any rate, Mrs. Latimer looked no less beautiful.

She went up the steps of the nursing-home and pressed the bell. After a minute the door was opened by a nurse in starched white. She hesitated, then stepped back as Mrs. Latimer, without a word, walked straight in.

'Is Doctor Bennett here, please?'

She smiled at the nurse with great and calculating sweetness, her fine eyes softly grey and luminous. The nurse, young and rather plain, responded eagerly to that smile and gentle tone.

'I'm afraid not, Madam — was he expecting you to call here?'

'No — no.' Mrs. Latimer seemed to droop. Her voice, still huskily soft, was faltering. 'I just — prayed he *would* be here. When are you expecting him?'

She gazed at the nurse, apparently hanging on her next words. The nurse looked somewhat anxious.

'He'll be at his own house, I expect. I — I'm afraid I don't expect him here before five o'clock. But if it is anything urgent, I might be able to contact him by telephone — '

'Don't do that.'

Mrs. Latimer's distress deepened. She gestured towards the half-open door of the waiting-room and moved towards it, murmuring: 'May I?'

In the waiting-room she crossed to the big, polished mahogany table in the centre and rested her hands on it, leaning a little. She pulled off her gloves. Her hands looked long and slender, white and beautifully fragile, against the dark table.

The nurse watched her in puzzled distress. There was something infinitely appealing and rather tragic in this beautiful, superbly dressed woman, who seemed to be struggling under some great emotion. The nurse's private life was monotonous enough for her to be glad of the glow brought into it by so glamorous a visitor.

Cleo Latimer, shrewd psychologist, had not been unaware of the effect she produced upon the other the moment the front door had opened and she saw the plain, kindly face of the nurse. It needed but a minute or two for her first impression to be confirmed.

Suddenly, Mrs. Latimer faced the nurse with eyes that were brimming. With a catch in her voice she said:

'I am a close friend — a very close friend — of Sir Hugh Albany. Tell me — how is he? The truth, please. Do not spare my feelings!'

The other's eyes widened.

Here, she scented, was Romance! The idea sent thrills running up and down her spine. Sir Hugh Albany, young, rich and handsome, the nurse recollected from her avid study of the glossy magazines, was going to marry the young and lovely Sherry Carfax. And now, out of some mysterious and glamorous past, stepped this beautiful woman — a 'very close friend!'

'Don't worry,' the nurse breathed. 'He'll be all right. I'm sure of it. The operation was quite successful. He will be awake very soon.'

Mrs. Latimer leaned forward eagerly, lips parted, hands clasped. She was laying it on thick and heavy.

'May I see him?' she whispered. 'Only for a minute?'

'Oh, no,' was the shocked reply. 'He's in no fit state to receive visitors yet. Those were strict orders of Sir David Owen and Doctor Bennett — '

'You don't know what you're denying me!' Mrs. Latimer exclaimed, her voice low and intense. She dropped into a chair gracefully, twisting and turning a scrap of handkerchief in her slender fingers.

'I'm sorry,' the nurse faltered. 'I'm only

obeying orders — '

'How often has that been said to a wretched victim!' Mrs. Latimer interrupted her bitterly. 'I am a victim! A victim of terrible circumstances.'

She broke off while the other stared at her, wide-eyed.

Cleo Latimer decided she could go ahead with confidence. She said:

'At this moment you hold a great deal of my future happiness in your hands. Perhaps more than mere happiness — peace of mind. I came to say good-bye to Sir Hugh. Today, I am going out of his life — forever. Once, he and I were . . . ' She paused, artistically. The nurse swallowed hard, her rapt gaze upon the beautiful face, like a rabbit fascinated by a snake.

'Never mind the past,' Mrs. Latimer continued, and her hands fluttered, speaking volumes of renunciation. 'That is gone. There can only be memories for me. The memory I would most like to treasure would be that of saying good-bye. I leave for America this evening, and I am never returning. Surely you can't deny me a minute with him.'

The other blinked.

'But — but,' she stammered uneasily, 'there were such strict orders. It was such a delicate operation . . .'

But she was weakening. Mrs. Latimer was quick to press her advantage.

'More reason why I should see him!' she said. 'And no one will know. No one will ever know.'

Magically, a couple of crisp notes rustled and were pressed quickly into the reluctant hand of the nurse.

'Oh, but I couldn't — '

'Don't misunderstand this little gift, please. What I would like you to do is to buy some little thing for yourself as a memento of a moment in your life when you were able to bring a moment of happiness to an anguished woman. A secret between you and I. Quickly, quickly!'

The nurse was lost.

It had nothing to do with the two crisp five-pound notes. She was hardly aware that she clutched them. She was bemused by Mrs. Latimer. She was in that condition of false entrancement as when she sat damp-eyed and starry-faced through some emotional movie in which her favourite stars performed. For her this was life — in the raw.

'All right,' she whispered. 'Come along.'

She led the way quickly up the wide staircase, along a thickly carpeted corridor. Outside a door she paused, her hand on the handle, and gave a conspiratorial glance, to which Mrs. Latimer responded appropriately.

The nurse opened the door and Cleo Latimer followed her.

The room was not large, with two windows looking down on to the street. Pale linen curtains were half-drawn across them. The same linen covered a screen which half-hid the white-painted hospital bed from the doorway. A large bowl of flowers stood on a narrow table between the two windows.

The nurse advanced silently to the bed. Mrs. Latimer stood beside her. Her face was quite pale now, and her eyes brilliant and hard as she stared at the man lying motionless before her.

Albany lay like a figure carved in marble. His head was heavily bandaged and his young, good-looking face was pale as the bandages. For a moment Mrs. Latimer stared intently at the closed eyes, as if by the very force of her will she would awaken him.

There was an atmosphere of tension which awed the nurse. In her romantic mind she had formed a nebulous sort of story about these two, a conglomeration of all the rubbish she had read and seen on the movies and which was her escape from life.

She was not surprised when the beautiful, glamorous woman at her side turned commandingly and said in a still, hushed voice:

'Leave us!'

True, for a moment she looked dismayed and uncertain, but Mrs. Latimer gripped her arm and repeated in a voice of tense command:

'Leave us. I do not ask more than a few precious moments with him.'

There was a compulsion about her too

strong for the other to resist. As she left, from the tail of her eye she saw Mrs. Latimer drop to her knees by the bedside. With a tremulous sigh, the nurse quietly closed the door behind her.

30

The Patient Whispers

The moment Cleo Latimer heard the door close, her hands shot out and gripped the shoulders of the sleeping man. The long, fragile fingers were like steel. She shook him gently but insistently, hissing his name in a menacing sibilant.

'Hugh! Hugh, wake up! Wake up! Listen to me, you fool!'

If the nurse could have seen the expression on Mrs. Latimer's face as she sought desperately to arouse Albany from his condition of half-stupor, half-sleep, she would have been shocked and horrified. She would have believed she was either in a nightmare or Mrs. Latimer had gone mad.

Gone now was the air of drooping tragedy, of beautiful wistfulness. Cleo Latimer seemed like a tigress. She knew she was working against time. Against desperate seconds. So long as she could get Albany to utter one brief sentence, his life meant nothing to her.

The man's eyes slowly opened.

He stared without focus or recognition at the beautiful face bent over him. The woman drew back a little.

'Hugh!' Her whisper was tense. 'It's Cleo! Hugh, listen to me!'

The blank eyes were fixed on her, but they remained dreamlike and unseeing.

'The picture!'

Mrs. Latimer uttered the words in a low, deliberate voice, a voice taut and harsh. 'The picture of the Purple Lake. Where was it painted? The Purple Lake!'

The man's lips moved. He spoke in a voice which was scarcely audible.

'The Purple Lake? Oh yes. The Purple Lake. Father painted that years ago.'

'Where?'

He closed his eyes. She bent over him. There was murder on her face now.

'Where? Where was it painted?'

Her voice was almost a suppressed scream.

'Where? Damn you, damn you! Where did he paint it?'

'I remember.'

Very slowly and with a fading clarity Albany spoke again. 'The Purple Lake. Father painted it, years ago . . . '

His voice faltered. The sentence trailed off into an almost incoherent whisper. The woman bent lower to catch the last few words. They barely reached her, and then his lips closed. Albany's face settled into a carved, graven expression.

But Mrs. Latimer drew back, her hands dropped to her sides. On her face was an expression amounting almost to exaltation. She drew in a great breath, one clenched hand pressed against her heart. She moved away from the bed with difficulty, gasping a little. The nurse, who had been waiting in agonized uncertainty outside, now opened the door and hurried towards her.

'It's been too much for you,' she said remorsefully. 'I really shouldn't have let you.'

Mrs. Latimer allowed herself to be half supported to the corridor. At the end, by the landing, there was a settee against the wall.

'Rest here for a minute. I'll just slip back and see if the patient is all right.'

Cleo Latimer nodded, her eyes half closed. As the other hurried back to the sick-room, Mrs. Latimer slipped her hand into her bag and drew out the little gold box. From it she took one of the tablets Doctor Morelle had given her.

The nurse tiptoed to her patient and regarded him critically. She took his pulse, frowned a little, slipped her large watch back into the pocket of her apron, and fussed with the already impeccably smooth bedclothes.

Well, no harm had been done, she thought. But she'd never do a thing like this again. Though she *might* be aiding the greatest love-story of the age, it wasn't worth the emotional strain. And, judging from the look of the woman, it had been too much of an emotional effort for her, too. Poor thing had looked real ill.

She bustled quietly out of the room, hurrying along the corridor to the landing. She stopped short by the settee in utter surprise. The woman wasn't there. The nurse glanced back uncertainly along the corridor, then reached the head of the stairs.

As she stood there, she heard the faint click of the front door closing.

Cleo Latimer had gone.

31

The Watcher

Miss Frayle was at that point in an argument where she was on the verge of talking to herself since, as she was arguing with herself, there was no one else to talk to.

With none too good a grace she had returned to Harley Street as the Doctor had instructed her, leaving him and Inspector Hood to go on to Scotland Yard to pick up the dossier on Chalmers and also any information they could rake in on the lovely Mrs. Latimer.

Miss Frayle would like to have gone with them.

She enjoyed visiting Scotland Yard, she liked Inspector Hood, and she was just becoming the tiniest bit weary of always being the one who had the shock of finding the body, then being sent into the corner and told to twiddle her thumbs and not interfere while the experts got on with the job of investigating the crime.

The experts certainly didn't seem to have got very far in this case, she reflected. The murderer seemed to be one jump ahead the whole time. Even Doctor Morelle appeared not to have reached any definite conclusion. Excepting, of course, his deduction that the picture of the Purple Lake was a definite clue. That *had* been quite smart of him, she told herself magnanimously, completely confirmed by the telegram she had found.

Relaxed comfortably in a deep armchair in Doctor Morelle's study, Miss Frayle was reaching a point now where she not so much argued as dogmatized. For it was quite obvious, she thought with a mental sniff, Cleo Latimer was the guilty party.

Miss Frayle had not the slightest doubt about it and, if she were a Scotland Yard detective, Mrs. Latimer would have been under lock and key almost from the minute Miss Frayle had set eyes on that richly expensive coat. The fact that her convictions were based entirely on feminine mistrust of the glamorous Cleo Latimer was not allowed to affect Miss Frayle's calculations. She knew she was right, and that was the end of it so far as she was concerned. If Doctor Morelle and Inspector Hood wished to behave stupidly just because they were men dealing with an attractive woman — if you *liked* that kind of attractiveness — then they could get on with it.

All that was needed was a clue to the motive of the murders.

Why had Gresham tried to murder Albany?

What was the significance of the telegram Gresham had obviously taken from his hapless victim?

And if — Miss Frayle pursued the somewhat tangled thread of her reflections — if Mrs. Latimer had killed Stefan Zusky, what was her motive?

Or had, as Inspector Hood had hinted, Baron Xavier killed him? If so, why?

Miss Frayle frowned.

Admittedly, it was far easier to pin a motive on the Baron than on Cleo Latimer. He might have a dozen reasons for wanting his secretary out of the way.

They might have had a personal quarrel. They might have had terrific political differences which necessitated the Baron eliminating Zusky, even so drastically. Zusky might be blackmailing Xavier.

Miss Frayle's spectacles had slid down to the end of her nose.

The line of thought she was pursuing inevitably and immediately took her back to Mrs. Latimer. She had denied knowing Zusky, then had afterwards confessed she had lied. She *had* known him all along. Hence she and Zusky could have been in league against the Baron. That might have been the motive for Baron Xavier shooting Zusky. Cleo Latimer and Gresham were associates — Miss Frayle preferred to think of them as confederates — and now Gresham had been killed.

Was it possible, then, that Mrs. Latimer was next on the list?

Miss Frayle sat up with a jerk. Although she disliked the woman very much indeed, she had no wish for her, too, to fall victim to a desperate and ruthless killer.

Miss Frayle wondered if the possibility

of Cleo Latimer being next on the list had occurred either to Inspector Hood or Doctor Morelle. She didn't think it had, otherwise they would have said so, and taken steps to have her guarded.

She rose quickly from the armchair and crossed to the telephone. As her hand went to lift the receiver, the instrument jangled into life.

The quick and unexpected stab of sound made her jump like a cat.

Miss Frayle stared at the telephone for several moments while it continued to shrill.

'If it's *her* saying she wants to see me, I shan't go!' she murmured half aloud. 'I won't!'

She had a frightening vision of going to see Mrs. Latimer and then finding yet another body. That would be more than she could bear!

The telephone continued to ring.

Gingerly she lifted the receiver, and in a high, strained voice said: 'Hullo? This is Doctor Morelle's residence.'

She gasped with relief as she heard Sherry Carfax's voice.

'Miss Frayle?' Sherry sounded eager and excited. 'Miss Frayle, is he there? The Doctor?'

'I'm afraid not. I was going to telephone you — '

'I'm glad he's not!' was the excited response. 'Listen — can you come along and see me at once? I — I can't talk to you about it over the telephone — but it's terribly important!'

'Has anything happened?'

'Yes! Something quite extraordinary. Please come as quickly as you can — I can't say anything more now. Too risky. But I think we may have an answer to everything we want to know — fairly soon.'

'Be there quick as I can,' Miss Frayle squeaked.

She hung up, stared at the telephone as if it were going to leap up and bite her. Then, with a murmured: 'Oh, dear — oh, *dear* me!' snatched up hat, bag and gloves.

For once she was lucky in getting a taxi.

One had pulled up next door, and she

rushed up to it just as the passenger was paying it off. Hastily giving Sherry's address, she tumbled in.

Sherry Carfax was no less excited than Miss Frayle. As they greeted each other, her eyes were bright and sparkling with excitement, her pretty face alight with mingled eagerness and determination.

'What's happened?' Miss Frayle asked breathlessly. 'I got here as quickly as I could.'

'Doctor Morelle doesn't know you were coming here?'

'I told you he was out. I came right away.'

'Where is he? Will he be wanting you soon?'

'He's with Inspector Hood at the moment. They were going on to Scotland Yard to pick up a dossier about Charles Gresham.'

She broke off and paused for a moment. She suddenly realized Sherry Carfax didn't know Gresham had been killed.

'He was murdered this afternoon,' she said quietly.

'*What!*'

Sherry spung round and stared at her, her hand at her throat, her eyes wide. She asked in a calmer voice:

'Gresham — murdered? Oh, how dreadful! How — what happened?'

Briefly Miss Frayle acquainted her with the dramatic events of the afternoon. The eagerness left the other's face. It grew hard and cold.

'I didn't know Gresham well,' Sherry Carfax said slowly. 'I didn't like him. But I can't pretend to feel anything but horror.'

She stopped, then, after a moment, murmured as if musing to herself:

'Gresham dead. Another one. Did Doctor Morelle have any idea who had done it? Any theory?'

Miss Frayle looked round almost guiltily, as if afraid the Doctor might be within earshot.

'Never let him hear you say that,' she said. 'He says he never has a theory. Haven't you ever heard him say: 'To theorize is to conjecture'?' Miss Frayle gave a quite passable imitation of

Doctor Morelle's precise, icy mode of speech. ''And to conjecture upon crime is the inevitable path to a wrong conclusion. Conclusions must be based upon logic. Logic and evidence.' That's what he says,' she concluded.

'So many murders are illogical. And evidence is often circumstantial. Did Doctor Morelle offer any logical conclusion, then?'

'He confided nothing in me.' She hesitated, and then went on: 'Between you and me, I believe he's a bit stuck. Although,' she added with gloomy satisfaction, 'he's always right in the end. Always seems to manage to work it out.'

She glanced sharply at the other.

'But I'm sure,' she said, 'you didn't send for me to discuss Doctor Morelle's way of working, Sherry. You said something had happened. You said you had the answer to it all.'

'I did.'

Miss Frayle stared at her speculatively. There was something about the girl's voice that held a new note. It was a tone which struck Miss Frayle as being somehow taut. Scared? Miss Frayle wondered.

Again she eyed Sherry Carfax.

Was she scared of something?

The other had dropped into a chair. It was a big, deep armchair that invited one to lie back in it and relax. Only Sherry Carfax wasn't relaxed.

She sat on the edge of the chair, her slim legs drawn under her. She was tense, the way she sat, her hands restless.

Miss Frayle frowned.

When she had first arrived, Sherry had been excited, eager. She was still excited, but now it seemed a nervous excitement. She looked definitely frightened. Miss Frayle realized the change had happened from the moment she had spoken of the death of Charles Gresham. She remembered she had described it in some detail. She was about to question Sherry and to reassure her. But before she could speak, the other was talking.

'Someone telephoned me this afternoon. It was a man with a sort of snuffly voice. And a Cockney accent. He asked me if I was interested in what had happened at Sir Hugh Albany's flat. I admitted I was.

Then I asked him who he was and what he wanted.'

She paused. Miss Frayle said eagerly:

'Yes, yes! What did he say to that?'

Sherry gave her a quick look.

'He told me not to worry who he was. 'I've got some information for anyone who's willing to pay for it,' he said. Then he went on that if I met him with five hundred pounds, he'd tell me who was in Hugh's flat when Stefan Zusky was murdered. He said he saw the man — '

'*Saw the man?*'

Miss Frayle could not help the interruption.

Sherry nodded and went on:

'He saw him and heard the shot.'

Miss Frayle's expression changed. It lost its eagerness. It grew dubious, then frankly sceptical.

'That old story!' She assumed a look of worldly scorn (copied unashamedly from Doctor Morelle). 'It's one any cheap crook can put over with the idea of getting easy money. After all,' she persisted judiciously, 'the murder's been in the papers. He's read all about the attack on Sir Hugh. And everyone knows you're engaged to him. It would be simple enough for a crook to make up some story — '

'No.'

Sherry stopped her abruptly. 'It's not as simple as that. This man more or less proved he was there.'

'How could he?'

'You know the flat underneath Hugh's?'

Miss Frayle cast her mind back. She recalled something the other had said about the flat below Albany's being occupied by a young man called Ward. He was away and the flat was empty.

Sherry nodded. 'That's exactly what this man said. He admitted he'd had his eye on it as a — a 'crib' for some time. He said he was actually in the flat below Hugh's when he saw someone go up the fire-escape. He had just broken in by the fire-escape himself. He heard footsteps, he said, and crouched down behind the window and watched. He saw this person — it was a man — clearly as he went up to Hugh's flat.'

'Who was it?'

'He wouldn't tell me any more. He said he told me enough to show he knew what he was talking about. If I wanted to know anything more, I'd have to pay him five hundred pounds in small notes.'

'What did you arrange?' Miss Frayle asked. 'Did you agree to pay him?'

'It was that or nothing. He told me if I didn't think it worth my while, he'd just keep his mouth closed. Let the police get on with it best they could. He said he wouldn't telephone me again. If I didn't turn up with the cash, nobody would know anything. And he rang off.'

There was a tense silence.

'Turn up where?' Miss Frayle finally asked.

'At Wapping. Seven o'clock tonight,' Sherry answered her. 'Wapping Old Stairs.'

'Oh, dear — oh, dear me!'

Miss Frayle gave a little shiver. 'What a place!' she groaned. 'So eerie. It'll be dark. Pitch dark, I know it! An exaggeration of every crime-book ever written!'

In spite of herself and her obvious

334

nervousness, Sherry smiled faintly.

'It sounds a pretty sinister spot,' she admitted. 'But I didn't have time to argue. He told me to come alone. I said I wouldn't — I was too frightened. He said I could bring a friend, but if I brought the police with me he'd know, and he wouldn't be there. I thought of you, Miss Frayle.' She hesitated, then asked simply: 'Would you come with me?'

32

Wapping Old Stairs

'Oh!'

Miss Frayle's voice was blank.

Her mind ran back over the past events, two of them outstandingly touched with horror. She had discovered Zusky. And then, this afternoon, Charles Gresham. Now she was being urged to set out on another adventure. To meet a self-confessed criminal, her only companion to be a frightened girl who carried the sum of five hundred pounds.

She had often been down to London's water-front, but always in company with Doctor Morelle. So far as the romance of that locality was concerned, she preferred to find it in books or at the cinema. Both of which, she invariably discovered, presented a far from accurate and realistic picture.

Wapping Old Stairs. She visualized the

dark, dank alley-way flanked by high black walls, and the hump of stone steps that led down to the mournful lapping of the river. Wapping Old Stairs — *at night, too.* Miss Frayle shivered involuntarily and glanced at Sherry's pale, set face.

A faint smile touched the girl's lips.

'You needn't come if you don't want to. I confess I'm frightened, too. I wasn't until you told me about Gresham's murder. It's that that makes it all the more menacing. It seems just as if the murderer, whoever he is, knows everything that goes on. But even though I'm scared, I'm going. I've made up my mind. Whatever he may have been involved in, I love Hugh. I can't rest until I know what the threat is that hangs over him.'

That got Miss Frayle.

A wave of sympathy engulfed her. Behind her horn-rimmed spectacles, her eyes grew misty. If the Doctor could have analysed her feelings at that moment, he would undoubtedly have been nauseated. But in this mysterious affair of murder, blackmail and violence, sordid enough and unpleasant as it was, Miss Frayle clung sentimentallly to the romance between her friend and Sir Hugh Albany.

She looked earnestly at Sherry Carfax. There was no doubt about it — whether or not she, Miss Frayle, made the journey to Wapping, Sherry would go.

'Have you got the money?' she asked.

From a large hand-bag with a shoulder-strap the other took some packets of notes.

'The banks were closed and it was difficult to get such a large sum quickly,' she said. 'But I got on to my jewellers. They lent me the money.'

When you were well off, it was as easy as that, Miss Frayle thought fleetingly. Then she made up her mind.

'I'm coming with you. I couldn't let you go alone. And in any case, I don't see how anything *more* frightening can happen!' And added fervently: 'I hope!'

By all the rules, there should have been a murky, yellow fog swirling eerily over the river. But in fact it was a singularly clear evening.

Nevertheless, it was dark enough.

Presently there would be a moon to lighten the sky, but now it hung over London, a vast black celestial dome spangled with a scattering of stars.

The tide was running in. The river was busy, its ebony surface reflecting the jewelled lights of tugs and lighters, chugging in ghostly swirls of white. Strings of barges lay quiescent, slumbering monsters, dark, primeval shapes against the blacker walls of the high wharves, docilely awaiting loading or unloading.

Wapping High Street was a chasm engorged between over-hanging walls, lighted at long intervals by old-fashioned lamps. There was little traffic now — pedestrians were few and far between. It was a study in grey light and stark shadow, over which hung reminders of the heavy, exotic atmosphere engendered by centuries-old shipments of spices from the four corners of the world.

'It's a bit overdone!' Sherry Carfax whispered to Miss Frayle, as they hurried along the deserted, stone paved street. 'Like a film-set. Too eerie to be real!'

'I — I suppose so,' Miss Frayle gulped. 'I wish we were seeing it from the one-and-threes!'

She was, as she frankly admitted to herself, afraid. What made it worse was that she didn't quite know what she was afraid of. She tried to tell herself it was simply because of the rather sinister surroundings. They did play their part. She would not have felt like this if their rendezvous with the mysterious cat-burglar had been in the middle of Piccadilly.

Not that she regretted having accompanied Sherry. It would have been unthinkable to have allowed her to come here alone. All the same, Miss Frayle ardently wished she might have the reassuring presence of Doctor Morelle beside her. Even at the cost of having to endure his sarcasm had he detected — as he unfailingly would — her timorousness.

Abruptly the great wall of a warehouse, beneath whose lowering frown they hurried, gave way to a public house. It made an oasis of genial humanity in this desert of uncertain shadows. Yellow light gleamed warmly from the windows. Within, a piano jangled with tinny gaiety. The heartening sound of voices reached their ears.

Their footsteps slowed, as if reluctant to leave this small radius for the bleakness beyond. Then Miss Frayle tightened her hand on Sherry's arm.

'There it is, along there,' she said. 'That second lamp, I think. I know the Stairs are somewhere in that direction.'

Suddenly a door of the public house swung open.

The light fell clear on them. The man framed in the doorway stared at them a moment. He was a creature of average height, but drooping, with drooping eyes and drooping mouth — even his clothes seemed to droop on him — and his arms drooped by his sides. He stared at them indifferently, then in a nasal voice threw over his shoulder:

'Garn, it ain't rainin'! I said it wasn't.' He went in again, the door swinging after him.

It was so unexpected, the way that door had swung open, that it set Miss Frayle's already tense nerves jangling. She almost screamed out when Sherry said, a quiet tense voice in her ear:

'I think that was him!'

'Oh, dear! Oh, dear me!' Miss Frayle stammered. 'Do you really? Why?'

'It sounded like the voice over the telephone.'

Her tone was curiously level and quiet.

'He'll follow us, if it is. D'you think we ought to go back?'

She thought wistfully of the lights and the cheerfulness they had left behind them. But Sherry impelled her on.

'What's the use? He wouldn't be sure I was the one he'd arranged to meet. The appointment was at the Old Stairs.'

They hurried on.

Fifty yards on a lamp gave out a sickly yellow-green light in a feeble effort to beat back the darkness. When they reached it, they saw it was at the entrance to a narrow, gloom-filled alley, hardly more than a crevice, through which they would have to creep. Faintly discernible in the narrow passage-way was a flight of stone steps leading up, then down the other side, the far side of which was lost in a black void.

'This is it.'

It seemed to Miss Frayle her voice was coming out of the top of her head. She glanced at her watch, peering short-sightedly at it in the glimmer from the lamp. It was exactly seven o'clock. In the distance, across the unseen river, clocks began to chime.

'We'll wait on the steps to make sure.'

Still Sherry's voice was quiet, controlled.

In spite of her own fear, Miss Frayle glanced curiously at her, wondering how she could apparently be so assured. Then she saw the other's face was deadly white, her mouth tightly compressed, that she had keyed herself to the last degree of nervous endurance.

It made her feel a little ashamed and, as they crossed into the shadows that engulfed the worn stone steps, her hand tightened on Sherry's arm again. She said, in a voice none too steady:

'Don't worry — we'll be all right. We'll see it through.'

Sherry nodded silently.

They ascended to the top. The alley led on for a dozen yards to the other side of the steps which ran down to the river. The tide was still flowing in, but slowly. It was nearly full. Some twenty or so steps down they felt and heard rather than saw the dark water swirling by, whispering, slapping, gurgling.

Far down-river a ship's siren bellowed moodily like a great, sleepy animal being awakened. Out towards midstream a large tug chugged upwards with the tide, a shadowy mass for a moment, then nothing more than a moving jewel of light. A pilot boat sped down on the far side, on its way to a big ship. Beyond it the lights of Rotherhithe twinkled, remote as a distant land.

For a minute or two they stared into the blackness, illumined only by occasional shimmering lances of gold reflected on the dark tide.

Then suddenly below them where the water lapped and crept up the steps came a faint bump and scrape. Something rattled softly.

Miss Frayle's fingers dug into Sherry's

arm. They waited tensely. There was a silence. Then, in a few seconds, another faint bump.

Miss Frayle sighed.

'It's only a moored boat, I think. Swinging on the tide. I can't see anything — '

She broke off with a little gasp as behind them, where the lamp gleamed at the entrance, a footstep sounded. They turned quickly, saw a dim figure flitting swiftly across the pool of uncertain light into the shadows of the alley. For a second the light gleamed on him. Both recognized him.

It was the man who had come out of the public house and watched them pass by. He crossed to the fringe of shadow where the street-lamp scarcely reached, and stood against the wall waiting, his white blur of face looking expectantly towards the steps.

'Come on,' Sherry whispered.

33

Voice in the Dark

Miss Frayle was not sorry to put the dark, sinister, chuckling river behind her. She moved down the steps again, keeping close to Sherry.

The man watched their approach, moving away from the wall, his back to the light and facing the steps. He continued to droop, yet there was about him an air of tense watchfulness.

'I'm Sherry Carfax.'

The man flicked her a quick glance, then looked suspiciously at Miss Frayle. He jerked his head towards her.

'Who's this?'

'A friend — I told you I wouldn't come here alone.'

He grunted. His expressionless eyes were fixed on Miss Frayle, and she gulped. A most unpleasant-looking man, she thought. There was something mean and weasley about him. A nasty little small-time crook, certainly a coward, but sure of himself at the moment because he had only two young women to deal with.

'Where's the doings?'

'I've brought the money all right.'

He licked his lips, then he rubbed the back of his hand across his mouth.

''And it over,' he said hoarsely.

Sherry shook her head. 'When you've given me the information you promised.'

Miss Frayle marvelled at the clear firmness of her voice.

'And 'ave you runnin' orf for the cops the minute I told yer? I don't trust no one. 'Alf now or the deal's orf!'

Sherry hesitated.

'Very well.'

She opened her hand-bag. Miss Frayle, making a vaguely defiant gesture at him, managed to say in a tight little voice:

'And don't you make any mistakes, like trying to snatch the rest and running away.'

He stared at her venomously, muttered something, then grabbed the packet of notes Sherry handed him. He glanced at them swiftly, pulled one out and rubbed it between finger and thumb. He held it up to the light, then, with a grunt of satisfaction, thrust the money into his pocket.

'Okay.'

He plunged immediately into his story. 'I bin watchin' that crib in Jermyn Street some time. That's my lay, round there. Toffs is careless, and they got the doings. That crib was dead easy, with that fire-escape. I seen the toff wot lives on the third floor go off in a taxi coupler days afore. I knowed 'e's goin' to be away some time — 'e's got plenty of luggage. So I just waits me time. Well, this evening I'm telling you of, when the copper's passed on 'is beat, I slip up the fire-escape.'

He paused and threw a suspicious glance round him. A ship's siren hung on the night and died away. He resumed:

'Then when I'm openin' the winder I 'ear a car pull up. 'Arf a minute later, footsteps is follerin' me up the fire-escape. I just manages ter get the winder open and 'op in.'

He halted for dramatic effect. Then wiped his hand across his mouth.

'I watches,' he continued hoarsely. 'Someone else on a lay, I thinks. And, blimey, I was right. The feller comes up quick, but not 'urryin'.'

Another pause while his rat-like gaze flicked over them.

Miss Frayle could scarcely breathe. There was no doubting the veracity of the man's words. It was evident by his manner he was speaking the truth.

'I saw 'im,' he said. 'Saw 'is face more clear even than wot I can see yours now . . .'

And then suddenly, on the steps behind Miss Frayle and Sherry, a footstep scraped softly. The man's head jerked up, his eyes staring.

'*Don't turn round. Remain exactly as you are without moving!*'

From the darkness behind, the voice sounded metallic, full of ugly menace.

The little crook's jaw dropped so that his mouth hung wide. His eyes strained towards the steps. Then he swore bitterly at Miss Frayle and Sherry. 'You done it on me,' he whined. 'You done me — '

'You've done yourself!'

The voice from the darkness was impersonal. Not daring to move, Miss Frayle and Sherry remained with their backs turned, motionless.

'Remember?' the horrible tones went on softly. 'You said if I changed my mind about paying you I'd find you at Wapping Old Stairs at seven. And here I am — a little early — to pay you. But not what you asked — '

'No!' The little crook's voice rose to a scream. 'For Gawd's sake, guv'nor, don't shoot! Don't — !'

There was a single, sharp report. From behind the two girls a stab of flame spat out.

The cringing figure before them said: 'Oh!' in a surprised voice and rocked back on his heels. ''E did it,' he murmured, as his legs buckled and he fell on his face.

Impulsively Miss Frayle swung round. She caught a glimpse of a figure racing up the steps, then he was swallowed in the darkness. She dropped to her knees beside the creature on the ground. His face was a drawn blur. A little thread of blood trickled from the corner of his lips. He opened his mouth and she bent her head.

He was choking in a strangled voice:

'Baron . . . the Bar-ahh — !'

Suddenly he was silent. His jaw sagged, his head fell forward on his chest.

Miss Frayle drew back slowly, then straightened. She looked at Sherry. Sherry Carfax hadn't moved. She stood as if turned to stone, staring in front of her. And then suddenly she screamed, scream after scream that split the night.

There came the sound of running footsteps, of someone shouting, and then the narrow, dark alley seemed clamorous with voices rushing in upon them. Miss Frayle saw burly figures hurrying towards her. Questions filled the air. Sherry was sobbing hysterically now, and Miss Frayle remembered wishing passionately that Doctor Morelle was among these rescuers.

Then everything turned black, and she dropped neatly to the ground in a dead faint.

34

The Two Dossiers

Doctor Morelle and Inspector Hood reached Scotland Yard, both silent and thoughtful.

To say that Gresham's murder had shaken the Inspector would be somewhat of an understatement. Beneath his mask of studied preoccupation he was sorely nonplussed. More than once he cast an anticipatory, sideway glance at his equally silent companion in the hope that the Doctor would, in manner no matter how caustic, be forthcoming with a suggestion which would offer some sort of lead.

Whatever analysis Doctor Morelle might have regarding this new murder, however, he was keeping it to himself behind a reserve even colder and more formidable than the other's.

They went into Hood's office.

After indicating a chair, into which

Doctor Morelle silently sank, the Inspector slumped behind his desk and stared gloomily at the scattered papers upon it. The Doctor regarded him with an attitude of cold detachment, through a cloud of smoke from an inevitable Le Sphinx. After a few moments of silence which was beginning to grow oppressive, Hood suddenly straightened himself, sniffed, sighed, reached for his pipe and began filling it from a tin on his desk.

'But what's the motive?'

He put the question slowly and heavily. 'Zusky. Gresham. What's the tie-up? Obviously the two are connected. Gresham. Zusky. The attempt on Albany. They all tie up.'

He threw a look at Doctor Morelle from beneath lowered lids.

'Aren't they?' he asked hopefully, puffing an acrid cloud of tobacco-smoke ceilingwards.

Doctor Morelle's finely chiselled nostrils flared as the fumes from the other's blackened briar billowed in his direction.

'In view of the fact that Zusky was found murdered in Albany's flat,' he said judiciously, 'and that we have established Gresham was on the scene at the time of the shooting of Albany, and that he subsequently telephoned my house to inform me he had evidence concerning Zusky's demise, it would be ridiculous to surmise that none of them is connected. If the motive for the first homicide is established, I fancy the motive for Gresham's murder will follow as a natural corollary.'

'Yes?'

There was a hopefully interrogative note in Hood's voice.

The Doctor unobligingly failed to embroider further, however. Instead, fixing the Inspector with a somewhat ironic look, he murmured:

'I was under the impression that you were going to obtain a dossier on Gresham's past activities for our perusal.'

The other grunted and reached for the telephone.

'Give me Records.' After a pause: 'Hood here. See if you've got anything on Gresham, will you? Yes — the new one — this afternoon. Charles Gresham.

Quickly as possible. Oh, and while you're about it, have a dekko and see if you've got anything about a Mrs. Latimer. Cleo Latimer.'

He hung up and drew noisily at his pipe, slumping back into his chair again with an unaccustomed scowl. Presently he jerked up and said abruptly:

'That clue you pointed out at the flat, Doctor.'

Doctor Morelle lifted an eyebrow inquiringly.

'That picture, the Purple Lake.'

The Doctor nodded silently.

With gloomy relish the other went on: 'I don't think there's anything in it myself. Hang on a minute.'

He crossed the office to a communicating door through which he poked his head and called: 'The picture we brought from Albany's flat. Purple Lake thing.'

He returned carrying the picture, which he propped up on the mantelpiece so that the light fell on it fully. He stepped back, squinted at it, then cocked a look at Doctor Morelle. The Doctor glanced at the picture without the slightest interest.

'The telegram Miss Frayle found,' Hood grunted, 'and which you were good enough to hand on to me, said: 'If anything happens see Purple Lake.' Obviously Gresham had got possession of it from Albany and he thought it would put him on to something. Your deduction was brilliant enough and perfectly correct. Gresham went to the flat, and first thing he did was to go for the picture. But where did it get him?'

Doctor Morelle glanced idly at his watch.

'Not very far, possibly,' he murmured politely.

Hood's pipe bubbled furiously. 'I began to form a theory,' he said. 'I decided Gresham was after something in the flat, something to do with the Purple Lake. Zusky surprised him there, and Gresham shot him. But that theory doesn't lead anywhere now, does it?'

Still the Doctor remained unobligingly and obdurately uncommunicative.

'Because,' the other proceeded, 'who killed Gresham? Anyway, I brought the damn' picture back here. I've had it subjected to every expert and every scientific examination. Had the frame taken to pieces and the picture X-rayed, and we can't find a damn' thing. Not a sausage. I thought maybe the picture had been painted over an Old Master or something like that, but there's nothing. It's my opinion that the sentence in the telegram about the Purple Lake hasn't got anything to do with this picture at all. Just a coincidence.'

Doctor Morelle shot him a narrowed glance.

'An exceedingly bizarre coincidence,' he said blandly.

'Anyway,' Hood added with finality, 'there's nothing in that picture.' He fixed Doctor Morelle with a challenging stare. 'Or do you really think there is?' he asked bluntly.

The Doctor put his head slightly on one side and studied the picture for a moment.

'It possesses some artistic merit,' he observed. 'The chiaroscuro is good. Quite good. I would say it was painted some fifty or sixty years ago by a talented amateur, influenced by the pre-Raphael-ites —'

An eloquent sigh from Hood interrupted Doctor Morelle's critical analysis.

'Spare us, Doctor! I'm not in the art business and this isn't an art gallery. I couldn't care less if it was painted by Michelangelo himself. I just thought you must have a line on the picture since you were so keen on picking it up as a clue. That's all. But I take it you're not ready to talk yet, is that it?'

A knock at the door spared the Doctor having to make some reply. A messenger entered the room and he turned with a murmured: 'Ah, the dossier!'

'Two.' Hood dismissed the messenger with a nod. 'So we've got something on Mrs. Latimer, too. That's a help, maybe. We'll take Gresham first.'

Charles Gresham's dossier was not large, but it was revealing.

The Inspector read from it while Doctor Morelle sat apparently absorbed in watching the unwavering blue thread of smoke that coiled up from his cigarette.

Gresham's age was given as forty-one. A good education had been followed by a commission in the Army when he was twenty. Two years later he was court-martialled for falsifying a mess account, found guilty and cashiered. Two years after that he was in trouble in connection with a share-pushing concern, and received twelve months' imprisonment. From then on, he appeared to have embarked on a career of unspectacular crime, specializing for the most part in fraud of one form or another. Later he became suspected of widening his criminal experience, becoming involved in blackmail, but no real evidence had ever been produced against him. After his last sentence of three years, he had contrived to keep clear of the police during the last ten years. It was known he paid several visits to France, most frequently to the Riviera, Cannes particularly. His visits, however, appeared to be in a legitimate capacity as agent for a motor-car firm and a totalizator company respectively.

The pages of the dossier rustled. Hood's voice droned on, interrupted only by the spasmodic gurgles from his pipe.

It seemed Gresham's family had long since ceased to have anything to do with him. Nevertheless, he had a certain *entrée* which enabled him to pursue his activities, particularly those of suspected blackmail, among so-called Society.

While in Cannes he had come under the notice of the Sûreté in connection with a fraud perpetrated on some wealthy Americans. For an unspecified reason, his victims had been reluctant to take up charges, and Gresham had wriggled out.

That incident was the last entry against him.

Inspector Hood closed the dossier and cocked a quizzical glance at Doctor Morelle.

'What d'you think of it?'

The Doctor contemplated his cigarette.

'From your narrative, the implication that there are at large a number of persons, each a potential murderer of Gresham, each with a different motive, would, I think, be sound. I assume Scotland Yard was, in fact, aware of his blackmailing activities, though not possessing actual proof?'

The other nodded.

'To know is one thing, to be able to prove what you know, another. I don't have to tell you how tricky evidence of blackmail is to nail. Especially among the people he got around with. They'd rather pay than talk.'

'Any indication of his associates? Any names?'

'Half a dozen,' Hood chuckled. 'Three of 'em are serving time now. I personally don't know anything about two more who are mentioned, but we can check up on them if necessary. And one other name has recently been added. You can guess who.'

The Doctor frowned impatiently, he was in no mood for playing guessing games. He observed drily:

'It needs little powers of ratiocination to estimate the name to be that of Mrs. Latimer. I offer the estimation, however, based upon inference rather than direct evidence —'

Hood raised his hand in good-humoured surrender. 'All right, all right, Doctor!' he chuckled. 'I asked for it!'

'More time would be gained if we were to proceed immediately into the question of her dossier rather than merely accepting her former associates as a postulate.'

The Inspector gave him a dizzy look, then nodded. He pushed Gresham's dossier to one side and picked up the other.

'This is stuff the Sûreté supplied us with. We've no dope of our own on her at all.'

Doctor Morelle contrived to refrain from an expression of pain at the other's use of slang, and waited without comment.

The picture of Cleo Latimer as drawn by the French police authorities was, if somewhat sketchy, at any rate dramatic.

If ever there had existed a *Mr.* Latimer, he was an entirely unknown quantity, and it had been broadmindedly assumed that the 'Mrs.' was a courtesy title.

Cleo Latimer was the daughter of a colourful personality who had emigrated to America, finding work in Chicago as a meat-packer, and subsequently blossoming forth under the glamorous if phoney title of Colonel Tom O'Hara. His end was the one expected. He was found dead with a knife in his back after he had outrageously bamboozled another crook of a very considerable sum of money.

It was this affair which had first brought Cleo to the notice of the American authorities. For a few years after that there was nothing recorded. She was never heard of in Paris, which city she had been unofficially but very firmly asked to leave after a scandal involving a young, wealthy Middle Eastern prince who had attempted to commit suicide.

Reaching this point in Cleo Latimer's biography, Hood grunted.

'I smell a strong scent of blackmail about the lady from now on!'

'Undoubtedly,' Doctor Morelle agreed.

Staring absently at the dossier, the other mused:

'Hard to think the expensive-looking, beautiful woman we saw today was once little Cleo — she was probably Connie then! — skipping about the pavements of Chicago while her father packed meat.'

'Apply yourself to the story of the

female throughout history and you will cease to be surprised at any feminine achievement.'

Hood grinned at him.

'You've probably got something there, Doctor, I shouldn't wonder. Well, let's get on.'

Following the episode of the Middle Eastern prince, Mrs. Latimer appeared to have been adequately supplied with money, since she travelled extensively, visiting most of the Middle European capitals.

Then, abruptly, she returned to America. remaining there for three or four years. Until, in one of New York's clean-ups, she was exposed as the hostess at a notorious gambling-house. She was arrested as she was preparing to fly for Europe, convicted, but shortly after sentence released on parole.

A year later, she reappeared in the South of France. It was here her name was first associated with that of Charles Gresham. She was involved with him in the fraud on the Americans who had not pressed the charge.

After that, she had either been very careful or very lucky, contriving to escape further attention of the police. It was believed she had eventually transferred her activities to London. But there was no record of her by Scotland Yard.

'There it is.'

Inspector Hood threw the dossier on to the desk. 'Fills in a picture of the lady, but doesn't tell us anything with a bearing on either of the murders. No tie-up between her and the Baron. Though, at a guess, I'd say she bumped into him some time during her travels around the Continent.'

'Circumstances could point in that direction,' Doctor Morelle conceded. 'However, that is not definite —'

'It can pretty soon be made definite,' Hood interrupted him, a hint of grimness in his usually genial tones. 'I think the time is approaching when Mrs. Latimer might be asked one or two leading questions.' He tapped the dossier. 'This alone is good enough reason.'

The Doctor glanced at his watch.

'It is six thirty,' he observed. 'I wonder if I may use your telephone?'

The Inspector looked at him sharply, then laughed.

'Go ahead.' As Doctor Morelle lifted the receiver: 'Just what have you got up your sleeve? Evidently you and I are thinking along quite different lines —' He broke off, a note of alarm in his voice, as he added: 'Not going to telephone the lovely Mrs. L., are you?'

'I would not dream of depriving you of that pleasure! At the present juncture Mrs. Latimer does not fit into place in my analysis. Which is not to say,' he added carefully, 'that she may not yet do so.'

The other's pipe bubbled, and a cloud of smoke billowed upwards. Moodily: 'So you have got something up your sleeve?'

Doctor Morelle smiled frostily. Then he spoke into the telephone.

'This is Doctor Morelle. I wish to speak to Doctor Bennett.'

35

The Perfumed Clue

Inspector Hood paused with his pipe in mid-air, eyeing Doctor Morelle shrewdly.

'Bennett, eh? So that's the line you're taking! Going to try and talk to Albany?'

'Doctor Bennett?' Doctor Morelle was saying into the telephone. 'As a result of my investigations, it is vital for me to speak to your patient. I have but one question to ask him. He shall not be disturbed by me more than that. You will be at the nursing-home? Thank you. Oh' — he glanced sardonically over the telephone at Hood, who was frowning at him thoughtfully — 'I shall be accompanied by Detective-Inspector Hood of Scotland Yard. His presence will not disturb your patient either, I can assure you.'

And as Hood raised his eyebrows sharply at this ambiguous remark, he replaced the receiver.

Hood snorted.

'What makes you think I'm going on a wild-goose chase with you to ask a semi-conscious man a lot of questions?'

'A single question,' Doctor Morelle corrected him smoothly, 'which may save us considerable time and trouble.' He gave a look at the picture of the Purple Lake which stood propped up on the mantelpiece and nodded at it. 'In regard to our clue.'

'That damned picture!' the Inspector exploded disgustedly. 'I'm going after Mrs. L. She'll have to answer more than one question, I'm telling you. And I'll get more out of her than you will asking your one question about that daub!'

Doctor Morelle shrugged.

'As you wish, my dear Inspector.'

He stalked imperturbably towards the door. He was halfway out of the office when Hood caught up with him.

'Hey! Where's the fire! What is this question you're going to ask Albany?'

The Doctor's smile was faintly enigmatic.

'It has occurred to me, I confess

somewhat belatedly, that much time might be saved if we discover the source of inspiration for the painting.'

Hood stared at him, frankly puzzled.

'Source of inspiration?'

'I merely wish to learn where the subject of the picture is located,' Doctor Morelle said patiently.

'Subject of the picture located . . . ?'

Then light dawned on the other's face.

'Of course!' he exclaimed. 'Of course! I'm a fool not to have thought of it myself. It could give us a real lead if we can find out that!'

'Precisely. In fact,' Doctor Morelle said, quietly, 'I believe it will supply us with the motive for the crimes.'

'You do, do you?'

Hood spoke with elaborate carelessness. 'One of your logical conclusions, eh?'

But if he thought he was going to trap the Doctor into any further admissions, he was mistaken. Doctor Morelle merely smiled at him. 'Going to seek Mrs. Latimer? Or will you be accompanying me?'

'I'm going to make sure of everything,' was the grim rejoinder. 'I'll tag along with you, yes. But if you'll wait a second, I'll have a man keep an eye on the lady.'

A thought struck him and he added: 'And just to make doubly sure, I'll put another man on to see Baron Xavier doesn't suddenly check out of his hotel!'

'It might be a precaution,' Doctor Morelle agreed, non-committally.

A police-car bore them rapidly to Doctor Bennett's house.

Doctor Morelle sat in a corner, upright and inscrutable, his hawk-like face betraying no vestige of eagerness or anticipation. Hood sat slumped back, frowning and gloomily chewing a pipe gone cold, obviously marshalling events and reviewing them in his mind.

Presently he said: 'This isn't a case with any political angle, I'm pretty sure, anyway. Crooks like our friends aren't interested in politics unless there's plenty of pounds, shillings and pence at the end of it.'

'Have you only just arrived at that conclusion?'

The Inspector shot Doctor Morelle a quick, suspicious look. But there was nothing in the Doctor's expression to show whether or not he was indulging in sarcasm.

'With the murder of Zusky, and this Xavier chap being involved, I began to think it was,' he admitted. 'I worked on those lines. But Gresham getting his this afternoon changed my opinion. Gresham was a crook. Mrs. Latimer's on the shady side of the street, too.'

He gave a faint snort of ironic laughter. 'We'll find a nice fat crock of gold or something very like it at the end of this little rainbow,' he said, 'if ever we do reach the end of it.'

The police-car pulled up outside the nursing-home. A clock near by was striking seven as Doctor Morelle and the Inspector got out of the car. Hood told the driver to wait for them, and followed the Doctor up the steps to the front door.

'Nice part, this,' he observed conversationally as they waited. He glanced up and down the street. The tall, fine old houses made an uneven pattern against the dark sky. A Rolls-Royce swept past with a purring whisper; a taxi honked impertinently, carrying a couple in evening dress to the theatre.

'Like a nice little flat around here,' Hood said. 'Something not too expensive,' he added sarcastically. 'About two thousand a year . . . '

The door opened. The plain-faced nurse, who had earlier opened the door to Mrs. Latimer, looked at them in a scared way.

'I am Doctor Morelle.'

The Doctor spoke without any conscious attempt at grandeur. It was as if the mere pronouncement of his identity explained all. He stepped into the hall, the other beside him. 'This is Inspector Hood of Scotland Yard. Doctor Bennett is expecting us.'

'Yes, Doctor Morelle.'

The nurse managed to produce a nervous whisper. She turned and led the way. 'Will — will you come this way, please?'

She held open a door and they went in. She closed the door quietly behind them.

Doctor Morelle glanced around appraisingly. It was a pleasant, quietly decorated room, with cream walls and a dark, fitted carpet. Heavy yellow brocade curtains hung from the windows; under the crystal chandelier a graceful mahogany table gleamed.

Hood whistled softly.

'Reminds me of the waiting-room in a hospital on one of my beats — I *don't* think! Green paint and whitewash —!' He broke off. 'What's the matter? Got a cold?'

Doctor Morelle gave him a disdainful look. His high-bridged nose was tilted as he sniffed the air delicately.

'There is an aroma which is not — ah — unfamiliar. I am trying to place it.'

The other wrinkled his nose and sniffed somewhat less delicately.

'All these dumps smell the same to me,' he remarked. 'Ills and pills. This is not so strong as some. What sort of a smell?'

'Indefinable. Yet it lingers.'

Frowning, he gave the room a searching scrutiny. Then suddenly, with a slight exclamation, crossed quickly to the table and stooped down.

Scarcely visible in the shadow and against the dark carpet, lay a slender glove. He picked it up and held it delicately to his twitching nose. Inspector Hood watched him in blank amazement.

'You ought to go careful,' he grunted. 'You might catch something!'

Doctor Morelle frowned and held out the glove to him. The other took it gingerly, then sniffed with enthusiasm as a faint, remembered fragrance arose from it. He looked startled.

'Mrs. Latimer, for a million!'

The Doctor nodded grimly. 'She has been here today.'

Hood pursed his lips.

'Looks like it all right. Not that she would have been allowed to see Albany —'

'Don't underestimate her. She is not the type of woman to leave here without fulfilling whatever purpose she came to achieve.'

The door opened and Doctor Bennett came in. The nurse appeared in the doorway behind him, her eyes anxiously scanning Doctor Morelle and the Scotland Yard man. 'I am somewhat disturbed,' Doctor Morelle began. 'A Mrs. Latimer has called here today. I trust she was not allowed to see your patient?'

Bennett smiled and shook his head.

'There are strict instructions that nobody may see him. Even Miss Carfax has been barred, though I am, as a matter of fact, expecting her at any moment.'

'You are quite sure of this?'

The other betrayed some resentment at Doctor Morelle's insistence.

'My orders in regard to my patients are obeyed implicity, as I expect yours are.'

He glanced to where the nurse stood as if rooted by the door.

'You might reassure Doctor Morelle on that point,' he said to her coldly.

Her plain face went red, then white, her eyes were startled and scared. Too late she was beginning to realize the enormity of her ghastly mistake in allowing her glamorously persuasive visitor to overrule her.

'Well?'

Bennett glanced at her in surprise.

Doctor Morelle's thin lips tightened. Slowly the nurse came forward, her eyes now turned upon him as if in hypnotic fascination.

'A Mrs. Latimer called here today, did she not?' Doctor Morelle asked icily.

She nodded wretchedly.

'She begged to be allowed to see him. She — she was in love with him. She said she was leaving for America tonight — that she would never see him again. She pleaded with me — '

Doctor Morelle gave an exclamation of nauseated disgust, and waved the other back as if her approach was unendurable.

'Spare us the more sickly details.' His gaze bore upon her. 'You permitted her to see Sir Hugh Albany?'

'Only for a minute or two.'

'Long enough! You were in the room with her, of course?'

The woman gulped and looked as if she devoutly wished the floor would open up and swallow her.

'I left them alone — for a minute,' she muttered, her voice no more than a whisper. 'I had to. She — she *made* me!'

'Under threat of instant death, I suppose!'

Doctor Morelle addressed Bennett:

'It might be as well if the staff here was reorganized somewhat.'

Inspector Hood, who had been chewing his pipe-stem thoughtfully, hands clasped behind his back, interjected mildly:

'How is Albany, anyway?'

'Well enough for you to see,' Bennett said, curtly. 'Providing you don't ask too many questions.' To the wretched nurse he added significantly: 'I shall have more to say about this,' and led Doctor Morelle and Hood out.

Albany gave them the listless, disinterested look of one too ill to have any care for outside matters, then he asked faintly:

'Where is Miss Carfax? You said she would be here —'

'She will be,' Bennett spoke reassuringly. 'We told her it would not be possible for her to see you until this evening. She understands that.'

Hood said, quietly:

'Sorry to trouble you at such a time, I'm sure. I am Detective-Inspector Hood of Scotland Yard. This gentleman is Doctor Morelle.'

A faint smile touched the patient's pale lips.

'Heard about you, Doctor . . . Been thinking of coming to see you, matter of fact. Thought you might give me some help . . . '

'You are the one most able to help us in this investigation,' Doctor Morelle replied. 'I do not propose to trouble you now with details — unless there is any question you wish to ask relative to anything especially worrying *you*.' He paused. The other made no comment.

'In the sitting-room of your Jermyn Street flat,' the Doctor proceeded, 'is a picture called the Purple Lake. Can you tell me where the subject of that picture is located?'

A faintly perplexed expression crossed the other's haggard features.

'Funny you should ask that. Been thinking about it before you came in. Someone — someone — has asked me that same question already. Can't quite remember, though —'

'Mrs. Latimer!' exclaimed Hood. 'That's what she was after — !'

Doctor Morelle silenced him as Albany sighed and began muttering incoherently to himself. The Doctor eyed him narrowly, glanced at Bennett, who reached out and with sensitive fingers took the mumbling figure's wrist.

36

The Getaway

'I'm — I'm — all right,' Albany muttered
faintly. 'What was it you were asking?'

'The origin of the picture called the
Purple Lake.'

'Oh, yes.' His eyelids flickered and
closed again, but he continued: 'It was
painted by my father. The lake at
Stormhaven Towers. At sunset, trees
round it make it look purple.' His voice
trailed off.

'You received a telegram from a certain
Stefan Zusky,' Doctor Morelle resumed,
'making an appointment at your flat with
him and Baron Xavier. In that telegram
was a reference to the Purple Lake. 'If
anything happens see Purple Lake', it
said. Have you any idea what that
reference means?'

A short silence, then: 'I know it's
something between Zusky and Xavier,

but that's all,' was the muttered reply. 'Zusky had to clear out of his own country. I offered to let him stay at Stormhaven Towers as long as he liked. He'd have to fend for himself. There were no servants . . . ' Again he broke off, to ask, more urgently: 'Sherry? Is she all right? Why isn't she here . . . ?'

'Miss Carfax is perfectly safe. She is with my secretary. You have no need to worry.'

'You here — and this chap from Scotland Yard — what's happened?'

'Stefan Zusky kept that appointment at your flat last night, and was shot dead. We are investigating his murder.'

'Zusky dead!'

'The assailants subjected your flat to a close search. Can you suggest to us what they might have been seeking?'

Again a pause.

Albany closed his eyes. He opened them and said quietly: 'Might have been chap named Gresham, looking for my diary — though I don't know how he could have known about it . . . '

A little hiss of anticipation escaped

Doctor Morelle's thin lips. The other continued:

'I — I've been trying to break with him and Cleo Latimer. They'd got a hold on me — I unwittingly involved myself with Gresham in a swindle on a friend of mine. It was too late for me to do any good anyway, and I was afraid the scandal might mean I'd lose Sherry.'

Once more his eyes flickered open and closed again.

'Then I discovered Gresham and Cleo were nothing more than a couple of blackmailers. I told them I was through and gave them twenty-four hours to get out of the country before I went to the police. I was prepared to tell all I knew against them myself.'

Doctor Morelle nodded thoughtfully to himself. Then:

'That was the motive, then, for Gresham's attempt on your life? To silence you?'

'I suppose so. It was a lucky escape for me. I don't remember what happened after the shot. I think I hid in a garage and he must have been unable to find me.

382

I was in a pretty bad way, but I had a dim recollection of a Doctor Bennett living near by — I'd once been to his house with a friend of mine — and I started off to him. It was dark by then and I don't know how I made it, but I did. That's — that's just about all I can tell you . . . ' His voice trailed off.

'Must you ask him any further questions?' Bennett cut in quietly. 'He's already talked long enough.'

'Just one or two more, if I may.'

'Make them brief, please.'

'I'm — I'm all right,' Albany muttered, as if with renewed strength. 'Glad to help all I can.'

'It would appear you acted as an intermediary between Baron Xavier and this person Zusky?' Doctor Morelle asked him.

'Xavier wanted him kept under cover for some reason. I don't know why — he said he didn't want to bother me with his political troubles that wouldn't mean anything to me anyway.'

'You passed on the contents of the telegram to the Baron?'

'I gave him the message over the 'phone.'

'You're sure it was Baron Xavier to whom you spoke?'

'Positive.'

'Do you believe it possible anyone else could have intercepted the message between the time of your receiving the telegram and Zusky's arrival at your flat?'

Albany thought for a moment, then:

'I lost the telegram after Gresham put me out. Probably he found it. It wouldn't mean anything to him. He knew nothing about Zusky or Baron Xavier — '

'And Mrs. Latimer?'

The other gave a startled gasp.

'She — she knew them both. She met them in the South of France two years ago . . . '

His voice was fading once more, and Bennett stepped between him and Doctor Morelle.

'No more!'

Followed by Inspector Hood, Doctor Morelle quitted the room, deep in thought.

'Didn't it occur to him it was all very

odd?' the Inspector muttered, following close behind Doctor Morelle. 'I mean, all this business going on between the Baron and this Zusky chap? You'd have thought he'd have wondered a bit what it was all in aid of.'

The Doctor regarded him coolly.

'That's easily explained. They were close friends — though they had not seen much of each other lately — and Albany accepted Baron Xavier's actions as a matter of course. He realized he was involved in complicated political problems which were no concern of his. If he could help his friend in any way, he was only too glad to do so.'

'I wonder,' Hood grunted, 'if he knew whether the scheme Xavier was planning to pull off with Zusky involved any money?'

'In my opinion, he has been completely frank with us,' was Doctor Morelle's judicious reply. 'His account of his relationship with Gresham and Mrs. Latimer seemed to me to have been offered with sincerity and cognizance of an unfortunate lapse on his part. He is obviously not a strong character, but he had undoubtedly attempted to overcome his inherent weakness, even to the extent of risking his life for the sake of his principles.'

'And his girl,' Hood added succinctly.

The Doctor regarded him with faint displeasure.

'It is conceivable that Miss Carfax exerted an influence upon him, that caused him to appraise afresh the sinister significance of the situation in which he had involved himself.'

Hood nodded.

'You mean facing up to those two bright beauties and telling 'em he was going to see they'd get what they'd been asking for — unless . . . ?'

'Words to that effect,' Doctor Morelle said, drily. But the other missed the sarcasm as he massaged his chin thoughtfully.

'Which still seems to leave us with the Purple Lake business,' he muttered.

They went on downstairs.

'I'll rope in our friends the Baron and Mrs. Latimer right away,' Inspector Hood said. 'And I'll get on to Haywards Heath and have 'em send a couple of men to keep an eye on Stormhaven Towers till we get down there — ' He broke off.

They had reached the foot of the stairs as there came a sharp, insistent ring at the front door. The nurse appeared and hurriedly admitted two plain-clothes officers. Hood glanced at the faces of the two men sharply.

'Well,' he demanded, 'what's new?'

While he advanced upon them, Doctor Morelle lit a cigarette and examined the end of it with an air of absorbed interest. The first plain-clothes man was saying:

'He's gone, sir. Checked out of the hotel an hour before I got there.'

Hood grunted grimly.

'What then?'

'Not much. Left no forwarding address. He came back in the afternoon for a little while. His private secretary paid the bill after Baron Xavier had gone.'

Hood grunted again, then turned inquiringly to the second man.

'Mrs. Latimer's flat appears to be shut up,' he said. 'I checked with a mechanic working at a garage near by. He knew her and said he'd seen her leave in her car about six o'clock. She was dressed for travelling, and he noticed a light suit-case she put in the back of the car. An Invicta, registered number CMC 498, hooded tourer, painted black.'

'Anyone with her?'

The man shook his head.

Inspector Hood glanced at Doctor Morelle. The Doctor tapped the ash off his cigarette, said to the first detective:

'You say the Baron's secretary paid the bill? Had he remained behind?'

'No. They'd both hopped it.'

Doctor Morelle regarded him with a faintly disapproving expression before turning to Hood.

'In which case we have no further time to lose,' he murmured. 'I suggest you do not bother with telephone calls to Haywards Heath, but that we reach Stormhaven Towers with all possible speed. I will just telephone Miss Frayle to be ready, and we can pick her up without loss of time — '

Doctor Bennett's appearance at the door interrupted him. He was looking harassed and displeased. His glance at the two plain-clothes men was by no means friendly.

'You're turning the place into a police-station!' he remarked bitterly. 'There's a 'phone call for you, Inspector,' adding hopefully: 'Will you and your friends be leaving soon?'

'The 'phone call can wait,' Hood snapped. 'We're on our way. Sorry to have been such a nuisance to you — '

The other shrugged then, as Hood brushed past, he said:

'Perhaps I should mention it's an urgent call from Wapping police-station. It's been passed on here by Scotland Yard.'

37

Hood's Suspect

'Wapping police-station,' Hood muttered, stopping in his tracks. 'What now?'

Followed by Doctor Morelle, he hurried across the hall to another room.

'Inspector Hood speaking.'

He listened intently for some moments, giving one or two grunts. The Doctor stood by impassively, apparently interested in the books which lined the walls. He gave a nod of appreciation as he noted one of his own works, *Study of Deep Analysis in Drug Addiction*,[1] in a conspicuous position. He turned inquiringly as the Inspector gave a stifled groan.

'I've no time to waste on them now,'

---

[1] Published by Manning and Hopper, London. (Also published by Karter, New York, and translated into French, Russian and Spanish.)

Hood grumbled into the 'phone. 'Miss Frayle and Miss Carfax can cool their heels with you a bit longer. Hold 'em until you hear from me.'

He hung up and swung round on Doctor Morelle. Even the Doctor's customarily impassive features wore a look of some surprise.

'More trouble!' Hood exploded. 'Your Miss Frayle and Miss Carfax went off on a private wild-goose chase of their very own to Wapping. They've been picked up there by the police — Miss Frayle in a dead faint and the other one screaming her head off. Evidently they'd got a date with some small-time crook. Seems he was shot dead while they were talking to him.' He blew out his cheeks. 'Another murder!'

Doctor Morelle's austere countenance was a study of keen displeasure.

'Wapping,' he murmured. Then: 'Was any indication offered as to their reason for meeting this man?'

'Far as I can make out, they thought they were doing a smart bit of following-up on the Zusky business.'

'Yes, indeed.' The Doctor nodded thoughtfully. 'It would be possible . . . '

'However, we've got no time to waste on them.' Hood was moving towards the door. 'I don't know if you're coming, too, but I'm off to Haywards Heath . . . '

'Just a moment,' Doctor Morelle's eyes were narrowed speculatively. 'This is no time for hasty action — '

'But you said just now we've no time to waste getting down to Stormhaven Towers!'

'This incident at Wapping tends to suggest another train of thought,' the Doctor replied equably. 'We might be better advised to proceed to Wapping *first*, and hear what these two ridiculous females have to say.'

The other hesitated a moment.

He was extremely eager to follow up the trail of Baron Xavier and Cleo Latimer with the fullest speed. On the other hand, he was more than reluctant to dispense with the Doctor's invaluable help. It occurred to him this case, involving as it did highly-placed and important people, might become somewhat complex. He was anxious to make no mistakes, and all during the investigation he had been conscious of a sneaking suspicion Doctor Morelle was not altogether seeing eye to eye with him. Above all things, he had a vast respect for the Doctor's judgment.

Inspector Hood glanced worriedly at his watch.

'Well,' he muttered uneasily, 'it shouldn't take us more than half an hour to pick them up, anyway. Perhaps you're right, Doctor. We'd better do as you say.'

'I happen to know I am right.'

And with that bland pronouncement, Doctor Morelle led the way out to the police-car.

Hood told the driver:

'Get to Wapping police-station quick as you can make it!' To the plain-clothes men: 'You'd better stick with us.'

As the car raced off, Hood slumped moodily back in his seat, shot a dark look at Doctor Morelle. The Doctor was reclining comfortably, his hands crossed over the handle of his sword-stick, looking for all the world as if he were merely paying some social call.

The Inspector shrugged helplessly to himself. 'Only hope you're right about all this, Doctor. Because if Baron X. and Mrs. L. slip through my fingers, I'm not going to hear the end of it for a long time.'

'We are pursuing the wiser course,' Doctor Morelle reassured him. 'That conclusion I arrived at by a process of simple reasoning. I gave Miss Frayle instructions she was to remain in the Carfax girl's company at all times until the latter visited the nursing-home. It is clear at some time since we last saw her, the young woman received a message prompting her to arrange a meeting with this man whom, you say, is a petty criminal.'

The other nodded.

'Name of Lugg. Well-known to the police, he is. Shifty character, but too easily scared for any big stuff.'

'Such an individual might well obtain possession of certain information. Information which, because of his acquaintance with the police, he would not be prepared to vouchsafe them. But which, nevertheless, he would seek to sell to the highest bidder.'

'Sounds reasonable.'

'It remains the only possible explanation for Miss Frayle and her companion being found where they were tonight,' Doctor Morelle retorted. 'This person, Lugg, was shot dead presumably while in the act of imparting his information. From which may be drawn the conclusion that his murderer had reason to suspect him of possessing this information and — ah — eliminated him to ensure his silence. This crime is, I feel convinced, inexorably connected with the two earlier murders and its solution will point to the elucidation of the other homicides.'

Hood sighed heavily and started to chew his pipe-stem like a dog gnawing a bone.

'I hope you're right,' he muttered again.

Doctor Morelle sniffed delicately and, in a gentle but ironic voice, replied:

'I always am, my dear Inspector.'

A small knot of morbid sightseers still hung outside the police-station, for the excitement of the shooting at Wapping Old Stairs had not yet died down. Inspector Hood and the Doctor brushed past them. Poor Miss Frayle, sitting on an extremely hard bench, Sherry Carfax beside her, felt her heart sink even lower as she saw the forbidding expression on Doctor Morelle's face as he advanced towards them.

Miss Frayle did not exactly cower as he approached. She merely wore the wan and abject look of a rabbit held in fascinated thrall by the hypnotic stare of some deadly snake. She did not rise from the hard bench, although she had been longing to for some time past, for it was excessively uncomfortable. She simply sat, hands clasped in her lap and, with a rising feeling of hysteria, waited.

'My *dear* Miss Frayle!' There was an inevitable razor's edge to his voice. 'It would appear that, not satisfied with your role of my amanuensis, you have to take upon yourself that of a detective. I should have imagined you had sufficient work on your hands — '

Suddenly, as if released by a spring, she

shot to her feet. Her eyes gleamed wildly behind her horn-rimmed spectacles, her mouth was half-open.

'I can't bear it!' she cried desperately. 'I can't bear any more! If you're going to be angry with me, I shall burst into tears! I shall scream the place down! You're made of ice, or iron — anyway something that isn't flesh and blood! You don't seem to realize what I've been through. Since last night — three dead men practically one after the other! Zusky — I found him! Gresham, this afternoon — I found him. This evening, this other horrible little man — !'

'Miss Frayle!'

His voice was like a whiplash. Immediately, Miss Frayle collapsed on to the bench again, Sherry Carfax taking her hand sympathetically. Hood looked on quizzically, the desk-sergeant mopped his forehead with an enormous handkerchief, and a constable in the background blew out his lips and rolled his eyes to the ceiling.

There was a quivering, indrawn breath from Miss Frayle, no more than a small sigh. Then Doctor Morelle observed quietly: 'I was merely about to congratulate you upon your devotion to my instructions in not leaving Miss Carfax. Perhaps,' he conceded stiffly, 'I made my approach too clumsily. I am, however, fully aware of the tension your nervous system has been subjected to during the past twenty-four hours.'

'Oh, Doctor! I didn't think you realized — ' She broke off, face wreathed in smiles. 'I — I feel so much better now.'

Indeed, the colour was returning to her cheeks, the wild expression vanishing from her eye. Except for a certain wanness, she was becoming, quite magically, her old self again.

'And now, perhaps, you will give the Inspector and myself a brief account of the circumstances that brought you both to this locality, and exactly what transpired subsequently.'

'Statement, Sergeant?' Hood asked the officer at the desk.

The Sergeant pinched his nose.

'Well, both ladies was a bit — ah — high-strung, sir,' he said. 'Hysterical, you might say. So I thought I'd wait till you come along.'

'Just as well we did!' Hood grunted.

'Oh,' the desk-sergeant replied, 'Miss Frayle seemed certain Doctor Morelle was bound to turn up.'

Hood could picture Miss Frayle's serene confidence that the Doctor would not fail to arrive and extricate her and her companion in distress from their difficulties. Hiding a half grin behind his hand, he snapped: 'What steps have you taken?'

''Phoned Scotland Yard to broadcast to police-cars in the neighbourhood,' the other answered promptly. 'Got the river-patrol working — according to Miss Frayle and Miss Carfax the attack was made from the steps themselves, which could only have been approached from the river.'

'Witnesses?'

'Only Miss Frayle and Miss Carfax witnessed the actual shooting. No one else. Couple of chaps were in the pub down the road, they heard the shot and then Miss Carfax yelling her head off.'

'Where's the body?'

The Sergeant graphically jerked a thumb over his shoulder.

'Identify him?'

'Lugg, his name is. Small-time sneak-thief. Lives down this part, but works the West End. Been out on ticket of leave six weeks.'

'Any associates?'

The desk-sergeant shook his head.

'He worked alone.'

Inspector Hood grunted, swung round to the Doctor who, during the Inspector's conversation with the sergeant, had been 'elucidating the salient facts' from Miss Frayle and Sherry. Hood pricked up his ears as he heard Miss Frayle graphically describing Lugg's sudden demise.

'He slumped to the ground,' Miss Frayle was quite unconscious of her melodramatic attitude as she clutched her heart in imitation of the little crook's last spasm, 'after he'd said: 'He did it!' — meaning, of course, the man who'd shot him. I dropped to my knees beside him. I caught his last words clearly. 'Baron', he said, 'The Baron . . . ''

Her voice faltered. 'I — I couldn't

think what he meant at the time,' she went on. 'I was confused and upset. But now — '

'The Baron, eh!' Hood echoed. 'The Baron! Doctor, that just about clinches it. The poor devil's helped us with his last breath!'

The telephone rang sharply.

'It's the river-patrol, sir. They've found an empty skiff floating on the Rotherhithe side. Bringing it over for inspection.'

Hood nodded his satisfaction, and turned back to Miss Frayle and Sherry. 'Now then, Miss Frayle. After he'd fired, you must have caught a glimpse of the murderer. I don't mean his face necessarily. But you got a general impression of him?'

'I — I did — get a fleeting glance,' Miss Frayle agreed slowly.

'Tall, short, thin, fat . . . ?'

'Tall.'

'He wore a raincoat,' Sherry Carfax put in. 'And a soft hat pulled low over his eyes.'

'Either of you recognize his voice?'

Sherry frowned.

'I can only say — it — seemed

familiar,' she said at length.

Miss Frayle nodded vigorously. 'It did — it did sound familiar to me. I can't quite place it — '

'Probably disguised.'

'Yes,' Miss Frayle agreed, 'it may have been.'

Hood rubbed his hands.

'Doctor Morelle,' he exclaimed breezily, 'I'm off! Don't know if you want to come along, but I'm off to Haywards Heath, and if I don't pick up a certain titled gentleman there, I'll take that empty skiff and row out to sea in it!'

Doctor Morelle turned to Miss Frayle.

'Do you think, my *dear* Miss Frayle, your nerves will stand the strain sufficiently to witness the termination of this particular case?'

Miss Frayle glanced at him, blushingly pleased at his invitation.

'I think I would like to be in at the finish.'

'Right!' Hood snapped. 'Let's go. Sergeant, arrange for Miss Carfax to be taken home at once.' To Sherry: 'Sir Hugh Albany's doing pretty well, but getting a bit anxious about you. You'd better look in at the nursing-home and leave a message you're still in the land of the living. Or — if they'll let you,' he grinned widely, 'tell him yourself. In person!'

38

Stormhaven Towers

Between Cuckfield and Haywards Heath a narrow road, shadowed in the moonlight on one side by an ancient wall of Horsham stone some ten feet high, led to the gates of Stormhaven Towers. On the other side of the road fields stretched out, rising to a copse. A signpost, old and unpainted for many a year, pointed the way to Stormhaven Towers.

'Take it slowly,' Inspector Hood instructed the driver.

The car slowed, rolled almost noiselessly along the road with only the sidelights gleaming. At the narrowest point of the road, Doctor Morelle said quietly: 'I think we should stop here and proceed the remainder of the way on foot. It would be advisable to leave the car in such a position that it cannot be passed by another.'

Hood instructed the car to be pulled up in the centre of the road. The driver cut the engine, and immediately the stillness and night-silence of the countryside rushed in on them.

By now the moon had risen and was beginning to soar in the sky, remote and tranquil, making the scene eerie with cold light and contrasting stark black shadow. A hundred yards down the road the high, ancient gates of Stormhaven Towers traced a delicate black pattern against the moonlight.

For a moment, none of the occupants of the car made a move. It might be the scene, the night-silence, held them in its grip. Then faint sounds crept upon them. Somewhere near by an owl hooted, the breeze tapped one twig against another, and from the distant village a dog barked. The sounds emphasized the cold, moonlit silence.

Inspector Hood cleared his throat.

'Well, what are we waiting for? You,' he spoke to one of the plain-clothes men, 'you stay with the driver and keep your eyes skinned, both of you.' He nodded towards the second plain-clothes man. 'You'd better come with us.'

Miss Frayle felt her heart beating more quickly as Doctor Morelle helped her out of the car, and she shivered a little.

'I trust you will contrive to keep your nerves under close control, Miss Frayle,' the Doctor murmured. 'This is no time for fainting fits.'

She glared at him reproachfully. His countenance seemed longer and more saturnine than ever in the pale light of the moon. Nevertheless, there was something comforting in his presence.

Quietly they followed Hood and the other officer towards the gates. Then suddenly Miss Frayle jumped and clutched at Doctor Morelle's arm.

From near by came the sharp, unmistakable crack of a fire-arm. It cut the silence and echoed against the copse on the hill and back to the high stone wall. Inspector Hood glanced across the fields, then at the Doctor.

'Poachers?'

'A revolver shot.'

Doctor Morelle led the way, moving

quickly, but silently, towards the gates. Miss Frayle fluttered along close behind. Before they reached the gates, another shot rang out.

The Doctor halted abruptly at the stone pillar of the gate. Miss Frayle bumped into him and, though her nose tingled from the sudden, painful contact with his shoulder, she was comforted at its muscular hardness.

'Th — that was a second shot!' she gasped. 'Is — is — he firing at us?'

He glared at her. Then to Hood, in a low voice: 'The first was a .38, I fancy. The second was a smaller calibre.'

'Sounded much alike to me.'

Doctor Morelle shrugged his shoulders then, with a nod which was at once a signal for silence and to follow him, led the way.

One of the gates stood open. A flagged drive, overgrown and unkempt, led to the house. It was a fine old Queen Anne mansion, shimmering in the bright radiance of the moon. At the foot of the wide, shallow stone steps up to the terrace, the drive divided right and left in a sweeping circle round the house. From each wing of the house gardens stretched on either side.

This, thought Miss Frayle, sentimentally, is one of the stately homes of England.

Hurrying alongside Doctor Morelle, she speculated romantically on whether Sir Hugh and Sherry would live here when they were married. It looked beautiful, but silent and still, and with an ineffable melancholy, forlornness and neglect. Miss Frayle felt, with a tautening of nerves, a certain sinister atmosphere about it, companion of its decay.

Everywhere the feeling of decay lay on the air. Thick moss, black and sprawling in the moonlight, encroached upon the drive. Rank grasses had grown, splitting the ancient stones.

Miss Frayle shivered. The romantic speculation and sentimental dream she had been indulging in suddenly gave place to a cold feeling of oppression. She began to wish she was safe back in Harley Street, with the familiar, heartening sounds of London all around.

She gulped as Doctor Morelle halted

suddenly and pointed to a long, dark shape, hardly discernible in the deep shadow of a tree just off the drive. They crossed to it. It was the car described by the garage-hand as the one in which he had seen Mrs. Latimer driving away. It had been backed up to the tree and its long black bonnet was pointing towards the gates of the drive.

The bonnet was still quite warm under the Doctor's touch. A scarf lay on the driver's seat and he picked it up. A faint, remembered fragrance rose from it, bringing to Miss Frayle's mind as she bent forward and sniffed the memory of that tall, glamorous woman in the superlative coat.

She glanced quickly at Doctor Morelle, a sudden, unreasonable irritation nagging at her as he held on to the scarf. But his pale, austere face was unreadable. His thin mouth was shadowed, the keen eyes veiled.

Hood, meanwhile, had been nosing around beside him. He turned to Doctor Morelle, his face set and grim.

'Don't like it. Too damned quiet. I want

to find the lake, but I don't want to be seen.' He nodded towards the car. 'Obviously she's here. She picked up the Baron and brought him along. They're in it together. But who fired those shots?' He shrugged irritably. 'Maybe it *was* poachers.'

'I cannot subscribe to the theory that poachers would use revolvers in their unlawful pursuits. And although it was difficult to judge the exact direction of those revolver-shots, I suggest it was within the grounds.' His arm made a sweeping gesture.

'All right,' the other agreed. 'But we can assume Mrs. L. and the Baron are here. That's clear enough from the car. Maybe they had a quarrel over the loot and blazed away at each other, and that's what we heard!' He shook his head sadly. 'Sounds terrible, doesn't it!'

'What loot, Inspector?' Miss Frayle asked.

He grinned broadly. 'I don't know,' he admitted. 'What I'm trying to say is that frankly I don't care a brass farthing if she's got a bazooka and he's got anti-tank artillery — I'm going to find the lake!'

'Are you aware of the lake's exact situation?' the Doctor queried.

'Do you know where it is?' the other countered. 'If you do, you might save me the trouble of mooching round —'

'It is my intention to gain access to the house,' was the grim reply. 'From there we should be in a position to view the grounds over a wide area.'

He set off towards the house without deigning to glance back to see if the others were following. Miss Frayle hurried in his wake. Hood rubbed his chin, muttering: 'I must be a bit jumpy or I'd have thought of that myself!'

The Doctor kept to the overgrown grass of the park, using the shadows as much as possible as he approached the terrace. The others followed close on his heels. None of them quite knew what danger lay ahead of them, but a sense of foreboding hung heavily on the atmosphere.

Since the second shot there had not been another sound. The silence was vast, with an emptiness that almost seemed to ring. In that silence Miss Frayle could hear the quick beat of her heart.

As they approached the house, its melancholy was even more apparent. The steps of the terrace were crumbling, the stones cracked and overgrown with coarse grass and multitudinous weeds. A loose flagstone caused Miss Frayle to stumble, and she gasped at the rattle the stone made.

A short flight of wide, shallow steps led up to the pillared doorway. The once white doors were dusty and grimed, deeply shadowed in the recess. The door opened at the Doctor's touch with what seemed to Miss Frayle a ghostly creak.

The hall ahead appeared a ghostly cavern, its limits lost in a gloom emphasized rather than relieved by the shafts of moonlight filtering through spacious windows. At the far end could dimly be discerned a stairway mounting in a tall slender curve into the darkness.

Doctor Morelle led the way forward. The floor was bare parquet, yet their footsteps were quiet in the thick dust which lay upon it. Miss Frayle had the

412

uneasy feeling she was intruding upon the old house.

On their right, folding doors were rolled back upon a dim room, hardly more than a deeper shadow in the shadows of the hall, but hinting at a promise of grandeur from the faint, dusty gleam of a crystal chandelier. Beyond it were the outlines of three french windows, the moonlight flooding in, leading out to that part of the terrace which ran along the side of the house.

It would not have surprised Miss Frayle in the least to have heard the phantom strains of a Viennese waltz or a prim minuet. As she followed the Doctor, it seemed to her that from the shadows might materialize elegant shapes clad in satin coats and taffeta gowns, treading a stately measure.

It was quite evident Doctor Morelle entertained no such romantic and whimsical fancies. There was a decisive briskness about him as he turned into the gloomy room, a questing air, as of one approaching the end of a search.

It was evidently the drawing-room. The

carpet had been taken up and the furniture was shrouded in dust-sheets accentuating its ghostly aspect. But, despite its pervading sense of decay, there lingered an echo of past grandeur and elegance.

Doctor Morelle crossed to the nearest window, the others, except Miss Frayle, close on his heels. For some reason, perhaps because she was still caught up in her romantic fancies of the past, Miss Frayle hesitated on the threshold, staring about her. Then she started after the Doctor. Suddenly she halted, gaping in the direction of the window at the far end of the room.

As if rooted to the spot, Miss Frayle continued to stare. She tried to speak, but no sound came. Her eyes riveted to a moonlit patch on the floor, she heard Doctor Morelle engaged with Hood and the other detective before the near window, and heard the Inspector utter a grunt of satisfaction.

The Doctor glanced back with an exclamation of annoyance, as he beheld Miss Frayle fixedly engrossed upon a problem of her own.

'At this juncture, my dear Miss Frayle, it should not be necessary for me to inform you that your attention here might be of some . . . '

His biting tone trailed off as he turned and followed the direction of her wide-eyed gaze.

'Oh . . . ' she gasped at length and, with a supreme effort, pointed dramatically.

Outstretched before the window, the moonlight pouring down on her, lay Mrs. Latimer. One arm was outflung, her face waxen, her lips dark and reposed. Her eyes were closed. A foot or two away from her, a small revolver glittered balefully.

39

The Man in the Shadow

'Kindly control yourself, Miss Frayle!' Doctor Morelle snapped ominously. 'By this time you should be accustomed to the unusual and macabre. I have no time to waste on hysterics or fainting attacks. Pull yourself together!'

His voice acted upon her like a bucket of cold water. She gasped and spluttered, then said breathlessly:

'I'm all right, Doctor. It was the shock, seeing her like that . . . '

She grasped the arm of a covered chair near by to steady herself, while Doctor Morelle knelt by the inert figure, the other two men joining him quickly. Miss Frayle muttered tremulously:

'It always seems to be me who finds them!'

'She's dead all right.' Inspector Hood was saying, his voice puzzled. 'But not a

416

mark on her. What d'you say, Doctor?'

Doctor Morelle rose slowly to his feet. His face, shadowed as he gazed down at the limp body of Mrs. Latimer, seemed strangely set and inscrutable. In a voice so low the others scarcely heard, he pronounced: 'A woman of wit and despair. Natural causes. She died of heart-failure.'

'Heart-failure!'

'Death ensued within the last fifteen minutes — I should estimate within a few moments of our hearing the second shot.'

Hood's gaze fell on the small revolver. He whipped out his handkerchief and picked it up carefully.

'The second shot,' he growled, still perplexed. 'What you getting at? You just said she died of natural causes.' He lifted the revolver, sniffed and exclaimed: 'This has just been fired!'

'Precisely.'

Miss Frayle stared at the Doctor. Did she discern an unwonted gentleness in his voice? A faint smile played about his lips, enigmatic as ever, yet, it seemed to her, holding a faint melancholy. She frowned and compressed her lips. She was about to speak when he answered Hood.

'I was aware upon meeting her that she suffered from an acutely morbid condition of the heart. Had she consulted me, it would have been my duty, in fact, to warn her if she wished to preserve her life she must at all costs relinquish her mode of life, avoid every kind of excitement. In brief, retire into what would have been for her complete obscurity.'

Miss Frayle said, her voice unusually snappy:

'Why didn't you tell her?'

'Mrs. Latimer did not elect to consult me as a physician. In any case, had I offered her my advice, I doubt if she would have heeded it. She was equally well aware of her danger —'

'Her fainting attacks!' Miss Frayle exclaimed. 'That's how you knew she'd have those things in her hand-bag when she fainted at the flat . . .'

He nodded.

'Although she realized she was risking her life, she could not give up. There was too much at stake.'

'What?' Hood queried. 'What was at stake?'

'What else but a fortune? Look.'

They followed the direction of his pointing finger. The french windows were wide open upon the terrace. Beyond, tangled and overgrown, the lawn stretched into the silver and the shadows. And beyond the stretch of lawn, something shimmered. It was a small, ornamental lake, its surface gleaming where the moonlight struck it, and purplish-black where the shadows of a semicircle of dark trees fell across it.

'By God!' Inspector Hood shouted. 'That's it! The Purple Lake!'

He stared down at the revolver he still grasped.

'She must have fired it,' he muttered. 'Yes, that'd be it. She was standing here by the window —' He broke off. 'But who was she shooting at? The Baron?'

'Baron Xavier?' Miss Frayle asked. 'Why ever should she be shooting at him?'

'The old story of thieves falling out. Eh, Doctor?'

Doctor Morelle gave a little shrug.

'Why should we waste time in conjecture when the solution may be so near?'

He stepped through on to the terrace.

Hood instructed the plain-clothes men to remain behind, then followed the Doctor. Miss Frayle refrained from glancing again at the lifeless figure at her feet. The strain was beginning to tell on her. She was glad when she stood out on the open terrace, though the night air was cold.

Doctor Morelle remained motionless for a moment at the head of the shallow steps leading down to the lawn. Though it was neglected and overgrown, Miss Frayle did not find it difficult to imagine its beauty on a summer's day, with the flower-beds in full bloom, smooth and velvet green stretching to the semicircular balustrade at the edge of the lake.

'Come on,' Hood grunted. 'Let's see what the lake can tell us.'

Down the steps to the lawn he went, moving quickly in his eagerness. The grass was tangled and almost knee-high.

Doctor Morelle had paused, frowning

slightly, and glanced back at the house. By now they were half-way between the terrace and the lake. Miss Frayle followed the Doctor's glance. She wondered what had brought that puzzled expression to his face. She kept close to him, the heavy, cold silence which surrounded them causing her a curious uneasiness.

Hood had halted and awaited the Doctor impatiently. It seemed as if for a moment the whole world was in suspense, that time had ceased. Then a faint rustle sounded near by. Miss Frayle's eyes widened, she pressed one clenched hand against her mouth and, with the other, gripped Doctor Morelle's arm. A low, eerie cry sounded suddenly, echoing out from the dark background of trees. A ghostly white shape soared out.

'Blinking owl!' Hood grumbled. 'Come on!'

But Doctor Morelle gave a little hissing exclamation. Hood paused, riveted by the Doctor's intent attitude. Suddenly there came a gasp, a moan that was hardly more than a whisper.

'Over there!' Hood breathed.

Where flower-beds had bloomed long ago, an ancient beech-tree flung a black shadow across the lawn. It was from here, almost in line with where they were standing, that the noise had come.

They hurried towards the place, Doctor Morelle moving with rapid, raking strides, his face now dark and anticipatory. Hitherto he had trod stealthily, but now he appeared heedless of being heard.

He spoke sharply, so that Miss Frayle jumped; his voice was so loud in comparison with the whispers in which they had conversed ever since their arrival at the old house.

'Have you a torch, Inspector? It would simplify matters if you were to produce it.'

Hood obliged, and the beam cut a white swathe through the blackness.

'Permit me to borrow it.'

The Doctor flashed the light over the tangled grass. A faint path showed through the tangle, as if something had been dragged through the grass, leaving a trail. Flashing the torch ahead, Doctor Morelle followed the trail. Then suddenly he gave an exclamation of satisfaction and Miss Frayle cried out involuntarily:

'Another one!'

Two or three yards ahead of them, almost hidden in the thick grass, a figure sprawled face downwards. As the light from the torch shone on it, it gave that faint moan which they had heard before.

'It's a man!' Miss Frayle cried unnecessarily.

'Take this,' the Doctor snapped, pushing the torch towards her. Then he and Hood were beside the prone man. Doctor Morelle turned him over gently.

Miss Frayle directed the white beam on to the face of Baron Xavier.

40

Doctor Morelle's Manoeuvre

The Baron's eyes were closed, his face ghastly, but there was no mistaking his young, good-looking features. Another faint moan escaped his lips.

'Well, well!' Hood commented with satisfaction. 'So it looks as if Mrs. Latimer got him first!'

Baron Xavier was unconscious. The torch showed blood on Doctor Morelle's hands as he gently unfastened the Baron's coat. A widening patch of blood darkened his shirt.

'Bring the light closer, Miss Frayle.'

The Doctor ripped the shirt away, examining the wound intently, then made a pad and bound it into place by the expedient of ripping the shirt into lengths. He worked quickly and deftly. Over his shoulder he told Hood:

'He will survive this. Bullet lodged

above the heart. Lost a good deal of blood, no doubt due to the exertion of attempting to crawl away from his assailant.'

Hood bent his head in agreement. 'Anyhow, we finally caught up with him — hullo!' He stooped suddenly and picked up a nickel-plated revolver the movement of the torch revealed lying in the grass.

'It's a .38,' he muttered. He snapped open the breech. 'And one round fired. Just recently, too. Accounts for the other shot we heard. Humph! Whole set-up speaks for itself. We'll get the full story from him later, but it's clear enough what happened. He and the woman came down here together. Then she took a pot at him. In other words, Mrs. L. double-crossed him, or he —'

Doctor Morelle straightened and interrupted him.

'It would be advisable to convey him to the hospital at Haywards Heath forthwith. I suggest you send your man for your car. It can drive up to the terrace and we can transfer Baron Xavier to it.

We do not wish to risk undue delay.'

Miss Frayle threw the inert figure a sympathetic glance while Inspector Hood gave a shout for the officer in the house, who came on the run. He received his instructions and went off. Doctor Morelle pulled out his cigarette-case and the Inspector produced his pipe which he proceeded to fill.

He studied the Doctor quizzically in the flame of his cigarette-lighter. In the yellow glow the aquiline sombre features showed no elation, no triumph at finding Baron Xavier. He murmured:

'I fear, my dear Hood, your reasoning is not altogether accurate.'

Miss Frayle had moved uneasily from one foot to the other and said in a shaky voice: 'I didn't realize how terribly tired I am. Can I sit down somewhere?'

The Doctor shot her a swift, sardonic look.

'You will find the grass somewhat damp; it will be more prudent for you to remain standing.'

She sighed and drooped. There were a lot of questions she wanted to ask, but she was too exhausted. She had hardly known what to expect, but she hadn't anticipated this, at any rate. It seemed such an anti-climax. Doctor Morelle seemed not in the least surprised at the dramatic discovery of Baron Xavier.

She glanced at Inspector Hood. He, too, seemed subdued, as if the end of his long and patient chase had proved somewhat of an anti-climax for him also.

He put into words what she felt too fatigued to express.

'If you don't think much of my reasoning, Doctor, what's your own idea? I must say you led us here as if the Baron was the very man you expected to find.'

'I expected to find him in the vicinity,' was the smooth reply. 'There were traces of blood on the trampled grass where he fell which evidently escaped your attention. Since he had been wounded, yet was not there, it was clear he must have removed himself elsewhere. Tracks led towards the shadow of the tree — with the rest you are acquainted.'

'All right, all right,' Hood sighed. 'But what's your theory? I've given you my idea and you say it's wrong —'

'The car awaits us,' the Doctor broke in, as they heard the police-car pulled up at the steps of the terrace.

The still unconscious Baron Xavier was carried to the car. As Miss Frayle trailed after the others, the sense of anti-climax continued. The stealthy approach to the house, the amazing discovery of Mrs. Latimer, the silence that had hemmed them in, everyone's carefully lowered voices. Now this sudden, almost casual, manner in which they were returning with Baron Xavier seemed somehow out of keeping with what had happened before, with yet the eerie and dramatic atmosphere still remaining.

It seemed a strange, unfinished end to the mystery, she thought. The threads of the case seemed to have become lost to her. She was too tired to think clearly, but only felt a vague dissatisfaction. Mrs. Latimer and the Baron. Had it been he, then, who had shot Lugg down in cold blood at Wapping Old Stairs? The Baron who had strangled Charles Gresham?

These conjectures were flitting hazily through her mind as she saw the Baron placed in the car, then Hood indicated to take her seat. She started to climb in — suddenly a grip of steel clasped her arm. Doctor Morelle was beside her, shaking his head. To her surprise she saw he was also gripping the Inspector, who looked up at him with an expression of almost comical surprise. Doctor Morelle spoke clearly and loudly to the driver:

'Keep your headlights on. Take us to the hospital first, then on to the police-station. We shall have to return for Mrs. Latimer.'

He slammed the door of the car shut with his foot. The driver and the two plain-clothes men eyed him questioningly. He inclined his head and, as if in a trance, the driver nodded. The engine started, the car rolled off, leaving Miss Frayle and the Inspector gaping at the Doctor in frank bewilderment.

As the car receded, Hood opened his mouth to speak but, with a quick, warning movement, Doctor Morelle drew him and Miss Frayle back into the shadows cast by the terrace.

'Not a sound, either of you,' he hissed. 'I have been observing the geography of the lake. Follow me closely, keep under cover at all costs and, above all, silence.'

Miss Frayle's eyes grew saucer-like behind her horn-rims. In a whisper no less menacing for its deadly quietness, the Doctor's voice was in her ear: 'No questions at this juncture, I warn you!'

He turned away from her and began to move swiftly, but with the stealth of a cat, towards the lawn. Instead of crossing the lawn, he now kept to the shadows of the shrubberies which bordered it as it stretched to the lake.

Cautiously, Miss Frayle and Hood followed.

The sound of the police-car had died away by the time they reached the end of the shrubbery, which mingled with the semicircle of trees forming the background to the lake. Beneath a tall overspreading tree Doctor Morelle paused, motionless and silent, taking his bearings.

The house and the lawn now lay behind them. The high shrubbery on their right, the lake immediately to their left. It shimmered smooth and silver where the moonlight shone down upon it, dark as gun-metal where the black shadows of the trees fell.

It was a rough oval shape, perhaps fifty yards across at its widest point and thirty at the narrowest. The half-circle balustrade round it framed a kind of terrace, and a flagged path, cracked and overgrown with weeds, ran round the lake. On the wooded side, not far from where they stood, a small, semi-ruined temple stood at the foot of the trees that grew by the water's edge, no more than a marble dome upon weed-clad pillars, a miniature sun-temple beloved of Georgian landscape gardeners. Like a ghostly legend of past glories, it showed no more than a fragile ruin in mingled shadow and moonlight.

It was soon clear from Doctor Morelle's quiescent attitude that he intended to wait in the dark shadow of the tree, so near the lake that they could hear the faint whisper of the water and feel its cold dankness on their faces.

The Doctor's intentions, so far as they

could judge them, utterly mystified Hood and Miss Frayle. Yet so evident was it that he had some purpose known to him, though hidden from them, that they could do nothing but wait unquestioningly, uncomprehending and expectant.

Despite the discomfort of the damp air and of feeling cramped as the long minutes passed, Miss Frayle felt a tense excitement mounting. Fatigue which she had thought overwhelming but a little while back had unaccountably dropped away. Firmly she straightened her spectacles upon her nose. She felt ready for anything. She glanced at Inspector Hood. He, too, stood motionless, caught up in the contagion of excitement which was heightened by the Doctor's attitude of patient watchfulness.

Miss Frayle felt rather than heard Hood give a small sigh. She saw him looking uncertainly at Doctor Morelle's tall, immobile figure, as if he were conjecturing whether or not to risk speaking to him. She felt her left foot beginning to ache with cramp. She moved it cautiously and Morelle's head whipped round angrily. He glared at her with dark and saturnine intensity, then his gaze turned back to the lake once more.

Time ceased to have meaning for Miss Frayle. The minutes ticked by interminably. Nothing moved. No other noise than the faint gurgles and whisperings made by the water disturbed the stillness. It seemed as if all around had fallen into a silence that might never be broken.

Then suddenly Doctor Morelle's head lifted. He tensed like a coiled spring. Through the dank silence a faint sound reached Miss Frayle's ears and icy chills crawled under her scalp. Her heart began to thud violently.

There was a slither, the water splashed a little more noisily. A thread of silver flashed across the surface of the lake. Miss Frayle gave a sudden gasp. Instantly her arm was in such a grip from the Doctor's fingers that she had to bite back a cry. Beside her she felt Hood crane forward.

Something black, snake-like, writhed across the path ahead of them and grew taut. There followed a queer, scraping noise. The water swirled uneasily, making little eddies of white foam.

They saw then that the taut, snake-like object was a rope, a rope which had lain slack and unseen, but which now, with some heavy object submerged in the lake on the end of it, was writhing towards the ruined sun-temple.

Near the edge of the lake the surface of the water suddenly broke. The moonlight revealed the square black shape of a box being rapidly hauled in on the end of the rope. The box caught on the stone coping of the flagged path. The rope slackened, tightened again.

From the shadowed ruins of the sun-temple a figure emerged, moved quickly and silently down to the water. It crouched over the box and hauled it up.

A cold thrill of horror chilled Miss Frayle as she saw the crouching figure wore the dark coat and pulled-down hat of the man who had appeared from the darkness behind her at Wapping Old Stairs.

It was too much for her. This was the climax and it was more than she could bear. She screamed. At the same moment,

Doctor Morelle raised his voice:

'Come on, Hood! At him!'

Not more than a dozen yards separated them from the man lifting the box up to the path. The Doctor leapt towards him, followed closely by Inspector Hood.

The man's head jerked up and twisted at their approach, one hand dragging at the pocket of his coat, the other hanging uselessly at his side.

'Stand back! Stand back, or I'll shoot!'

He had fallen across the dripping box as though to guard it with his body, a revolver glinting as he levelled it at them.

But Hood bore down on him in a fierce rush, grabbed his wrist as the revolver exploded harmlessly upwards. There was a flash of steel and Doctor Morelle's sword-stick pointed menacingly against the crouching man's chest. The Inspector gave a twist, the revolver dropped with a clatter and, with a gasping cry, the man collapsed.

With mingled horror and disbelief, Miss Frayle stared into the distorted face of Richard Whitmore, the pleasant and agreeable secretary to Baron Xavier.

41

The Purple Lake gives up its Secret

Miss Frayle found it difficult to believe that this creature, mouthing with impotent fury, was the nonchalant young man who had danced and talked with her so pleasantly at Lady Tonbridge's party only a night or two ago.

Hood had dragged him upright, holding him securely, but the other seemed in need of support rather than a detaining grip. The once lazy, amused blue eyes were now glaring; the smiling lips drawn back in a writhing grimace, a maniacal babble streaming from them.

'A million! A million! Cleo — for you and me! A million between us! Cleo! Cleo!'

He uttered the name in a final, despairing cry. Hood shook him hard. 'She won't answer you, Whitmore! Any more than Zusky, Gresham or Lugg!'

The other groaned. The wild expression

died from his face. For a moment he stared at them blankly. Then he suddenly sagged forward and would have fallen but that Hood caught him in time and laid him down. Over his shoulder he warned Doctor Morelle, 'Watch out for tricks.'

'He has fainted. He has lost a considerable amount of blood. Observe.'

He lifted Whitmore's useless arm, to reveal a bullet wound from which blood was oozing. With a rolled handkerchief he tied a tourniquet above the wound, observing drily:

'As I prognosticated, your conjecture proved to be wrong. You did not take into account the possibility that someone other than the Baron and Mrs. Latimer might be here. Hence your assumption that she had attempted to shoot him.'

'You — you mean you *knew* this other chap was going to be here?'

'Certainly. It has been clear to me for some time that he was implicated and that your suspicions regarding Xavier were unfounded. At least, insofar as murder was concerned. He was merely guarding what will doubtless prove to be his own property.'

He completed the tourniquet, rose and touched the box with his foot.

'This contains the secret of the Purple Lake. A secret of which the Baron was well aware. Of which Richard Whitmore and Mrs. Latimer also became aware when they ascertained the contents of Zusky's telegram.'

Miss Frayle could control her patience no longer.

'But what's in the box, Doctor?' she cried. 'What's in it?'

Without answering, he stooped over the box while Hood directed his torch on it. It was of the size of a small suit-case, covered in water-proofed canvas. Morelle ripped the canvas away with his sword-stick to reveal a heavy leather case fitted with a stout lock. Inserting the sword-stick under the lock, he glanced up at Miss Frayle and, with a sardonic smile:

'Your insatiable feminine curiosity is about to be satisfied. No doubt you are entitled to some compensation for a somewhat strenuous and possibly nerve-racking evening.'

He gave a quick twist of his wrist, which wrenched the lock open, and lifted the lid. Folds of oiled silk gleamed in the torchlight. Inspector Hood leaned forward. Miss Frayle, her eyes wide open and eager, watched Doctor Morelle unfold the wrappings.

The Doctor produced thick wads of banknotes and bonds. A japanned tin document box glistened dully. Tucked beside it was a chamois-leather bag. Doctor Morelle opened the neck and poured a shimmering glitter of precious stones into his palm.

'For such as this, men lose their heads and commit murder.'

He glanced with bitter distaste at the sparkling heap he had spilled out of the bag. Then he poured them back, retied the bag, replaced it in the case and closed the lid. He raised his head intently.

'I hear the car returning,' he said.

Miss Frayle turned and caught the flash of headlamps from the drive as the police-car approached.

42

Summing Up

Miss Frayle sat at her desk in Doctor Morelle's study amid a litter of papers and unopened correspondence.

Although there were one or two interesting-looking envelopes which she ardently wished to open, she had been too busily engaged upon a task which occupied her interest even more and from which, anyway, she had no respite.

Doctor Morelle was working on his case-book. Invisible, sunk in a deep armchair, his precise, modulated voice reached her as if it were disembodied.

'The primary difficulty in the case lay, of course, in the motive for Zusky's murder. Several possibilities presented themselves, since he was a man engaged in political activities and machinations. It became more and more apparent as I learned the natures of the protagonists most closely concerned that mere mundane gain was the most likely motive. The greatest difficulty in the elucidation of the mystery lay in the fact that much relative to it had been planned long ago. It was only by patient sifting of facts and their correct interpretation that I was able to reach the first definite conclusions. In this respect, I was struck by the coincidence of Richard Whitmore having entered Baron Xavier's employ when the latter was in the South of France, and that also there at the time were the remarkable Mrs. Latimer and Gresham.

'It was at this time that Xavier contrived to begin the conversion of certain of his properties in his country into negotiable bonds and easily portable wealth. It was a matter which required gradual careful negotiating for fear of precipitating the revolution which eventually did, in fact, take place and drove him to seek refuge here. Zusky, faithful friend and secretary, was the means by which that wealth was transferred to this country.

'The key to the motive for the first

murder lay in the telegram Zusky sent Albany. It was evident that the former had urgent need to see Xavier in order to impart a warning, which a third party — Whitmore — was anxious the Baron should not receive, regarding the treasure secreted in the lake. Possibly he knew Whitmore had somehow stumbled on the secret. The telegram hinted at this danger threatening his employer's fortune.'

Doctor Morelle paused to take an inevitable Le Sphinx from the human skull which served as a cigarette-box, and light it. Through a cloud of smoke, he continued:

'Whom did we know for certain was aware of the contents of the telegram? One: the recipient, Albany. Two: Baron Xavier himself. Three: Gresham, since the telegram was found by Miss Frayle in his flat after his demise. Furthermore, it could be assumed the knowledge of the message might also be shared by Mrs. Latimer.'

Miss Frayle's flying pencil paused. She frowned a little at him.

'Why Richard Whitmore, Doctor? We

knew all the others were mixed up in it, but how about him?'

He sighed long-sufferingly.

'Syntax is not your strong point, Miss Frayle. However . . . ' He drew at his cigarette.

'During my interview with Whitmore,' he went on, 'he stated that Albany had telephoned Xavier. Whitmore passed the telephone call on to the Baron. I subsequently satisfied myself of the fact that it was possible for Whitmore to listen-in to any telephone calls Baron Xavier received. In questioning him, I asked him if he knew if the Baron had left Lady Tonbridge's house at any time during that evening. It was at this point that he made his fatal mistake. He answered that he did not know. Later, however, when I questioned the butler, that individual stated quite clearly that Whitmore had approached him earlier in the evening instructing him to be discreet regarding Baron Xavier's wish to slip out for a quarter of an hour or so, unobserved.

'The butler was explicit, his word could

not be doubted. Why had Whitmore deliberately lied to me? Obviously there was a definite reason for such a palpable falsehood. It led me to review my interview with him, and I gained the impression that he had implied by suggestion, very skilfully and obliquely, never by definite statement, that there was a quarrel between the Baron and Zusky.

'I checked the time the butler had witnessed Baron Xavier leave the reception and the time he next saw him. The interval proved to be not more than ten minutes — in which time it would have been humanly impossible for him to have reached Jermyn Street, murdered Zusky, and returned. I was not unaware, however, of a certain superficial physical resemblance between the Baron and Whitmore, and, bearing that in mind, it occurred to me it would have been relatively simple for the latter to plant in the butler's mind that the Baron wished to leave for a brief while. In fact Whitmore *himself* intended to slip away, safe in the knowledge that the butler would believe him to be the Baron, and murder Zusky. Which, as we now know, is what actually occurred. He arrived a few moments after Gresham had left, just in time to admit his victim into the flat.

'However, as is so often the case with premeditated homicide, the unforeseen happened. The murderer was observed by the sneak-thief, Lugg. He had not witnessed Gresham's arrival or departure. Lugg subsequently followed and attempted to blackmail Whitmore, with unfortunate results for himself. His last words as he died were no doubt an attempt to reveal it was the Baron's man who had followed him to Wapping Old Stairs and shot him.

'Turning to Gresham, he was no more than a catspaw for Mrs. Latimer. Aware he was losing his nerve and was liable to break, she telephoned Whitmore, warning him. In fact she telephoned him while I myself was conversing with Whitmore. Without compunction, he set out to silence Gresham, even as he subsequently silenced Lugg. By now, Mrs. Latimer had discovered the meaning of the reference in the telegram to the Purple Lake.

Together with Whitmore, she drove down to Stormhaven Towers following Lugg's murder. At the same time, Baron Xavier suspected an attempt was being made to rob him of his property and he determined to guard it, no matter what suspicion might fall on him as a result.

'Therefore we have the arrival at Stormhaven Towers first of Baron Xavier, then Mrs. Latimer and Whitmore. The latter, foreseeing the Baron might be there, took the precaution of placing Mrs. Latimer on guard at the house, then proceeded to the lake. Mrs. Latimer saw the Baron attempt to intercept him and fired, wounding him. This effort proved too much for her. Suffering, as she was, from a fatal heart affection, the intense excitement and strain which had been imposed upon it within twenty-four hours, plus the final shock of the shooting, was too much, and she succumbed. Whitmore was in turn shot in the arm by Baron Xavier, who then collapsed from his own wound. Before Whitmore could reach the house, Inspector Hood and I, accompanied by Miss

Frayle, were upon the scene. Whitmore concealed himself, and I deliberately led him to believe we were going off with the Baron in the police-car.'

Doctor Morelle paused and stubbed out his cigarette.

'That will suffice for now, Miss Frayle.'

With a sigh she closed her notebook. She glanced at him for a moment, hesitated, then, fixing her glasses firmly on her nose and her lips tightening with resolution, she rose from her chair, took something from the desk and crossed to the Doctor.

'I had occasion to go to the safe just now.'

Her voice was tight and slightly shrill.

He raised an eyebrow. She held out a hand towards him.

'And I found this!'

Under his nose she thrust a light, frothy scarf from which a faint, remembered fragrance arose. 'It's hers! You kept it!'

For a moment he regarded her with a long, dark stare. She returned it without flinching until, at length, he broke into a sardonic chuckle.

'It occurred to me,' he murmured, 'it might serve as a memento of a very remarkable woman, my *dear* Miss Frayle —'

'It occurs to *me* it will be more appropriate in Inspector Hood's keeping at Scotland Yard,' she snapped. 'And I'll see he gets it! Myself!'

She whipped the scarf away from him and marched back to her desk, features glowing, eyes glinting behind her horn-rims. For a moment there was silence as she sat down and began industriously to busy herself with the correspondence. Then, from the shadowed depths of his armchair, the Doctor's voice came, bitter, sardonic.

'Kindly advise me if there is anything of importance among that accumulated mail.'

'Yes, Doctor.'

She was her prim, secretarial self once more. Fussily she opened envelopes, read out the contents: invitations to lecture, a request to attend a medical conference, then read a note which brought from her an exclamation of pleasure.

★ ★ ★

'*Dear Miss Frayle* [she read it very loudly].

'*Hugh is going on marvellously and we plan to be married in a few weeks' time and do hope you will come to the wedding. I am wondering if you can possibly persuade Doctor Morelle to be best man —* '

A muffled snort from the armchair.

'Emphatically not!'

Miss Frayle sighed wistfully, her expression softening as she drew a mental picture of cloudy-white wedding-dresses, smiling bridesmaids and cherubic pages and immaculately attired bridegroom. She could almost smell the orange blossom and hear the great organ pealing out the Wedding March. If only the Doctor would show an interest in such romantic diversions. If only he could be prevailed upon to leave his case-books and macabre exhibits for a while and refresh his spirit in an atmosphere of blissful happiness.

You never know, he might enjoy it, she told herself, allowing a roseate optimism to wing her on loftier flights of fancy. He might even make a habit of attending weddings, like those other people who became inveterate theatrical first-nighters. And if only she could inveigle him into interesting himself to that extent, who knows, but one day — She broke off, a blush suffusing her cheek, her heart beating quickly.

'What are you mooning over now, my *dear* Miss Frayle? Surely I may be permitted to know the nature of the remainder of the correspondence? Or is it addressed entirely and privately to you?'

His icy tones cracked her reverie like a pickaxe driving through ice.

'I — I — ' she stammered.

'Kindly deal with the rest of the mail!' he snapped.

'Yes, Doctor.'

She took up an envelope, heavily crested. 'An invitation to another party,' she exclaimed. 'From the Dowager Duchess of —'

'*Most* emphatically not!'

Doctor Morelle's voice rose in a positive snarl as he went on: 'I would rather act as a best man — whatever extraordinary function that might be!'

Miss Frayle darted a sudden, eager look towards him and with hope renewed her romantic dreams began roseately to shape themselves in her mind once more.

THE END